*Here's what some bestselling authors
are saying about Diana Whitney:*

"Diana Whitney is that rare talent who can blend
irrepressible humor with heart-tugging pathos for a
joyous, emotional roller coaster of a read! If you
want to laugh and cry and be fabulously
entertained, you'll love Diana Whitney."
—Bestselling author Suzanne Forster

"Diana Whitney brings you characters you can
laugh and cry with in a story you will never forget.
A book by Diana Whitney will steal your heart and
leave you chuckling in delight."
—Bestselling author Christine Rimmer

"A unique and gifted writer, Diana Whitney
knows how to wring emotion from the first scene
to the last."
—Bestselling author Pat Warren

Dear Reader,

Whether or not it's back to school—for you *or* the kids—Special Edition this month is the place to return to for romance!

Our THAT SPECIAL WOMAN!, Serena Fanon, is heading straight for a Montana wedding in Jackie Merritt's *Montana Passion,* the second title in Jackie's MADE IN MONTANA miniseries. But that's not the only wedding this month—in Christine Flynn's *The Black Sheep's Bride,* another blushing bride joins the family in the latest installment of THE WHITAKER BRIDES. And three little matchmakers scheme to bring their unsuspecting parents back together again in *Daddy of the House,* book one of Diana Whitney's new miniseries, PARENTHOOD.

This month, the special cross-line miniseries DADDY KNOWS LAST comes to Special Edition. In *Married... With Twins!,* Jennifer Mikels tells the tale of a couple on the brink of a breakup—that is, until they become instant parents to two adorable girls. September brings two Silhouette authors to the Special Edition family for the first time. Shirley Larson's *A Cowboy Is Forever* is a reunion ranch story not to be missed, and in Ingrid Weaver's latest, *The Wolf and the Woman's Touch,* a sexy loner agrees to help a woman find her missing niece—but only if she'll give him one night of passion.

I hope you enjoy each and every story to come!

Sincerely,

Tara Gavin,
Senior Editor

Please address questions and book requests to:
Silhouette Reader Service
U.S.: 3010 Walden Ave., P.O. Box 1325, Buffalo, NY 14269
Canadian: P.O. Box 609, Fort Erie, Ont. L2A 5X3

DIANA WHITNEY

DADDY OF THE HOUSE

Published by Silhouette Books
America's Publisher of Contemporary Romance

To Cristine Niessner, with gratitude
and deep appreciation.

 SILHOUETTE BOOKS

ISBN 0-373-24052-X

DADDY OF THE HOUSE

Copyright © 1996 by Diana Hinz

Printed in U.S.A.

Books by Diana Whitney

DIANA WHITNEY

says she loves "fat babies and warm puppies, mountain streams and California sunshine, camping, hiking and gold prospecting. Not to mention strong romantic heroes!" She married her own real-life hero over twenty years ago. With his encouragement, she left her longtime career as a municipal finance director and pursued the dream that had haunted her since childhood—writing. To Diana, writing is a joy, the ultimate satisfaction. Reading, too, is her passion, from spine-chilling thrillers to sweeping sagas, but nothing can compare to the magic and wonder of romance.

My Family

by David Murdock
age 9

My mom and dad got divorsed last year.
I was real ad. So was my little sister Laurie
and baby Nathan. Mom moved us all to a
punkin farm a ~~mill~~ miLion miles away
from dad so Laurie and me knew it was
up to us to get them back together ~~agin~~
agin. Only first we had to get rid
of moms stuffy old boyfriend so we
locked him in the barn with a
really mean goat, ✳ then we...

Chapter One

He only took his eyes off the winding rural road for a moment, just long enough to glance at the map in his lap. Certainly he should have known better, despite the physical toll taken by a grueling, nine-hour drive.

Bone-tired and anxious, he was irritable, distracted and completely out of his element, cursing the potholed path that country folk actually considered to be drivable. Los Angeles freeways may not be perfect, but they had big green signs to let people know where they were, and lanes wide enough that he didn't feel like sucking in his breath to pass another car. And not once in twenty years of city driving had he ever seen a cow in the road.

Until now.

Blurting a word he wouldn't use in front of his children, J. D. Murdock stomped on the brake, wrenched the wheel and plunged into a drainage ditch tangled with wild blackberries. His chin bounced off the steering wheel so hard he saw stars.

Fat, round, yellow stars.

Blinking, he squeezed his eyes shut, shook his head and realized that he wasn't seeing stars at all. He was staring at pumpkins, acres and acres of them sprawled just beyond the barbed wire fence that was now wrapped around the crushed fender of his beloved Jeep Cherokee.

At that defining moment, with his chin throbbing and his ankle screaming in pain, Jay realized just how much he hated this uncivilized wilderness. He hated everything about it, from the weed-encrusted hills to the odious creatures dotting the landscape with foul calling cards. It was, he decided, an absolutely miserable place, hot and noisy, with the constant cacophony of squawking, chirping, humming and squealing emanating from an unnerving assortment of bugs, birds and mysterious unidentified beasties.

And the air smelled weird, too, a peculiar hybrid of scents that reminded him of an acorn-studded Christmas tree plopped in the middle of a freshly manured lawn. Disgusting, Jay thought, and so primitive he couldn't believe any rational person would chose to live in such a godforsaken place.

Clearly, his ex-wife had moved here just to spite him.

Several hours later, Jay sat on the edge of an emergency room cot, sporting six stitches in his chin along with a roaring headache and a rotten attitude. What really ticked him off, aside from his own stupidity, was the fractured left ankle that throbbed with percussive intensity. From the knee down, his leg was swathed in a thick plaster cocoon that weighed about a thousand pounds and made him feel like he was chained to the floor.

He was trapped, claustrophobic enough to gnaw off the damned cast and angry enough to spit chewed plaster in the smug, bovine face of the suicidal cow that had caused all this grief. The worst part of his ordeal would be telling his kids that their long-awaited camping trip had to be postponed. Again.

Jay was glumly mulling that thought when a childish shout echoed through the hospital's sterile halls. "Here he is, Mom!"

A moment later, the quiet emergency room was besieged by a churning mass of chattering energy. "Dad, Dad, your car's all squished. Mom got real sick when she saw it and, like, I figured she was gonna faint and stuff, but Archie made her drink water—"

Archie? Jay stiffened.

The boy continued without missing a beat. "But when he told her you were gonna be okay, she got better, so we all got in the van and came straight here, on account of she said you wouldn't mind having company, even if you were kinda sad about your car and everything."

As Jay continued to ponder who this Archie person could be, the exuberant nine-year-old paused for a gulp of air. David's frantic gaze settled on his father's entombed leg. "Wow," he whispered, eyes wide with envy. "That's so totally cool. How come your pants are all ripped?"

"Because I wouldn't take them off," Jay grumbled, regarding the slit pant leg with frustration. The jeans were brand new, and had set him back thirty bucks.

"Can I write my name on it?"

"Hmm?"

"Your cast," David explained patiently. "Can I, like, sign it or something?"

"Oh. Yeah, sure." At the same moment, Jay's attention was diverted by his sobbing seven-year-old daughter, who'd just appeared in the doorway clutching a raggedy stuffed rabbit. "Laurel, honey, it's okay." He opened his arms, reaching out to the terrified child. "I'm fine, really."

With a choked sob, the little girl dashed across the room, clamored onto the cot and flung herself against her father's chest. Jay hugged her, murmuring softly as he stroked her fine blond hair. "There, there, sweetie. Everything's okay. Everything's going to be just fine."

Laurel hiccupped, resting her wet cheek against Jay's rib cage as she tilted her head to peer through thick, blue-rimmed glasses. Aqua eyes the same shade as his own were reddened, brimming with tears. She regarded him with unabashed terror. "Are you hurt real bad, Daddy?"

"Nah. Barely a scratch."

The girl's gaze settled on his swollen chin. She gingerly touched the bandage. "You look like Popeye."

Jay laughed, as amused by his son's indignant expression as by his daughter's unflattering but unfortunately accurate observation.

Crossing his skinny arms, David fixed his sister with a hard stare. "Geez, Laurie, that's really mean. Like, Dad coulda been *killed,* and you go and make fun of him."

"I wasn't making fun—honest!" Horrified by the implication that she might have hurt her beloved daddy's feelings, Laurel clutched Jay's T-shirt and blurted, "I *love* Popeye! He's my absolute favorite!"

"I know, sweetie," Jay soothed, massaging her tense little back. "I'm not upset. Laurie? What is it, honey?"

Every trace of color had drained from the child's face. Her mouth twisted, quivering, and a fresh flood of tears streamed down her freckled cheeks. "Y-you're never gonna d-die, are you, Daddy?"

Before Jay could respond, David answered. "Everybody dies," the boy said with a nonchalant shrug that belied the stark terror in his young eyes. "But only after they get all old and wrinkly. Besides," he added, affectionately patting his sister's bare leg, "Mom says that Dad is the smartest and strongest cop on the whole force, and no matter what happens he can always take care of himself. That's right, isn't it, Dad?"

The question was posed with a tremor of desperation that raised a lump in Jay's throat. He tried to cough it away.

Failing, he paused to gather his composure while slipping a comforting arm around his son's thin shoulders.

After taking a few shaky breaths, Jay hugged both his oldest children tightly. "Don't worry," he whispered. "Nothing's going to happen to me. I plan to be around for a long, long time."

Although the children seemed somewhat consoled by the reassurance, Jay's thoughts took a distinctly darker turn. Despite the dangers of his profession, he'd never thought much about dying. He couldn't afford to. A fearful cop is ineffective at best, and at worst a hazard to himself and others. As an undercover officer, Jay was especially cautious about keeping a tight wrap on his nerves, which was why this sudden surge of emotion was so unsettling. After all, the accident was minor, as were his injuries.

But what if it had been serious? What if, God forbid, he *had* been killed? The thought of never seeing his children again—of never seeing Bethany—knotted his stomach and chilled him to the bone.

Bethany. Sweet, beautiful Bethany.

In his mind, Jay crooned her name like a love song. To him it was. Since the day he'd first seen Bethany Cornell giggling with her friends in their high-school hallway, J. D. Murdock—track star, all-star, senior athlete of the year and adolescent jock-of-all-trades—had been instantly, utterly, irrevocably in love.

Her image floated through his thoughts—an unmanageable swirl of dark curls framing a pixie-petite, freckled face, midnight eyes that sparkled with mischief and an impish grin infectious enough to make a grumpy goldfish giggle.

For twelve years, that radiant smile had been a beacon in the night. Bethany had been Jay's rock, his guiding light, his lifeline to sanity. Then suddenly she was gone, and his entire world had crumbled into darkness.

The lump in Jay's chest swelled to the point of pain. A worrisome prickle heated his eyelids, a sensation that had become depressingly familiar during the past year. But he couldn't indulge his emotions now. He had to be strong for his children.

Children who were suddenly squirming in his arms.

David pulled away first. "Hey, Mom! Dad's got a really neat cast. He says I can sign it and everything!"

Jay took a shuddering breath before opening his eyes. He knew what he'd see. Still, the sight of her nearly stopped his heart.

Bethany was in the doorway with Nathan propped on her hip. Ignoring the wriggling two-year-old, she stood there biting her lower lip, her face so pale that her freckles stood out like little brown soldiers. The thick mane that had once spread wild on Jay's pillow was now partially tamed, tied atop her head with something akin to a red sweatband. She wore denim bib overalls with muddy knees over a stained T-shirt that looked more like a used shop rag than an article of clothing.

She was without doubt the most beautiful woman in the world.

Ignoring the mad chatter of the older kids mingled with Nathan's stubborn screech to be released, Jay sat frozen, unable to speak, unable to breathe, unable to tear his gaze from the woman he'd loved all his life.

Their eyes met, his and Bethany's, speaking volumes in silence, a palpable message that each understood but neither dared to acknowledge.

Jay didn't know how much time passed; he was aware of nothing other than the woman who'd lit up the room, and his heart, by her presence.

Then little Nathan pounded his mother's shoulder while emitting a five-decibel shriek of displeasure. The spell was broken.

Bethany blinked once, then lowered the screaming toddler to the floor, at which time he promptly shot across the room to dismantle a wall-mounted blood-pressure machine, an activity his mother would have instantly squelched had her attention not been otherwise directed.

Her frightened gaze enveloped Jay, lingering on his bruised face, then performing a thorough scan of his body before stopping at the clunky cast on his left leg. She clasped her hands together, sucking in a shaky breath. "They told me your injuries weren't serious. I didn't expect you to be so...so battered."

Jay swallowed hard. The fear in his wife's—*ex*-wife's—eyes revved his protective instincts into high gear. Bethany had never been able to deal with a crisis, even a small one. She inevitably panicked. She used to beep him at work to solve the most minor problems. Once that had irritated him. Now that his pager had been silent for nearly a year, Jay would give just about anything he owned to hear that telltale squeak in his pocket, and to feel needed again.

Pasting on a reflexive smile, Jay managed a shrug that sent a shock wave of pain down his strained back. "Hey, I feel great," he lied. "It looks worse than it is."

Bethany sighed. "I know."

"Huh?"

"Your ankle will take time to heal, of course, and you have a mild concussion, but you're going to be just fine."

"Well...yeah, sure." Jay's smile faded as Bethany rushed past to unwind the rubber blood-pressure cuff from around Nathan's waist.

"Mustn't touch," she said, struggling to extract the inflation bulb from between the toddler's clamped teeth. "Turn loose, Nathan. It's not a toy."

With his mother distracted, David took the opportunity to reclaim his dad's attention. "So, I guess we're not gonna get to go camping, are we?"

"Hmm?" Jay focused on his son, who was staring up with great dark eyes that were exactly like his mother's. David was, in fact, the spitting image of Bethany except for the freckles—which poor Laurel, who otherwise resembled Jay, had received in abundance. He hugged his somber daughter and gave his son a reassuring grin. "Of course we're going camping. This is Labor Day weekend, isn't it? The minute they spring me from this here jail, we're going to pile in the car and—"

"I had it towed," Bethany announced.

"You . . . towed my car?"

"Not personally." Dropping the rescued cuff on the nightstand, she wiped the wet bulb on her overalls and scooped up her grinning son in a single fluid motion. "I called a funny-looking truck with a big hook on the back that specializes in that kind of thing. Laurel, will you run out and find that nice nurse we were talking to earlier? She has your father's crutches."

Jay reared forward, nearly lurching off the bed. *"You towed my car?"*

A frown puckered Bethany's perfectly arched brows. "Please calm down, Jay. You're upsetting the children."

He sat back, stunned. In all the years they'd been together, Bethany had never once told him to calm down. It had always been the other way around.

Now, however, she was speaking with the same slow, logical tone that she used with Nathan. "There wasn't any choice, Jay. The radiator was leaking, there's some kind of purple goop dripping out of the engine, the left fender was totally twisted into a tire, two of which are flat as road kill. Oh, and Archie thinks the axle is bent."

Archie again. Jay's eyes narrowed into mean little slits.

Bethany shifted the baby on her hip, wiping his soggy mouth with the back of her hand. "I asked the garage to put a rush on the repairs, but it's still going to take a few days to—"

"Who the devil is Archie?" Jay blurted with considerably more force than he intended.

Her eyes widened. "Archie Lunt, the deputy who helped you out of the car."

An image of florid jowls, a bald head and kind blue eyes popped into his mind. Jay mopped his forehead, mumbling. "Oh, yeah. That Archie."

A worried frown creased her forehead. "Maybe you hit the steering wheel harder than we thought."

Massively relieved to learn that the Archie in question wasn't some kind of dashing gigolo with lurid designs on his wife—ah, ex-wife—Jay just sat there, grinning stupidly.

David heaved a giant sigh. "So camping's out, huh?"

"I promised camping, and a'camping we will go." Jay tousled his son's ruffled hair. "I'll just rent a car and—"

"No driving," Bethany said firmly.

Jay glanced at his cast. "Only my left foot is out of commission," he reasoned. "I can still handle an automatic."

"You're not supposed to operate machinery while taking your medication."

"What medication?"

"The medication in my purse."

"Oh. Well, maybe I can find a motel with a pool and the kids can come—" Jay's shoulders slumped as Bethany shook her head. "Why not?"

"You can't be alone, at least not for a few days. The concussion, you know."

Confused, Jay frowned at David, who rocked back on his heels with a happy wink. "No problemo, Dad. Mom says you can stay with us."

"Yeah?" Buoyed by the thought of being under the same roof with his family, Jay felt a sudden surge of affection for the clunky cast.

"There's a futon in the sewing room," Bethany purred, her eyes sparkling. "I'm sure you'll be very comfortable."

Only slightly deflated, Jay shrugged. "Sure, it'll be fine. I'll have to call the lieutenant—"

"I spoke with him an hour ago. He says not to worry, you have plenty of sick time."

"Ah . . . okay. Thanks. Then I guess all I have to do is telephone my insurance agent—"

"Already done."

"It is?"

"Mmm . . . Don't pull Mommy's hair, Nathan." Bending to set the toddler down, she untangled her son's tiny fingers while skimming a glance at Jay. "I hope you don't mind."

"No, of course not."

It was no mystery that she knew Jay's insurance agent, since the guy had also been Bethany's agent until the divorce last year. Still, Jay scratched his head, wondering if this bundle of energetic efficiency could possibly be the lovable but undeniably high-strung woman who'd shared his life for over ten years.

"At any rate," Bethany continued, "I've had a copy of your policy faxed to my boss—he's an insurance agent— and the mechanic has agreed to direct-bill your insurance company. David, hold your brother's hand so I can help your father, okay?"

"Sure, Mom."

As soon as David had clamped onto his baby brother's fat little fist, Laurel reappeared dragging a pair of awkward wooden crutches.

Jay was horrified. "I don't need those."

"Just for a few days," Bethany crooned as if cajoling one of the children. "You'll get the hang of them in no time at all."

"I don't have to get the hang of them because I'm *not* going to use them," Jay growled, pressing his flattened palms against the mattress. "They call this thing a walking cast, and that's exactly what I'm going to do with it."

"Please, Jay, the doctor says—"

Muttering, he pushed himself into a standing position, wobbling there a moment while Bethany's lungs deflated with a long-suffering sigh.

Jay took a test step with his unfettered leg. "Aha. See? I told you."

His smug expression dissipated when he heaved the plastered foot forward, whereupon the cast's metal arch support hit polished linoleum like a ball bearing on grease. Flinging out both arms and his one good leg, he spun like a human top, then let out a surprised bellow as the momentum suddenly shifted. One minute he was skidding across the floor; the next, he was flat on his back, gasping and winded.

When his vision cleared, Bethany was standing over him, biting back a smile. "Forgive my skepticism. I now concede that you have the situation completely under control."

Ten minutes later, Jay hobbled out of the hospital, humbled, humiliated and using the damn crutches.

"David's looking at me," Laurel whined from her third-row seat at the back of the minivan. "Make him stop."

Bethany glanced in the rearview mirror. "Please don't tease your sister."

David lifted his chin from the backrest of the middle seat, turning to raise innocent eyes toward his mother. "I'm just looking out the back window."

"Choose another window," Bethany muttered, steering the van around a curve pocked with potholes. She winced as Nathan, securely fastened in a car seat immediately behind her, dropped his toy truck and emitted a screech of frustration. "David, honey—"

"Got it, Mom."

Another glance in the mirror confirmed that the older boy had unfastened his seat belt and ducked down to retrieve his brother's toy. A moment later, Nathan was happily rum-rumming his truck along the frame of his car seat while David leaned back and buckled himself in.

Bethany sighed, grateful for a momentary lull that most certainly wouldn't last. Children were at best a challenge. At worst, they were merciless chatter machines programmed to drive parents and siblings to the brink of utter insanity.

Thankfully, they were almost home.

After a conscious effort to loosen her taloned grip on the steering wheel, she angled a glance to the right. In the passenger seat, Jay sat stiff and motionless, the hated crutches splayed on the floor in the carpeted void beside the van's sliding side door. His arms were folded, his expression grim. He was staring straight ahead as if studying the passing scenery, although Bethany doubted he was admiring golden hills studded by ancient oaks, or the verdant landscape of irrigated pastures. She recognized the subtle twitch of his jaw, the rigid thrust of his stiff shoulders. He was angry.

And he was in pain.

Not that he'd ever admit it. Defender of justice, protector of innocence and consummate constituent of the masculine mystique, James David Murdock would rather die ugly than reveal even the slightest hint of human weakness. Feeling pain was a weakness, he'd simply grit his teeth, pretending it didn't exist. In his stringent view, to acknowledge pain was to lose control over it. Loss of control was, of course, another weakness.

But only for men. Jay charitably accepted, even encouraged, free expression of such pitiful behavior from children and females, classifications which, Bethany suspected, Jay viewed as interchangeable.

She sneaked a second glance at her husband—*ex*-husband—then quickly focused on the road while her heart pounded against her ribs. This wasn't safe, she thought, not safe at all.

Despite bruises and abrasions, Jay Murdock was still the handsomest man she'd ever known, and by far the sexiest. His sandy hair, worn collar length and shaggy to blend with the style of his vice squad cohorts, was so endearingly disheveled that Bethany longed to reach out and smooth it with her fingers.

She dared not, of course. Simply looking at him was difficult enough; touching him would be far too risky.

Because Bethany couldn't remember a time when she hadn't been in love with Jay Murdock. Leaving him had been the hardest thing she'd ever done, but staying away had been nearly impossible. Now with Jay under the same roof, she wondered how she'd ever be able to resist temptation.

Her grip on the wheel tightened again.

She *would* resist; she had no choice. Their marriage was over now. She couldn't afford to look back.

As the van passed the fateful ditch tangled with twisted fence wire, Bethany slipped a glance from the corner of her eye. Beside her, Jay's expression had flattened into one of pure venom. He said nothing.

After another hundred yards, she turned into the gravel drive cutting a swath through the pumpkin fields, at which time Jay uttered his first words since leaving the hospital. "These are *your* pumpkins?"

"Mine and the bank's." Even to her own ears, the airy reply seemed insultingly flippant. She hastened an explanation. "Apparently Uncle Horace had raised pumpkins on this land for decades. When he willed it to me, I'm sure he was hoping I'd keep up the tradition."

"You don't know the first thing about farming," Jay sputtered incredulously. "In fact, you're the only person I know who can kill a cactus."

"I didn't kill it," she snapped. "The cat knocked it off the shelf."

"Sure, after it had already dissolved into a putrefying yellow mass. I told you not to water it so much— Ouch!" Jay lurched forward, grabbing the dashboard as the car whipped around and jerked to a stop in front of a typical clapboard farmhouse, complete with covered porch and second story dormers.

"Sorry." Irritated and unrepentant, Bethany flipped off the ignition. Beside her, Jay groused and muttered, but she wasn't listening. Instead, she was staring at the telltale gleam of crimson metal extending beyond the side of the house, instantly recognizable as the trunk of her boss's extravagant luxury sedan. She swallowed a moan.

David, who also noticed the car, wasn't as charitable. "Aw, geez, what's he doing here?"

Jay's head swiveled around. "Who?"

"Him," David grumbled, jerking a thumb toward the porch.

Just then the screen door squeaked open. A tall blond man wearing a snappy double-breasted suit with a tie that reflected sunlight stepped onto the porch carrying a soda can and flashing a smarmy smile.

Bethany covered her eyes and took a deep breath. She should have known he wouldn't wait for her call. Now his impatience had turned a touchy situation into a potentially explosive one.

Peeking through her fingers, she saw Jay's stunned expression as the man ambled down the steps with a hospitable wave.

Jay swallowed so hard his Adam's apple bounced. "Who the devil is that?"

Bethany lowered her hand, forcing what she hoped was a convincing smile. "Roger Morris, the owner of Morris Insurance Agency. I work there. He's, ah, my boss."

A disgusted snort emanated from the back seat. "He thinks he's your boyfriend."

"That's enough, David." Avoiding her ex-husband's horrified stare, Bethany shoved the van door open, exiting so fast she nearly tripped on the side step. She hurried to the passenger side to unlatch the van's side door. The moment she slid it open, David and Laurel piled out.

As Bethany climbed inside to unbuckle Nathan from his car seat, she heard Jay's passenger door open. A glance over her shoulder confirmed her fears.

Roger had already poked his head into the passenger compartment and was introducing himself to Jay, who stared at the man's extended palm as if eyeing day-old fish.

After a long moment, Roger smoothly retrieved the rejected hand, using it to brush his spotless lapels. "Tough break, old man," he said, watching David drag the clunky crutches out of the van. "Quite fortunate, however, that you were adequately insured."

Jay snatched the crutches from his son. "Yeah, fortunate."

Clasping his hands behind him, Roger shifted on his imported leather heels, oblivious to the fact that he was blocking Jay's exit from the van. "Not to bring up unpleasantries," Roger said, seeming oddly pleased by Jay's misfortune, "but have you considered the possibility that this untoward incident might have had, shall we say, a decidedly permanent outcome?"

Jay stopped struggling with the crutches long enough to give Morris a perplexed stare. "Permanent?"

The man nodded somberly. "Frightening thought, I know, but one must consider the financial implications. Certainly, Jay—may I call you Jay—?"

"No."

The crisp reply was delivered with a withering stare noticed only by Bethany, who swallowed a groan and hauled Nathan out of the car while her competent if somewhat dense boss continued a well-rehearsed and oft-cited sales pitch without missing a beat. "Seriously, Jay, you strike me as a man who cares deeply for his children and desires only the best for them. Am I right?''

Trapped in his seat, Jay tossed a pleading glance toward the back of the minivan. It was empty. When his frantic gaze landed on Bethany, she was carrying Nathan up the porch steps, leaving him to deal with this pompous jerk on his own.

At that untimely moment, Roger leaned even farther into the van, gripping Jay's wrist. ''Have you provided for your children's education if, heaven forbid, something horrible were to happen?''

''Huh?''

Roger's face was mere inches away. ''Life insurance, Jay. Pennies a day to provide your children with the financial security they'll need in the event of your unfortunate demise.''

Apparently Jay's thunderous expression conveyed not only a lack of enthusiasm, but a silent suggestion that if the annoying fellow didn't shut up and move aside, there might be more than one unfortunate demise to discuss.

Roger straightened as a crutch tip whizzed past his nose, then stepped away from the van. His gaze darted toward Bethany as he gave his crisp, white collar a nervous tug. ''Perhaps we should discuss this another time.''

Without bothering to respond, Jay planted the crutch tips in the dirt, heaved his throbbing body forward and, grunting with effort, focused his concentration on the awkward struggle to exit the van without falling on his face.

By the time Jay was propped on solid ground, sweating as if he'd run a marathon, he realized that Nathan had been deposited on the porch and Bethany was escorting her boss around the house toward the gleaming red sedan. They were engaged in hushed conversation, an infuriating intimacy that shook Jay to the soles of his feet. Bethany whispered something to her boss, who responded with a grave expression, coupled with an empathetic glance that raised every hackle on the back of Jay's neck.

Jay eyed Morris's hand, which rested lightly on Bethany's shoulder and served as an unpleasant reminder of his son's warning that this pompous jerk wanted to be his wife's—ex-wife's—boyfriend. Instantly furious, Jay considered discouraging that idiotic intention by demonstrating a highly unique and decidedly uncomfortable use of crutches.

At that fortuitous moment, Morris called out, "Nice meeting you, old man. We'll, ah, talk soon." Then he spun on his polished loafers, climbed into his car and drove away so fast the tires spit gravel.

With Morris gone, Jay turned his attention to the porch steps, eyeing the obstacle with trepidation. The crutches chewed into his armpits as if issuing a challenge. Four small steps. To Jay, it might have well been a million.

He was vaguely aware of a sweet scent wafting around him. "Do you need help?" Bethany asked kindly.

Of course he needed help. Those damned wooden steps loomed like a cliff, although Jay would rather chew glass than admit it. Real men do not whine about problems; they defeat them.

After indicating that he did not in any way, shape or form require physical assistance, Jay licked his lips, blinking away a rush of stinging sweat from his eyes. His head was pounding, his vision blurred, and his leg felt like it was about to explode.

With some effort, he focused his mind to mentally calculate the rhythm of using the crutches as a lever and his uninjured leg as a landing zone. Thus fortified, Jay filled his lungs, swung the crutches forward and thunked his way up to the peeling porch, painfully aware that Bethany was watching with crossed arms and a skeptical expression.

Once on the porch, Jay stood, panting, while David scampered to open the screen door, allowing his father to swing himself inside the cluttered but otherwise roomy foyer. Jay vaguely noted a large parlor to his left, a staircase straight ahead, beside which a small hallway led toward the back of the house. An opening to the right of the hallway angled into what appeared to be the kitchen.

Laurel, having dashed straight from the van to the house, now ran downstairs, her chubby face flushed with excitement. "Wanna see my room, Daddy? It's real pretty. Mommy sewed pink curtains that match my bedspread, and I have a whole lot of shelves for my dolls, and my very own closet and everything!"

Fatigued to the point of collapse, Jay managed a thin smile. "Sure, sweetie. I'd love to see your room."

Behind him the screen door slapped shut. Nathan scurried across the hardwood floor to grab Jay's thighs in a baby-size bear hug. "Whoa, buddy. You'll knock Dad over." Teetering, Jay repositioned the crutches so he could reach down and stroke the boy's feathery blond hair. "You're getting big, aren't you? Last time I saw you, you couldn't reach higher than my knees."

Hooking a finger over his lower teeth, Nathan tilted his head back so far Jay feared he might fall over, then made a startling, if slightly garbled announcement. "Me go potty all by my-telf."

Jay chuckled and gave the proud toddler a thumbs-up. "That's my man."

Nathan was so tickled by the praise that he shoved both little fists against his mouth and ran up the stairs, giggling.

"Hey, Dad!"

"Hmm?" The movement of glancing over his shoulder made Jay dizzy. Ignoring a nauseous surge, he focused on David, who was bouncing from foot to foot, his arms flailing with animated gestures.

"Wanna see our pond? It's got real big catfish. Wanna go fishing?"

"Daddy doesn't want to go fishing," Laurel announced, taking umbrage at the intrusion. "He wants to see my room."

David gave his sister a withering stare. "Nobody wants to see your dumb room."

"It's not dumb!"

"Is, too."

"Is *not!*"

The rest of the argument swirled into a mass of white noise as Jay struggled to stay upright. He was woozy, his good leg felt like rubber and he must be going insane because he could swear there was a snarling lump of fur at his feet.

Just when Jay was certain that life as he knew it was about to end, that same sweet fragrance surrounded him again, and he was embraced by soft, loving arms.

"Go lay down, Leon," Bethany said to the snarling lump, which immediately fell silent and slunk away. Tightening her grip on Jay, she gently guided him toward a short hallway. "The tours will have to wait," she told the children. "Right now, your father needs rest."

Massively relieved, Jay had never loved Bethany more than he did at that moment.

Laurel, however, was not ready to give up without a fight. "I want to show Daddy my new doll!"

Fortunately, Bethany was adamant. "Not now."

"But, Mommy—"

A cooling breeze brushed Jay's face as David whizzed past on his way upstairs. The boy snagged his sister by the arm, nodding toward his parents. "Don't you get it, Laurie? They want to be *alone.*"

Laurie's bewildered expression brightened into a knowing grin. "Oh, yeah. *Alone.*"

Jay was vaguely aware that David hooked an arm around his sister's shoulders, whispered something that seemed to amuse her immensely, then hustled her upstairs. He was more acutely aware of Bethany, the feel of her fingers pressing against his ribs and her soothing voice in his ear.

"Easy now," she murmured, leading him into the short hallway to the right of the stairs. "Just a few more steps."

They passed through a doorway into a room lit by sunlight. A moment later, he was stretched out on a soft bed, moaning in relief. Efficient hands fluffed a pillow beneath his head. Something soft and cozy covered his body. A silky palm stroked his brow.

The last thing Jay imagined before slipping into a deep sleep was the warmth of sweet lips brushing his cheek.

Chapter Two

After scooping scrambled eggs onto David's plate, Bethany dropped the frying pan on the stove just in time to catch two pieces of toast as they popped out of the toaster slots.

"Use your spoon, Nathan." The maternal caution was firmly issued even though she knew it wouldn't do much good. Nathan was entering his food-sculpture stage and showing no small amount of talent. He was, in fact, the only one of her three children who enjoyed transforming a bowl of thick oatmeal into a tableau of the Grand Tetons so he could suck off the sugared peaks.

At the moment, he was struggling to squish scrambled eggs into his latest morning masterpiece, an endeavor Bethany disrupted after delivering buttered toast to Laurel.

"Please don't play with your food," she muttered, wiping his sticky hands before handing the disgruntled toddler a spoon. "Mommy will get your clay out after breakfast, okay?"

Nathan pushed his plate away and stuck out his lower lip. "No want clay."

"Eat your breakfast."

"No."

Bethany sighed, recognizing the stubborn tilt of the toddler's cleft chin. He was, she realized, just like his father. The thought made her smile.

"Mom?" David set down a glass of milk with one hand and wiped his mouth with another. "Can I wake Dad up now?"

"Daddy needs his rest."

"But he's gonna miss breakfast."

"I'll fix his breakfast later." Stifling a yawn, Bethany set David's empty plate in the sink and wished she, too, could catch a few more winks. To enforce a precaution suggested by the emergency room physician, she'd been up every two hours last night rousting Jay to make certain he hadn't lost consciousness. His irritation at the frequent interruptions hadn't bothered Bethany a bit. Jay always woke up grumpy. Usually his crankiness dissipated with his morning shower. Today, however, that normally predictable mood swing would be sorely tested.

The thought was interrupted when Laurel suddenly pushed her chair away from the table. "Mommy, can we make pancakes for Daddy's breakfast? He always says pancakes make him feel better."

Smiling, Bethany stroked her daughter's hair. Laurel was such a nurturing child, so compassionate and softhearted that once, after having accidently crushed a beetle beneath her bicycle tire, she'd had nightmares about the bug's distraught parents holding a mournful wake at the skid mark. "If your daddy wants pancakes, that's what we'll make, okay?"

Laurel nodded so vigorously that her glasses slid half-way down her nose. She poked them into place. "Can I be the flipper? I know how, honest. When the pancake is all full of bubble holes, it gets flipped, right? Can I do that, please, Mommy, please?"

"Yes, baby, you can be the designated flipper."

"Yay!"

Laurel jumped in place, clapping her hands, while Nathan poured an entire glass of milk onto his congealed eggs. Bethany snatched the sloppy plate away, moaning, and was about to dump the mess in the sink when a strange thud emanated from the guest room. She froze, listening.

David lit like neon. "Dad's up!"

Before Bethany could wipe her hands on a tea towel, she heard the squeak of a door hinge, followed by a rumbling canine snarl.

A moment later, Jay's furious bellow reverberated through the house. *"Beth!"*

"Oh, good grief. Stay here," she told David, who was already on his feet.

As the grumbling boy sat down, Bethany tossed the towel aside and sprinted through the living room. When she entered the hallway, she found Jay, his crutch propped against the doorjamb while he was locked in a visual stalemate with the growling hunk of black-and-white fur doggedly blocking his exit.

The scene was so comical Bethany nearly laughed out loud, but since she knew that any display of amusement would encourage Leon and infuriate Jay, she managed to contain herself. Placing her hands on her hips, she forced a stern tone. "You're not supposed to be out of bed," she told her plainly frustrated ex.

The dog, which resembled a medium-size Border collie with raggedy ears, issued a rumbling agreement.

Jay glared at Leon. "Call off this fur-faced menace or I'm going to make a hat out of him on the spot."

Bethany sighed. "Quiet, Leon."

Leon responded by glancing over his shoulder and twisting his head to focus his good eye on his mistress. He whined once, then whirled to face Jay, pleating his muzzle in silent challenge.

"That's enough. Go lay down." This time Bethany added more force to the command. The dog obeyed, albeit reluctantly, backing away from the door to sit sullenly at the end of the hall and fix Jay with a this-isn't-finished stare.

Puffing her cheeks, Bethany blew out a breath and angled a covert glance at the scowling man. "Sorry about that. Leon was my uncle's dog. We inherited him with the farm, so he tends to be a bit protective." She gave the animal an affectionate smile. "The local vet told me that Leon lost the sight in his left eye about four years ago, but it doesn't seem to slow him down or keep him from being a great little watchdog. He makes us feel safe."

Jay shifted on the single crutch he was using and gave the animal a derisive glower. "That moth-eaten mutt couldn't protect his own tail. If you want to feel safe, get a real dog."

With a pained sigh, Bethany glanced over her shoulder. "Leon, I think you've just been insulted."

Instantly Leon stood, bared his teeth and emitted a low, rolling growl. The hairs on his back stiffened, and what remained of his scarred ears flatted like a skullcap.

Jay's surprised blink quickly narrowed into a skeptical stare. "Okay, okay. I get the message." Leon, apparently taking umbrage with Jay's tone, snarled even louder. After a long moment, Jay tossed his free hand in a gesture of pure exasperation. "How do you turn the damned thing off?"

Bethany smiled sweetly. "Well, you might try apologizing."

"Give me a break."

She shrugged. Leon took a step forward.

"Oh, good grief." Totally frustrated, Jay slumped against his crutch, glowering at the furious animal that was now displaying its entire inventory of sharp little teeth. "I'm sorry, all right?"

Leon fell silent, plopping his bony rump on the floor and cocking his head to keep Jay in full view of his good eye.

"Well, then," Beth said cheerily. "Now that a proper truce has been established, let's get back to the original question. What are you doing out of bed?"

"Looking for the bathroom," Jay snapped. "I need a shower."

"Uh-uh. You can't get the cast wet. No showers."

His jaw dropped. "You're kidding, right?"

"I'm afraid not." She brightened. "But you can take a sponge bath."

"A *what?*" He shook his head, muttering. "No way, no damned way. A man can't be expected to function without a decent shower." He snapped his head up, eyes wide and horrified. "How the devil am I supposed to wash my hair?"

"In the sink."

"*Women* wash their hair in the sink."

"So do men with broken ankles."

"Not this man."

"Oh, for heaven's sake, we're not talking about castration. All you have to do is stick your head in the sink and turn on the faucet." She cleared her throat, avoiding his incredulous gaze. "I can, uh, help if you'd like."

His eyes narrowed into furious slits, indicating that he'd rather have his spleen removed by carnivorous rodents.

"Suit yourself." She sighed, jerking a thumb toward the end of the hall. "It's the last door on your left."

Lurching away from the jamb, Jay sidled into the hall, tossed Leon a sour look, then awkwardly clumped his way into the bathroom and slammed the door. A moment later,

Bethany heard water running. The faucet, she decided, not the shower.

Relief that he'd taken her warning seriously was upstaged by a dull throb situated between her shoulder blades. Rolling her head did little to alleviate the ache, which was no doubt caused by the tension of realizing that her ex-husband's extended presence would affect every aspect of the new life she was struggling to create—a life that was, in a word, chaotic.

In addition to the burden of single parenthood and holding a full-time job, Bethany also had the responsibility of a farm teeming with plant and animal life about which she knew less than nothing. Since Jay had always maintained that she'd never be able to make it without him, the last thing she wanted was him hanging around long enough to see just how true his prediction had been.

After all, she'd always yearned for independence. Now she had it. If rushing to the office each morning and doing housework half the night wasn't the satisfying experience she'd imagined, there was little choice now. Jay's generous child-support payments weren't enough to cover household expenses, property taxes and all the other costs associated with a growing family. There were also vet bills for the animals, doctor bills for the kids, new glasses for Laurel—and the equipment David needed to join the soccer team would cost more than a week's groceries.

Besides, Bethany's self-esteem was at stake here. For years, she'd felt helpless and useless, particularly as the older children's interests expanded beyond a need for continual mothering. Someday they'd be grown, and Bethany feared ending up like her own mother, a fragile, clingy woman who viewed herself only as an extension of others.

The troubling thoughts clung to her as she passed the kitchen, ignoring the chaos of her children's continual squabbling to wander through the parlor and gaze out over the pumpkin fields that were an admittedly bizarre representation of emotional freedom. Focusing on the past, Bethany remembered how frightened she'd once felt, and how lost. Like a nonperson, a mere appendage that was occasionally useful, but never particularly critical.

In retrospect, she wondered if that fear was one of the reasons she'd left Jay. It could have been, she supposed, but there were so many other problems, the most crucial of which was the emotional estrangement that had driven an inalienable wedge in their relationship.

Bethany turned away from the window, silently lamenting their broken family and the loss of the man who would always own a piece of her heart.

Dropping onto the worn sofa, she dragged a fat throw pillow into her lap, hugging it to her breast as if a piece of stuffed fabric could offer some slight comfort. Where had it all gone wrong? she wondered. Why hadn't love been enough?

She stared without seeing, her mind lost in the abyss of a past she couldn't reconcile and wasn't sure she even understood.

Their life together had begun with such promise. They'd been inseparable soul mates, planning the future with the guileless joy and unbridled passion of youth. The world had been a bright place then, a sunny landscape of color and hope and infinite possibilities.

Then they'd grown up. And they'd grown apart.

Jay had changed from an idealistic dreamer to a cynical pessimist, as jaded by his career as he was devoted to it. His transfer into the vice squad, which necessitated frequent undercover forays into the seamy side of life, left him exhausted and suspicious, exacerbating the problems in their marriage.

Early in Jay's career, he'd enjoyed sharing details of his day with Bethany. After the transfer, he became withdrawn and uncommunicative, refusing to discuss even the most mundane aspects of his job. The less he talked, the more desperate Bethany had become.

Feeling isolated and alone, Bethany had nonetheless recognized that she was in danger of becoming a merciless nag, exaggerating nuisance problems just to get her husband's attention. Jay had responded by spending even less time at home.

Deep down, Bethany hadn't really blamed him for that, but as his world continued to expand, hers had shrunk to claustrophobic dimensions. In the end, she'd been consumed by fear—fear for his safety; fear for her sanity; fear that by trying to pull him closer, she had actually driven him away. Jay had never understood her fear. He'd never understood her loneliness.

That's what had destroyed their marriage.

Tossing his soiled T-shirt over his shoulder, Jay hobbled out of the bathroom, nearly tripping over Leon, who'd planted himself in the center of the hallway and stubbornly refused to budge. Jay glowered at the dog. "Move it, bud."

Leon sat up, cocked his head and pleated his muzzle in a silent snarl.

Jay bared his teeth and growled.

Leon stood, snarling audibly now.

Jay leaned over his crutch, growling even louder.

It was silly, he knew, but for some primal reason he felt compelled to establish some territory here. Males have always had to compete, to fight for a rightful place in the world. Leon knew that. Jay knew it, too. They understood each other.

And so they stood there, dog and human, snarling and growling and snapping air until Leon's teeth dripped with liquid fury and Jay's upper lip curled high enough to brush the base of his flared nostrils. There could only be one winner here, only one champion—

"The first one to heist his leg will get swatted with a newspaper and tied to the porch."

At the sound of his mistress's voice, Leon backed away, whimpering, and laid down with his chin on his forepaws. Jay skimmed an embarrassed glance into the open living room where Bethany was watching, her arms crossed, her expression wry.

Except for what Jay fervently hoped was a sparkle of amusement in her eyes, Bethany's expression remained stern. "Nice role model, Dad. Thank heaven Nathan didn't see that or I'd spend the rest of my life trying to leash-train him."

Jay cleared his throat, opting for a smooth change of subject. "You know, sponge baths aren't half bad once you get the hang of them."

As the corner of her mouth quivered with a reluctant smile, her dark gaze slid suggestively down his bare chest, lingering at the unfastened waistband of his slit-legged jeans. "Actually I was beginning to wonder if you'd prefer a garden hose and a gallon of flea dip."

So much for distraction.

"He started it," Jay blurted, pointing at the hapless dog. "It was all his fault."

Rearing his head, Leon emitted a startled yip that Jay interpreted as the canine equivalent of "huh?"

Bethany tossed up her hands. "I don't care who started it, there will be no—I repeat, *no*—grunts, snarls, growls, or any other audible sounds of disrespect from either of you *ever again*. Do I make myself clear?"

Jay nodded. Leon whined.

Both males were absolutely silent as Bethany spun on her heel and marched into the kitchen. The moment she was out of sight, Jay and Leon exchanged soundless lip curls, then went their separate ways.

In the converted sewing room, Jay tossed his T-shirt on the floor beside the bulging duffel Bethany had thankfully rescued from his crunched car. Fortunately, he'd packed plenty of clothes for the now-canceled camping trip, so he wouldn't be stuck wearing shredded jeans for the rest of his stay here.

Which brought up the question of exactly how long that stay might be. The ankle would take weeks, perhaps months, to mend. He wondered if Bethany would let him stay that long.

No, of course not. But a couple of weeks, maybe. Assuming, of course, that he behaved himself and stopped harassing her dog.

The potential was plausible. Jay had more than enough sick leave accrued, and besides, his ankle would keep him on light duty for months. They'd stick him behind a desk, where he'd push papers until he was either street-fit or stark raving mad, whichever occurred first. Under those circumstances, he'd much prefer staying here, where he could quietly pretend that his family was whole again. It was a lie, of course, but it was such a comforting lie. At least, it was comforting to Jay.

A slow throb worked its way up his leg, reminding him that it was time to take his medicine. He glanced at the nightstand and chuckled. Bethany had laid out his morning dose beside a full water glass, against which a note had been propped. The note said, "Take these as soon as you wake up."

He tossed back the pills, washed them down, then painfully lowered himself onto the open futon which had, surprisingly enough, provided a relatively comfy bed. He glanced around the cluttered room, recognizing Bethany's beloved sewing machine, now neatly tucked into its cabinet and pushed against a wall. Beside it, the card table she'd always used to cut patterns was heaped with colorful thread caddies, stacks of fabric and the woven sewing basket that had been his gift to her about six Christmases ago.

The walls were covered with family pictures, bittersweet memories that brought a lump to Jay's chest. There was a snapshot of David holding his newborn sister, and another of Laurel on her third birthday, sobbing frantically because her big brother had blown out *her* candles.

Smiling, Jay recalled how Bethany had soothed their heartbroken daughter by relighting the candles so she could blow them out all by herself, which she did with utter glee, over and over and over again.

It had been a wonderful party.

Now, as Jay studied the remaining photos, he tried to remember details of the day each was taken. At first, the memories came easily. Then he realized that the later photographs, particularly those taken after Nathan was born, seemed alien to him.

The beach picture, for instance. David was holding Nathan's hand while the water swirled around their toes, but Jay couldn't recall ever having taken Nathan to the beach.

Assuming that Bethany and the kids must have gone on that particular trip while he'd been working, Jay frowned at another shot of the children at some kind of amusement park. He hadn't been with them then, either.

And there were more unfamiliar scenes, dozens of them. His children at the zoo; his children at the park; his children standing by a yellow bus on the first day of school; his children having a bike race in front of the house where Jay now lived alone.

Tears pricked his eyes. He'd missed so much of their lives, but there'd been no choice. A man had to support his family, supply them with food and clothing and shelter. That was a man's role, and by God, Jay had fulfilled it the best he could.

Bethany had never understood that role. She'd never understood the pressures of his job.

That's what had destroyed their marriage.

It took nearly an hour for Jay to change from his ruined jeans, which he'd slept in, to a pair of walking shorts and a clean T-shirt. Actually, the process of dressing lasted only about twenty minutes. Recovering from the ordeal, now that took some serious time.

He was weaker than he'd thought.

Still, Jay had managed to clothe himself, even if it had taken two tries to get his shorts on with the fly in front. Bethany had tapped on the door a while back to see if he was all right. He'd told her—between panting breaths—that he was perfectly fine. So she'd left, and he'd been too whipped to call her back and admit that he'd lied.

Now he was upright and breathing normally. He was also hungry enough to chew cardboard.

Leaving one crutch propped against the wall, he tucked the other one under his left arm and hobbled across the room. No sooner had he opened the door than the telephone rang.

A moment later, Laurel's voice rang out from the kitchen. "Mom! It's Mr. Morris."

Jay's shoulder blades drew together. Accepting that his wife had moved five hundred miles away was one thing; accepting her hormonal, obscenely handsome, Jeremy Irons look-alike boss was quite another.

A slight increase in hobble speed motivated him across the living room in time to see Bethany rush in the back door, sweaty, grubby and adorably disheveled. He flattened against the wall, obscuring himself yet still able to see her take the phone from Laurel, who skipped out the same door her mother had entered.

"Hello, Roger. Sorry, I was outside." Clamping the wall phone receiver under her chin, Bethany stretched the huge cord to the sink and rinsed her hands. "I couldn't possibly. Yes, I know you made plans, but everything has changed. I only agreed to accompany you because I assumed Laurel and David would be with their father—

Hmm?'' She turned off the faucet and snatched a paper towel from a roll hanging under the cupboard. "Yes, I suppose Nathan's sitter would agree to watch the older children, too, but I can't possibly leave Jay alone. He's still pretty shaky, and I think his leg's giving him a lot of pain."

Jay, concealed between a buffet cabinet and a potted palm, found himself nodding in approval. Actually, his leg didn't feel all that bad at the moment, but it would be rude to interrupt the conversation to point that out. Besides, the ankle would no doubt hurt like hell when the pain pills wore off, and he *was* feeling a bit woozy.

Bethany was right. He really shouldn't be left alone.

Parting the fronds, Jay peered through the foliage, noting that Bethany had propped her hip against the counter, closed her eyes and was listening with an expression that, much to Jay's delight, hovered between abject boredom and sublime irritation.

"Yes, I know how difficult it was to get tickets, and I really am sorry. You know, Margaret adores the theater. Why don't you give her a call. Hmm? Oh, I doubt she'd misunderstand your intentions, Roger. She's sixty-eight years old."

Jay's quiet chuckle dissolved as the stairs behind him began to vibrate. Before he could yank his face out of the palm tree, David was at the foot of the stairs, his eyes wide with disbelief. Jay sighed, laid a finger against his lips, then returned his attention to the kitchen just as Bethany stifled a yawn.

"No, I don't think anyone will assume you can't get a date if you go by yourself," Bethany muttered, rolling her eyes. "A lot of people go stag to the theater. Hmm? Of course I'm sure. I, ah, read an article in the *New Yorker*." Shifting impatiently, she glanced over her shoulder to look out the kitchen window. "Listen, Roger, I'm kind of in the middle of something. We'll talk later, okay? Right. Have a good time tonight."

With a pained sigh, Bethany replaced the receiver, rubbed the back of her neck and went outside.

David spoke the moment the kitchen door closed. "So how come you're spying on Mom?"

"I wasn't exactly spying," Jay replied lamely, struggling to extract himself from the palm fronds. "I just didn't want to interrupt her conversation with, er, Mr. Morris."

At the mention of his mother's boss, the boy opened his mouth and pretended to gag himself with his finger.

Sensing a potential alliance here, Jay seized the opportunity to elicit a bit more information about the slick insurance salesman who, he suspected, was interested in supplying his wife with something considerably more intimate than a policy and a paycheck. "May I assume that you're not particularly fond of Mr. Morris?"

"He's a dweeb."

"Ah." Bright boy, Jay thought proudly. "But your mother seems to like him."

"Mom likes everyone. She says people up here are friendlier than folks in L.A."

"Are they?"

Offering a loose shrug, David plopped onto a worn brown sofa brightened by doilies. "I dunno. Some are real nice, like Archie and Mr. O'Roarke—that was his cow you almost hit—and Danny Piper's mom, and the lady with orange hair who works at the supermarket. Mostly I think that people just seem friendlier on account of there not being as many of 'em, you know?"

Oddly enough, that made sense. Jay swung his crutch around the chunky maple coffee table, pivoted on his right foot and lowered himself carefully beside his son. "So what do you think of farm life, David?" he asked, laying the crutch on the floor beside the sofa. "Do you like living here?"

"Yeah, it's real cool. There's all kinds of animals and stuff, and ponds to swim in, and lots of roads to ride bikes with my friend Danny, and—'' David bit off the words, angling a wary glance at his father. "I mean, it's okay, but I wish things could be like they were.''

Jay tried to smile, but his cheeks felt like tanned leather. He coughed away the stiffness and slid a reassuring arm around his son's thin shoulders. "It's all right for you to be happy here. I *want* you to be happy.''

"You do?''

"Of course I do. You're my son, and I love you. All I've ever wanted for you, and for Laurel and Nathan, is that you're all safe and happy. So, what about your sister?''

"Laurie?'' David's nose wrinkled in concentration. "She likes the farm, but I think she's kinda scared about starting a new school next week. She's just a kid, you know, and it's, like, hard for her to make friends.''

Jay studied his son's sober face, amazed that a nine-year-old could be so perceptive. Laurel was indeed a quiet, sensitive child, shy to the point of being reclusive and terrified of new situations. The divorce, although difficult for everyone, had been particularly traumatic for his daughter.

"Your sister is going to need a lot of help," Jay said finally. "I know I can count on you to give it to her.''

"I'll take real good care of her,'' David assured him. "On account of you want her to be safe and happy, right?''

"Right.''

"'Cause you love Laurie, right?''

"Right.''

David considered this. "So what about Mom?''

A cautious fission tingled Jay's nape as he studied a loose thread on the hem of his tan shorts. "I'm not sure what you're asking.''

"Do you want her to be happy, too?''

"Yes.''

"And safe?''

"Of course.''

"And that's 'cause you still love her, too?''

The unexpected question, so forthrightly posed, knocked the breath out of Jay. A surge of pure panic tightened his stomach. He felt pinned against the cushions, impaled by his son's guileless gaze. How could Jay answer?

How could he not?

With the decision, cool air rushed into his lungs and a sense of peace settled over him. "Yes, son, I still love your mother. I'll always love her."

David leaned back, satisfied. "Yeah, I figured. So how come you didn't stay married?"

A fat bead of sweat slipped from Jay's brow to douse his eyelid. He blinked it away. "Things happen."

"What kind of things?"

"Grown-up things."

David muttered an explicit and shocking colloquialism commonly used to describe the decor of a cow pasture. Before Jay could respond to the inappropriate language, the boy fixed him with a hard share. "Man, that's so lame. How come you and Mom are always saying *we* hafta tell *you* the truth, but every time we ask you guys something, you're always shining us?"

Jay blinked. "'Shining us'?"

"You know, giving us—" David repeated the cow pasture comment.

Sighing, Jay shook his head. "Do me a favor and don't use that word anymore, okay?"

A mischievous sparkle danced in the boy's dark eyes. "So, you gonna tell me the truth, or what?"

Jay retrieved his arm from the back of the sofa and patted David's knee. "I don't know what the truth is, David. Your mother and I both changed, I guess. Maybe we were each looking for different things out of life. All I really know for certain is that your mom was looking for something she didn't think she could find while we were together."

"And you wanted her to be happy, right?"

"Right."

The boy's mouth scrunched up, and Jay could practically hear his little brain gears spinning. "So, like, if Mom wasn't happy now, you'd do something to fix it, wouldn't you?"

"Well, sure." Jay straightened. "Is something wrong with your mother? Has she decided that she doesn't like living on a farm?"

"Nah. Mom loves it here. Says it's peaceful and pretty."

"Oh." His hopes dented, if not completely dashed, Jay leaned back and forced a pained smile. "Well, that's good."

"Yeah." An unsettling smirk hovered at the corner of the boy's mouth. He stood abruptly, wiping his palms on his jeans. "Well, I gotta do my chores. Wanna come with me?"

Actually, he didn't. "What kind of chores?"

"Oh, cleaning the barn and feeding C.J., stuff like that."

"C.J.?"

"Yeah, Crazy Joe. He used to be my great-uncle's goat, only now he's ours. Thing is, he acts kinda screwy sometimes. Whenever he gets loose, he runs around butting everything until he knocks himself cuckoo. Mom says he's kinda—" David circled his index finger at his temple "—if you know what I mean."

Jay nodded to indicate that he did indeed know what the boy meant.

David snickered, slipping a quick glance toward the kitchen as if assuring himself that they were still alone. "Last week, Mom's boss got stuck in the barn with C.J., and you shoulda heard the commotion. Mr. Morris was hollering and there was all this crashing and thumping and stuff. Then Mom ran over to open the door and whoosh! The guy hauls out like his butt's on fire, then C.J. comes roaring out and, like, chases him all the way to his car. It was too much. You shoulda seen it."

Somehow Jay managed to suppress a grin at the image. He cleared his throat. "I don't suppose you know how Mr. Morris happened to find himself trapped with a lunatic goat, do you?"

David's gaze shifted. "Maybe someone told him Mom was in the barn."

"I see." The grin was just tearing at Jay's lips, making it almost impossible to hold back. He concealed it behind a curled fist. "And why do you suppose the man didn't leave as soon as he realized that there was a mad goat in the barn instead of your mother?"

Decidedly uncomfortable now, David stuffed his hands in his pockets and studied his sneakers. "Maybe the door accidentally got locked or something. Anyway, I gotta go." Yanking his hands out of his pockets, the boy spun around and sprinted into the kitchen. A moment later the back door slammed.

Jay leaned back, tucking his laced fingers behind his head. Here he was, feeling trapped and helpless, stuck in a godforsaken place where cows grazed in the road and a furry, one-eyed menace prowled the house with impunity.

And yet, just as Jay had decided that the only acceptable place for any animal was on his own dinner plate, he'd discovered a perceptive, clearly intelligent and highly astute horned mammal that not only despised his ex-wife's boss, but was also clever enough to display said displeasure in a distinctly direct and, to Jay's mind, highly appropriate manner.

Yes, indeed, Crazy Joe was definitely Jay's kind of goat. He hoped the little guy could find a good home when Bethany finally came to her senses and put this lousy, pumpkin-studded plot of dirt up for sale.

The day that happened, Jay would plant himself on the driveway with a moving van and a map leading home. Then they'd all be together again.

It was just a matter of time. Jay was certain of that. Or at least, he pretended to be certain of it.

Any doubt that his family would someday be reunited was instantly dismissed. Jay dared not recognize those doubts, or give credence to his secret fears. To do so would be tantamount to accepting that Bethany and the children were truly gone, lost to him forever.

As for what Jay had told his son about wanting nothing more than his family's happiness, that was absolutely true.

What Jay hadn't mentioned was his own refusal to believe, or even acknowledge, the possibility that his family could ever be happy without him.

Chapter Three

"Oh, Lord, what's this?" Dropping to her knees, Bethany inspected the discolored punctures dotting her precious pumpkin vines. Lifting a floppy leaf for closer investigation, she was horrified to note a yellowish slime oozing from one of the tiny holes.

Her distressed moan roused Leon from his shady napping spot in front of the house. He trundled over to investigate, poking his pointy nose into the vine for a vigorous sniff. Instantly he whined and backed away.

Bethany's heart sank. "It's bad, isn't it?"

Ears drooping, Leon heaved an empathetic sigh, bellied down and plopped his chin on the damp earth.

"But I just sprayed a couple of weeks ago," Bethany muttered. "That cost a small fortune, and now this... this—" Frowning, she realized that she didn't have a clue what "this" even was.

Poking at the plant, Bethany hunched down for a better look. It was a hole, all right, smack dab in the middle of the vine stem. Since there seemed nothing else to see, she scooted backward, sat on her haunches and wiped her hands on her overalls.

"Something is in there," she told Leon. "It's probably a gross-looking beast with feelers and pinchers and ugly, buggy eyeballs."

Leon raised his head but didn't dispute the ominous pronouncement. Instead, he cocked his head, quietly watching his mistress settle into a dry irrigation furrow and reach for the thick book tucked into the bucket of tools she always carried into the fields.

If not for her *Encyclopedia of Agriculture,* Bethany wouldn't know a cucumber beetle from fusarium wilt, and her poor pumpkins wouldn't have stood a chance. She was no farmer, after all. The sad truth was that Jay had been right about the cactus. She *had* killed it, but she hadn't meant to. It's just that the prickly little guy always looked so dry and thirsty that she hadn't been able to pass by without giving it a drink.

She still felt guilty about having committed cacticide, but despite inexperience and proven dearth of gardening talent, she was nonetheless determined to spare her pumpkin crop from a similar fate. She scrupulously inspected the fields every week, clipping samples of problem areas to review with local experts.

These pumpkin fields were considerably more than a fun hobby—they were Bethany's only hope of avoiding a financial disaster, because when she'd inherited her uncle's farm, she'd also inherited the mortgage he'd taken out to put this crop in the ground.

Fortunately, Bethany was also able to assume the contract Uncle Horace had with a local canning company, which promised to purchase her entire harvest for a fixed rate per pound. During a routine inspection last month, the canner's rep had estimated that the final crop poundage would be high enough to pay off the mortgage with enough left over to double next season's crop by planting barren acreage behind the house.

Assuming, of course, that she could solve her immediate problem, whatever the devil it was. She thumbed through the book, mumbling aloud. "Let's see, here... Wait." Squinting, she shaded the page with her hand, read for a moment, then grabbed a leaf and examined it before letting it snap into place. "No evidence of bacterial disease. That's good, I think."

Leon, seeming unimpressed by the revelation, opted for a quick nap while Bethany continued to flip through page after page of potential pumpkin eaters. Finally a particularly salient paragraph caught her attention. "By Jove, I think I've got it."

Leon opened one eye.

"Squash borers," she told the dog, pulling a small pocketknife from her overalls. "Watch this."

Holding a section of damaged stem in her palm, Bethany carefully slit the stalk and used the tip of the knife to scoop out a white, wormlike larva with a rust-colored bump that she assumed to be the head. She shuddered, dropping the ghastly creature in front of the dog's nose. "I told you it would be ugly."

Leon tilted his head, examining the squirmy little beast with apparent disgust, then stood and lumbered to his shady porch, leaving his mistress to handle the situation on her own.

Heaving a worried sigh, Bethany sat in the dirt, patting a fat little pumpkin. "Don't worry about a thing," she told it with more confidence than she felt. "I'm going to take good care of you, and you are going to repay my kindness by growing big and strong, aren't you?"

The pumpkin just sat there, so Bethany pulled the book onto her lap and glumly reread the encyclopedic segment on squash borers, which according to the article shouldn't even be attacking this late in the season. Apparently that tidbit of information hadn't been shared with the odious chewers that were tunneling through her precious vines.

The good news was that she probably wouldn't have to buy more spray, since pesticides weren't considered effective on larvae buried inside stems. The bad news was that the only suggested control was to individually remove the creatures by searching for bore holes and slitting the stalks, as she'd just done, after which she was supposed to heap a shovel of soil over the damaged area.

All well and good, except that Bethany had nearly ten acres of pumpkins. Even if only a small percentage of the vines were affected, the chore would still take forever.

She wondered if Roger would give her a few days off and decided he probably would. Despite a few aggravating propensities, Roger Morris was actually a very nice person. He was also an astute businessman, so any time off would naturally be docked from her paycheck. No way could Bethany afford that kind of loss. She was barely making ends meet as it was.

There was no choice, she finally decided, but to spend every spare minute rooting out squash borers, even if she had to haul out a flashlight and work all night.

Ignoring the din of explosions and horrid game music emanating from the television, Jay peered out the window watching Bethany toil in the midday heat. She'd been in the fields for hours, crawling through the vines as if inspecting every leaf. Every so often she'd stop, yank something out of her pocket and fiddle with one of the stupid bushes, then toss whatever she'd located into a small white bucket she was dragging through the rows. This odd procedure would be completed by moving a pile of dirt from one place to another, at which time she'd hunch like a prowling cat and start the entire process all over again.

Behind him, the television issued an ominous crescendo, followed by Laurel's gasp of dismay.

"Aw'right!" David chortled. "My dragon ate your knight!"

"You cheated," came the indignant reply. "I'm gonna tell."

"It's a video game, Laurie. You can't cheat on a video game. I'm just better than you."

"No, you're not!"

"Yes, I am."

Jay looked over his shoulder. "If you two don't stop bickering, I'm going to take the game home with me."

Clearly horrified by that possibility, Laurel dropped the game handset and leaped to her feet. "But you *gave* it us! You can't take presents back. It's not fair!"

"It's not fair to reward your daddy's generosity by driving him nuts, either. If you can't play nice with the game—"

"We can," David assured him, pulling his sister to her previous position on the floor. "I'll teach Laurie how to play better, then she won't get so mad, okay?"

Jay smiled. "Sounds like a plan."

Massively relieved, David hit the reset button to start a new game, and Laurel paid rapt attention to her brother's explanation of the furtive thumb movements necessary to control the animated screen creatures.

With harmony restored, Jay pivoted on his crutch and hobbled toward the kitchen door. "I'm going outside for a while," he told the children. "Call me if Nathan wakes up from his nap."

David glanced up. "Don't go into the back pasture," he warned. "C.J.'s tied out there."

"C.J.'s the goat, right?" Jay waited for his son's affirmative nod before asking, "Why is he tied up?"

"Because he's supposed to eat the weeds, only he likes Mom's pumpkins better. You can go say hi to him if you want, but don't let him loose or Mom will kill you."

"Trust me, I'm not about to let him loose."

Satisfied, David returned his attention to the game and Jay went out to the back porch. He thunked awkwardly toward the steps, vibrating the wooden porch planks and apparently disturbing Leon's nap. The dog looked up.

Jay curled a lip him. Leon responded by silently baring his teeth, after which Jay hobbled down the stairs and the dog went back to sleep.

Standing at the base of the steps, Jay gazed around the property, noting that the barn was about fifty yards west of the house, old but fairly well preserved. The huge doors were open, but Jay thought they'd been closed when he'd arrived yesterday.

Beside the barn was a roomy chain-link enclosure complete with water buckets, a feeding trough and an enclosed stall that resembled a huge, flat-roofed dog house. Judging by the size of the chained padlock on the gate, Jay assumed the pen to be old Crazy Joe's place. All in all, fairly nice digs for a goat.

Curiosity propelled Jay toward the back of the house, where he was greeted by a vast pasture overgrown with dry grass and weeds. A fire waiting to happen, Jay thought, eyeing the dead vegetation. This late in the summer, mechanical mowers couldn't be used because the spark of a metal blade striking a rock would ignite an instant inferno. Jay didn't know much about rural living, but he understood that residents frequently kept grazing animals in these wild pastures to nibble down the fuel. Unfortunately, if Bethany was relying on one little goat to make a dent in this thigh-high forage, she was in for a rude awakening.

Shading his eyes, Jay scanned the field. When he finally spotted the animal in question tied to a huge scrub oak, he nearly laughed out loud. From this distance, the bony beast looked like a hairy barrel on stilts, with jackrabbit ears and a pendulous lump drooping beneath its chin. It had been dehorned, which was fortunate if the description of its foul personality was even halfway accurate. At the moment, however, it was chewing benignly, which was, after all, its primary assignment.

Since old C.J. shared his own distrust of Roger Morris, Jay felt a certain affection for the homely creature, and found himself giving it a cheerful wave before heading toward the pumpkin fields that stretched from the front yard to the edge of the road.

Using the graded walking paths between fields, Jay found Bethany scooting between pumpkin hills, nose to the ground and bottom in the air, looking like a denim-clad hound on a blood trail. He stood silently, watching her move between plants, oblivious to his presence as she yanked out each vine stem for a scrupulous inspection.

Suddenly she mumbled something and sat up, reaching into her bib overalls. "Hold still," she told the plant, whipping a penknife out of her pocket. "This won't hurt a bit."

Stunned, Jay watched her expertly slit the stem and scoop out what appeared to be a small white grub, all in one fluid motion. He was amazed, not only by her unexpected proficiency, but by the mere fact that a woman so terrified of insects that she'd once heaved an entire pot of spaghetti at a June bug was now crawling through bug-infested dirt digging slimy white grubs out of pumpkin stems.

"There," she cooed, petting the top of a lumpy orange gourd. "Now, don't you feel better?"

Twisting at the waist, she shook the grub from the knife tip into the white bucket, then froze, staring at Jay's cast. Her face snapped up, and a crimson flush spread between freckles. "How long have you been there?"

"Long enough to hear your reassuring bedside manner," he replied, nodding at the pumpkin she'd been stroking. "I'm surprised you didn't give it an aspirin and put a cool cloth on its head."

"I would, if I thought it could help." Bethany stood, avoiding his gaze as she dropped the folded penknife into her pocket and brushed off her dusty knees. "Are you ready for lunch?"

"I grabbed a sandwich with the kids."

She looked up, startled. "You fed the children?"

Irritated by her stunned expression, Jay was also stung by the unpleasant realization that she had every reason to be surprised, considering he couldn't even remember the last time he'd fixed a meal for their children.

Before the move to this godforsaken plot of ground, the kids had visited Jay frequently, and he'd inevitably taken them to a restaurant or ordered take-out. Now he looked away, embarrassed by the dubious arc of his ex-wife's brow. "I *am* capable of slapping two pieces of bread together, you know."

"With something in the middle?"

He shifted on his crutch, scowling. "Peanut butter and jelly, if that meets with your approval."

"It does." A grateful smile sparkled in her eyes. "Thank you, Jay. I appreciate your help."

Now he really felt guilty. "I can bring you something, if you're hungry."

She glanced into the bucket of squiggly white creatures. "No, thanks. I lost my appetite hours ago."

Jay followed her gaze, wrinkling his nose. "What *are* those things?"

"Squash borer larvae, I think. Disgusting, aren't they?"

"What are you going to do with them?"

"Toss them into the pond and let my catfish have a feast."

Jay's ears perked. "Catfish?"

"Mmm. Fat ones, too. David caught one a couple of weeks ago and made me fry it for supper. Not bad, actually."

"I love fried catfish," he mumbled, salivating at the thought.

"You do?"

"Oh, yeah, especially when it's all crispy and coated with cornmeal."

"I didn't know that." She looked away, gazing pensively across the fields. "That's sad, don't you think? I mean, that two people can spend so many years together and still not know what the other one likes."

Distinctly uncomfortable with the intimate shift in conversation, Jay tried to shrug, but succeeded only in bruising his armpit on the crutch. "So I never mentioned a craving for catfish. So what? Don't make a big deal out of it."

She regarded him, her eyes wide and thoughtful. "Is that what I'm doing?"

"Well, no, not really." He swallowed hard, feeling like a first-class heel. "I mean, it was my fault. If I'd asked for catfish, you'd have fixed it, right?"

A dimple deepened at the corner of her mouth. "Only once, after which time I'd have learned that the little monsters must be skinned with pliers and have spiny whiskers sharper than roofing nails. From that point forward, you'd have been on your own as far as catfish was concerned."

"Even if I'd begged?"

She covered a snort of laughter with her hand. "Somehow, I can't imagine you begging for anything. From what I remember, you even considered the word 'please' distasteful, a sign of weakness never to be uttered by a *real* man."

The comment was accurate enough to be hurtful, so Jay responded by clamping his lips shut and glaring into thin air.

Bethany sighed. "I see you haven't refined your 'this conversation is over' signal. Fine with me. I don't really have time to chat anyway."

The abrupt change in her voice startled Jay, not because it wasn't familiar, but because it was.

A quick glance confirmed that she'd returned to inspecting stems, hunched over the vines just as he'd found her a few minutes earlier. Only now her expression had changed. Tight little lines bracketed her mouth, and ridges of tension puckered between her brows. The lovely brown eyes that only moments ago had been sparkling with humor were now dull, flat and angry.

It was, Jay realized, an expression she'd worn consistently during the final years of their marriage. Until this moment, it had never occurred to him that he might have been the cause of it.

That alarming concept was interrupted by a plume of dust at the mouth of the driveway, diverting his attention as well as Bethany's. She glanced up, wiping her moist forehead with the back of her wrist, then stood to wave at the vehicle that was tooling toward them, a white sedan Jay didn't recognize as a patrol unit until he noticed a county sheriff logo stenciled on the door.

The car pulled up parallel to the field where Bethany was working. A portly deputy emerged, hatless, and glanced around the field, removing his aviator-style sunglasses and hanging the earpiece on the flap of his breast pocket.

"Hey, Archie," Bethany called, pulling off her work gloves. "Can I get you a cold drink?"

"Sounds good," Archie replied, picking his way over the pumpkin plants. "Been a real scorcher, hasn't it?" He emphasized his discomfort by wiping two fingers across his pink forehead, then smoothing the few remaining strands of thin hair striping his otherwise bald scalp. When he reached the walking path, he grinned at Jay, extending a meaty hand. "Well, you're looking better than the last time I saw you. Beth taking good care of you, is she?"

"Real good, thanks." Jay shook the deputy's hand, remembering that the first time he'd seen those twinkling blue eyes, they'd been peering through the cracked window of his twisted Jeep. "Nice to see you again. I don't think I had the chance to thank you for peeling me out of that wreck."

"Lucky I was passing by," Archie said, giving Jay's hand a firm squeeze before releasing it. Shifting his ample weight, Archie crossed his bare arms, propping them on a belly that strained the buttons of his uniform. "So, Beth tells me you're a brother in blue."

"LAPD, twelve years."

"Patrol?"

"Vice."

The deputy winced. "Dirty business, that. Couldn't do it myself. I like dealing with real folks."

Jay nodded, understanding that law enforcement jargon divided the populace into two distinct and separate groups, bad guys—or gals, as the case may be—and real folks. "So did I," Jay agreed, recalling that he'd truly enjoyed traffic patrol early in his career. "But someone's got to sweep out the riffraff, and vice is a stepping-stone up the political ladder, so—" He ended with a shrug, to which Archie offered an empathetic nod.

"Know what you mean, lad," the deputy said. "Started off as a city cop myself, but riding herd on pimps and pushers gave me ulcers and damned near broke up my marriage."

From the corner of his eye, Jay saw Bethany stiffen. So did Archie, who instantly recognized the faux pas and tried to make amends. "Begging your pardon, Beth. I didn't mean any disrespect."

"None taken," Bethany said cheerfully.

Too cheerfully, Jay thought.

"So, what can I get you, Archie?" she asked, tossing her gloves beside the bucket of squirming grubs. "Iced tea, soda or lemonade?"

"Iced tea sounds real fine," Archie mumbled, eyeing the bucket. "What in the devil you got there?"

After Bethany offered a succinct summary of the situation, the old deputy levered on his boot heels, scratching a droopy earlobe. "That's a problem, all right. The farm bureau might be able to round up a work crew to give you a hand."

Bethany shook her head hard enough to vibrate the fuzzy spout of hair tied on top of her head. "I looked into that a few weeks ago, when the fields needed spraying. The hourly rate for a county work crew is ten times what I make at the office. I just can't afford it." A shout caught Bethany's attention. She turned, squinting at the house. "What is it, David?"

The boy was on the front steps, wringing his hands and dancing from one foot to the other. "Nathan woke up," he hollered. "Only Laurie and me didn't hear him on account of the video game, and...well, he sorta got into something he shouldn't have."

Bethany went white. "Oh, good Lord."

Before Jay could adjust his crutch to turn around, she'd sprinted halfway across the field.

"Go on, son," Archie said as Jay slid a glance over his shoulder. "I've got things that need doing, so you scoot and see what that young 'un is into this time."

There was something ominous in the way Archie stressed the phrase *this time*, although Jay was too anxious to give the comment more than a passing thought.

By the time he'd ka-thunked his way into the house, Laurel and David were standing in the living room, wincing at their mother's wail of distress emanating from somewhere upstairs.

"What happened?" Jay demanded.

"Nathan cleaned the bathroom," Laurel explained.

Alerted by his father's perplexed expression, David added, "Nathan really likes bathrooms. I mean, he *really* likes 'em."

Relieved that the situation seemed harmless, if still somewhat confusing, Jay eyed the stairway with trepidation and finally decided that by discarding the crutch, he could balance himself against the handrail and use the walking cast for the purpose it was intended.

That's exactly what he did, although the climb was a bit more arduous than expected. He emerged on the upstairs landing, winded but none the worse for wear, just as a tiny T-shirt flew out of an open door Jay presumed to be the bathroom entrance. A moment later, a pair of little overalls plopped onto the pile, creating an odd cloud of dust.

Jay hobbled down the short hallway, touching the wall to balance himself. He'd just reached the doorway when a pair of training pants whizzed past his knees, joining the growing heap of clothing.

He peeked inside. "Holy cow," he mumbled, stunned.

The entire bathroom, including towels, walls and floor, was coated with gritty white powder. An empty container of baby powder lay in a sink caked with a gloppy wet paste of the stuff. Wads of wet toilet paper clung to everything, with drier sheets looped around the sink, the toilet, the towel racks and heaped inside the tub as if the remainder of the roll had been unwound there.

Perched on the toilet seat was his naked son, grinning and oblivious to the fact that he, too, was smeared with the powder from the bottom of his wiggly toes up to the apex of his scalp.

"Me help Mommy," Nathan announced, seeming immensely pleased with his accomplishment.

Bethany, who was kneeling in the midst of the bedlam, shoveled a pile of toilet paper to one side, pushed a strand of hair out of her face and gave Jay a withering stare. "This is all your fault."

"*My* fault?"

"Absolutely. If you hadn't brought home a bottle of champagne to celebrate your promotion, none of this would have happened."

Since Nathan had indisputably been conceived on the night in question, Jay could do little more than offer a conciliatory shrug. "Can I, uh, do something to help? Or have I done quite enough?"

She slid him a weary glance, softened by the hint of a smile tugging the corner of her mouth. "I suppose you're thinking that half the responsibility is mine."

"Now that you mention it, I don't really recall that you offered much resistance."

Her smile broke free. "None whatsoever. Do you suppose this is my penance for having been such a wanton woman?"

"Nah. It's just Nature's way of livening things up, that's all. If it weren't for kids, think how bored parents would be."

"Boredom," she mused, still smiling. "I've heard that word before. I can't for the life of me remember what it means."

She looked up, meeting his eyes with a smoldering intensity that proved she, too, was remembering Nathan's conception with the same yearning that Jay felt.

They shared the look, and the moment, silently. A familiar heat stirred in his groin. He wanted to hold her again, to kiss her throat and nibble that sweet spot beneath her ear—

The image dissipated as Bethany turned away. "It could be worse, I suppose. Last week Nathan plugged up the sink with clay and turned on the water. That's when I discovered that my bedroom ceiling leaks and learned that plasterers charge more than brain surgeons. Do me a favor and have David bring a trash bag up here, will you? A big trash bag."

Jay licked his lips. "Sure. No problem."

"And a broom, please."

"Yeah, a broom." He blew out a breath, glancing around the chaos and realizing that there was no space for two people to work in the tiny room, even if he was capable of kneeling to scoop up wet toilet paper...which he wasn't. That wasn't to say he couldn't do something to help. He held out a hand to Nathan, who instantly slid off his perch to tuck a tiny hand in his father's large palm. "C'mon, buddy, let's get you cleaned up and give your mommy some breathing room."

Bethany stood, kicking aside a pile of soggy paper wads. "That will have to wait. This is the only tub in the house."

"There's a shower downstairs," Jay pointed out, referring to the facility situated between the sewing room and Bethany's bedroom.

"Yes, but the spray is pretty erratic. If you try to give him a shower, you'll end up soaked yourself, and you can't get—"

"My cast wet. I know. So we'll just have to implement Plan B."

She cocked a wary eye. "Which is?"

"I'll take him out front and hose him off."

Bethany started to protest, then thought better of it. Even if the nearest neighbor hadn't been a mile away, a nude toddler frolicking in his own front yard was hardly a crime. Besides, she could use all the help she could get.

"Go for it," she said, tossing her hands in defeat. "Laurel will show you where his clean clothes are."

Jay grinned at the giggling toddler. "Okay, kiddo, you're in for a real treat."

As they disappeared down the hall, Bethany called out, "Don't forget to scrub the powder out of his hair."

"Got it covered," came the reply.

"And for heaven's sake, don't turn your back on him, or he'll be halfway to town, mooning everyone on the road."

The only response she heard was a peculiar thumping as the two males descended the stairs. Sighing, she scooped up an armful of twisted toilet paper and tried not to think about the squash borers chewing up her bank account.

Forty-five minutes later, the trash bag was bulging and Bethany had finished rinsing the final cleanser bubbles down the sink when she heard the familiar ka-thunk on the stairs.

"Great, you're done," Jay said, poking his head in the doorway. "You'd better come downstairs."

She dropped the broom. "You've lost Nathan."

"Nathan's fine, clean, dry, decently attired, and happily eating a Popsicle."

"Where is he?"

"On the porch."

"Alone?"

A wrinkle of irritation creased Jay's forehead. "David and Laurel are watching him. Now are you going to come downstairs or not?"

"Why, what's wrong?"

"Nothing's wrong," he replied, reaching out to tug her hand. "I just want you to see something."

Her stomach sank. "Did Nathan flood C.J.'s pen with the water hose again?"

Jay stopped, eyeing her strangely. "When did you get so suspicious?"

"The day your youngest son learned how to crawl." Laying a palm over her pounding heart, Bethany took a deep breath. "Okay, I'm ready."

Shaking his head, Jay awkwardly clumped toward the stairs, chuckling. "You know, you're going to give yourself a coronary if you don't stop worrying so much."

"I'm a mother," she muttered. "Worrying is my job."

She followed Jay down the stairs, mentally recounting every potential disaster that could possibly await her. By the time they'd reached the foyer, she was a nervous wreck. Jay opened the front door, grinning smugly, then stood back, gesturing that she should go first.

She hesitated. "Want me to take the first bullet, huh?"

"Oh, for crying out loud."

"Just checking," she assured him, sidling through the door, her skittish gaze scanning the porch. Much to her relief, all three children were safe and sound, seated on the front stoop munching frozen treats.

David looked over his shoulder. "Look, Mom. Isn't this neat?"

"Isn't what—?" The question died on her lips as she glanced at the pumpkin fields, which were crawling with people.

Taking a wobbly step forward, she propped herself on the porch rail and rubbed her eyes. When she opened them again, the people were still there. In the midst of the activity stood Archie Lunt, directing workers like a plantation caretaker.

After a long moment, Bethany tested her voice. "What in the world is going on?"

"As soon as you went in the house, Archie called the station and relayed your situation." Jay hobbled over, joining her at the porch rail. "Apparently the dispatcher got on the phone and called some of your neighbors, who in turn called other neighbors, and so on. By the time I'd finished squirting Nathan off, truckloads of people were driving in armed with buckets and pocketknives. Archie figures the entire field should be larvae-free by sunset."

"Oh."

Jay saw her stifle a sniff with her palm and realized she was blinking back tears. His smile faded, and not because he thought she was sad. To the contrary, her wet eyes were shining with gratitude, her cheeks flushed with sudden joy.

It was her joy that hit Jay like a fist.

Since the divorce, he'd taken solace in convincing himself that Bethany would never be able to make it without him, that she'd never be truly happy unless he was an integral part of her life.

That belief had done more than soothe his ego; it had kept him sane. The certainty that Bethany would come back to him gave Jay a reason to face long, lonely days and agonizing nights.

But he'd been wrong. Now he realized that Bethany *was* happy, happier than she'd ever been during their years together.

The realization broke his heart.

Chapter Four

By midmorning on Sunday, Jay was ensconced on the porch bench swing with his cast propped on the rail, glumly gazing out over the lush acres of pest-free pumpkins. He was quiet and depressed and had been that way since yesterday afternoon when he'd suddenly discovered that the girl he'd loved all his life had evolved into a woman he hardly knew, a woman of strength and commitment and of a courage he hadn't realized she possessed.

The sad fact was that Bethany didn't need him any more. And if she didn't need him, how could he expect her to love him?

Jay understood that he'd been fooling himself. All he held dear—his children, his family, his beloved wife—were lost to him now, gone forever. Life as he'd known it was irrevocably over. It would be difficult to go on.

He would go on, of course. He wasn't a coward, ready to fold because he hadn't been dealt a winning hand. He had a responsibility to be there for his children, and for his children's children. And by God, he *would* be there for them, no matter what the emotional cost. No one would ever know of his pain, or of his struggle with despair.

A real man overcame adversity. A real man controlled emotion. A real man didn't need his wife to make him feel whole.

Then again, a real man never would have lost her in the first place.

The front door squeaked. A moment later, David and Laurel rushed toward the motionless swing. "Hey, Dad, y'know what me and Laurie were thinking?"

Jay forced a smile. "I haven't a clue."

"Well, what with tomorrow being Labor Day, it's kinda like our last day of vacation, on account of we have to start school on Tuesday, so me and Laurie were thinking, um…" David angled a glance at his sister, who'd crossed her fingers and was holding her breath. "We were thinking maybe we could go camping tonight, on account of us not being able to go again, like, for a whole entire year."

Taken by surprise, Jay just sat there, mute, glancing quizzically from David to little Laurel, who apparently took his silence as denial and launched into begging mode. "Please, Daddy. We could set up the tent and sleep out, just like we used to do a long time ago. Remember how you and Davie used to catch fish, and Mommy would cook them on that funny green stove? And when it got dark, we'd all roast marshmallows and sing songs and laugh and have so much fun?" The girl paused for breath, angling a desperate look at her brother.

Recognizing his sister's silent plea, David took over. "The tent and sleeping bags were all packed for the trip, so all we hafta do is take 'em down to the catfish pond and set everything up."

A spark of understanding glimmered in the back of Jay's mind. "The catfish pond behind the house?"

"Uh-huh." Laurel nodded vigorously, then poked her glasses back into place. "There's lots of trees and stuff. We can pretend we're up in the mountains."

"It'll be so great," David insisted, his eyes desperate as he clutched his father's arm. "We can go fishing and roast weenies and everything."

"Yeah, and besides—" Laurel ducked under Jay's propped leg to zip around the swing and flank him. "Nathan hasn't ever been camping before, not in his *whole* life." With her magnified eyes bigger than pie plates, she pinched Jay's hand so hard his fingers throbbed. "This could be his very last chance, and it would be awful if he missed it, just *awful!*"

Jay managed not to laugh. "Nathan's only two, honey. I think he's got a few good camping years left. Besides, your mother would never go along with this."

The children exchanged a telling glance, after which Laurel stared at her feet and David cleared his throat. "Mom thinks it's a swell idea."

That was news to Jay. "She does?"

"She said you like catfish," David replied carefully. "And she said every kid in the whole world deserves to sleep in a tent at least once. Didn't she, Laurie?"

Laurel nodded without looking up.

Jay absently rubbed his bandaged chin. "I don't know, son—"

"Please, Dad!" David lurched forward, and for a moment Jay feared the boy would grab him by the throat. Instead, he simply leaned over until he was nose to nose with his stunned father. "This was supposed to be our weekend with you. It's not fair for it to be all ruined on account of some dumb cow!"

"Well..."

Sensing weakness, David went in for the kill. "Laurie and me will do all the work, honest. We'll set up the tent and carry down the sleeping bags and fishing poles and everything.''

''Well, we certainly have enough bait,'' Jay added, with a rueful glance toward the white buckets of larvae lining the fields.

''So, is it okay?''

In the silence that followed, neither child issued a breath, and Laurel was so rigid, Jay feared her little spine might crack. Finally, he shrugged. ''If it's okay with your mother, it's okay with me.''

The children's tense expressions dissolved with relief. ''Aw'right!'' David hollered, yanking down a fistful of air while his gleeful sister hugged herself. ''C'mon, Laurie. We gotta get started.''

''Thank you, Daddy.'' Laurel swiped a damp kiss across her father's cheek, then dashed across the porch, following her brother into the house.

The children dodged the doily-decorated sofa, then sprinted through the living room and found their mother in the kitchen, preparing to mop the floor.

''Goodness, take a breath,'' Bethany told her winded kids. ''Now, what's all this excitement about?''

''Dad wants to go camping tonight,'' David blurted. ''Down by the catfish pond.''

Bethany couldn't have been more stunned if they'd told her that Jay had ripped off his cast and was leaping hurdles over the barn. ''That's ridiculous,'' she finally stammered. ''He can't possibly be serious.''

''Oh, he is,'' Laurel said somberly. ''He thinks every kid in the whole wide world deserves to sleep in a tent.''

''He thinks *what?*'' Straightening, Bethany flicked her hand as if swatting an insect. ''No, uh-uh, this is not going to happen.''

David leaped forward, squeezing her hand. ''Please, Mom. Tomorrow's our very last day of vacation and this was supposed to be our weekend with Dad. It's not fair for you to make us miss it."

"Not fair at all," Laurel agreed, bobbing her blond head.

Bethany plopped the mop into the bucket, crossed her arms and propped a hip against the counter, wondering exactly when her oldest children had figured out where her strings were and learned to pull them so effectively.

Sucking air into her cheeks, she considered the peculiar request. It wasn't as if Jay wanted to take the children a hundred miles away, after all. The pond was only a few yards behind the house, in the back pasture.

Still, Bethany was concerned about Jay himself. He seemed to be well on the road to recovery, but he tired easily, and she suspected that his ankle hurt more than he'd care to admit. "I'm not sure your father's up to an overnight camp out, even at the catfish pond."

"He is," David insisted. "He's never felt better, honest!" The quirk of his mother's brow clued the boy that he might have taken that a bit far. "I mean, he feels lots better than he did yesterday, and besides, he really *wants* to."

Bethany rubbed her neck. "Well, at least you'd be close enough to come get me if something went wrong."

The children exchanged a telling glance as Laurel cleared her throat. "Dad wants Nathan to come, too."

"*What?*" Bethany extended her flattened palms in a scissored movement, like an umpire's safe signal. "Now this is where I put my foot down. The only way your father could handle Nathan is if he was harnessed and tied to a tent stake."

"But, Mom—"

"No. Absolutely not."

"We, uh—" David coughed into his hand "—kinda figured you could watch Nathan."

"How am I supposed to do that, hang out the bedroom window with a pair of binoculars?" Bethany's dry laugh dissipated at the matching pair of innocent smiles. "Oh, no. I'm not, repeat *not* sleeping in a stupid tent."

"But Nathan's never gone camping before," Laurel whined. "It could be his only chance, forever and ever."

Bethany jammed one hand on her hip. "Now that's a bit dramatic, even for you, Laurie. Nathan will have lots of chances to go camping."

"Maybe not," David intoned with an ominous frown. "I mean, you guys are getting up there, you know?"

"Getting up there?" Bethany touched her throat and felt wrinkles fairly oozing from her skin. "Exactly what are you trying to say?"

Issuing a theatrical sigh, David laid a sympathetic hand on his mother's arm. "It's just that at your age, you never know when stuff is gonna start falling apart. By next summer, your hair might be all white and you might need a cane just to get up the stairs."

Bethany gave her son a withering stare. "At the rate things are going, my hair might be white by tomorrow."

"Which is why," David reasoned, "you hafta go camping tonight, before it's too late."

Bethany was already shaking her head when Laurel abruptly latched onto her waist. "Please, Mommy," she begged as a swell of tears spilled down her freckled cheeks. "Don't you want us to have fun? Don't you love us any more?"

"You know better than that, Laurie."

"But you *love* camping. You used to tell us it was like going to God's house for a visit." A lamentable sob shuddered the child's frail little body. "Please, Mommy. We'll never ask anything ever again. We won't ask Santa for anything and you won't have to buy us birthday presents—"

David's head snapped up. "Huh?"

"And you can keep our allowance for a whole year—"

"No allowance?" David squeaked.

Quelling her horrified brother with a squinty stare, Laurel continued without missing a beat. "And you'll never have to remind us about chores if only you'll let us do this one teensy-weensy little thing."

Bethany felt like a wrung-out rag. The house needed a thorough cleaning, laundry was heaped to perilous proportions, and despite having been rescued by her gracious neighbors, she still had a thousand things to do in preparation for next month's harvest. The last thing she needed right now was the pressure of supervising a quasi camp out with a physically challenged ex-husband.

Then again, the children hadn't spent time with their father in months. After all, they certainly hadn't asked to be uprooted from the only home they'd known and moved five hundred miles from the father they adored. That had been Bethany's decision, one that still pinched her with guilt. After all, she'd gotten what she wanted—or at least what she'd thought she wanted. In that context, a single night seemed a small exchange for the disruption she'd caused in her children's lives, and in Jay's.

Mellowing, Bethany finally closed her eyes and gritted her teeth. "Just one night, understand?"

Laurel tilted her wet face up. "Nathan, too?"

Bethany winced. She could already feel sharp rocks poking into her back. "Nathan, too."

"Yay!" Laurel gripped her mother's waist so tightly that Bethany could barely breathe. "It's going to be so fun, Mommy. We'll sing and tell camp fire stories and be a real live family again."

Bethany stiffened. "Honey, I think you're making something out of this that just isn't there."

But Laurel wasn't listening. She'd already released her mother, skipped across the kitchen and yanked open the back door.

"I'll get the fishing poles!" David hollered, shooting onto the back porch.

"I'll get the sleeping bags!" Tossing her mother a triumphant grin, Laurel dashed out, letting the door slam behind her.

The crafty youngsters slapped a high-five, emitted a whoop of victory and dashed toward the storage shed, while their browbeaten mother watched from the window, trying to swallow the massive lump lodged in her throat. She understood her children's desperate need to recapture happier times from the past. She also understood why it wouldn't, why it couldn't work. They could never go back, never become the loving family they'd once been.

The children didn't understand that now, but they soon would. Then their joyous smiles would fade, and their sweet young hopes would be dashed.

To their loving mother, that seemed the cruelest fate of all.

"*My* bed!" Nathan squealed, flopping backward onto the sleeping bag his mother had just unrolled.

Sitting back on her heels, Bethany crouched around the center pole to flatten the ends of the final bag, which consumed the last few inches of bare tent floor. "This is Daddy's bed," she told the excited toddler. "Yours is the little one here in the middle."

Nathan studied the cartoon-studded flannel, then clamped his tiny lips into a stubborn line. "No want that bed. Want *this* bed."

"Well, little man, we can't always have what we want."

Bethany blew at the damp tendril stuck to the corner of her mouth, wondering for the umpteenth time how on earth she'd ever let herself be talked into this silly excursion. It had taken half the afternoon just to lug all the equipment to a cleared area by the pond known as the beach, then she'd spent another hour hammering tent stakes in sweltering humidity.

Jay hadn't been much help since his cast kept him from assuming the kneeling position necessary for close-to-the-ground work. He had, however, been of serious assistance when it came time to raise the tent, which Bethany judged to weigh more than the average adult rhinoceros.

How *did* she get herself into these things?

Flexing her stiff shoulders, she realized that going along to avoid conflict was a habit ingrained since childhood. Her mother had provided the perfect role model of a helpless female, flitting between expectant family members in an endless quest to meet everyone's needs but her own.

It was a model Bethany was determined not to emulate, and yet she *had* emulated it. For years. Then one lonely afternoon she'd looked into a mirror, and seen her mother's pinched face staring back at her. At that moment, Beth finally realized that she, too, had ceased to be a person in her own right and had become an extension of those she loved most.

It had been the most terrifying instant of her life. It had also been the most liberating.

Or at least that's what she'd thought at the time.

Nathan interrupted the reverie, calling out, "Mommy, Mommy, watch me sleep."

When she glanced over her shoulder, the toddler shimmied between the folds of his father's sleeping bag and squinched his eyes so tightly that his entire face seemed to fold in on itself.

Bethany chuckled, overwhelmed by a surge of maternal love. Nathan was maddeningly mischievous, impossibly hyperactive and endearingly delightful. She absolutely adored him. "Okay, squirt, but sleep fast because Mommy's going to fix hot dogs for dinner."

Nathan faked an ear-splitting snore.

Shaking her head, Bethany stood carefully, ducking her head as drooping canvas brushed the top of her skull. She parted the netted opening, emerging into the makeshift campsite just as Laurel was rooting through a grocery bag beside the ice cooler.

The girl glanced up, frowning and anxious. "Where are the marshmallows? You didn't forget them, did you? We have to have marshmallows or it won't be like camping at all."

"The marshmallows are in there," she assured the nervous child. "Look under the potato chips."

Bending until her head was nearly inside the bag, Laurel yanked out the chips and issued a relieved sigh. "Oh, good. They're the fat, juicy ones."

Straightening, Laurel dropped the chips into the bag and skipped to the edge of the pond, where Jay was teaching David the finer points of pond fishing. So far, Bethany noted that neither fisherman had so much as dampened a hook, although if the tangle of line, lures and other angling paraphernalia were any clue, the final stage of preparation appeared to be at hand.

Jay, seated on a folding wood-and-canvas camp stool, had laid both poles on his lap and was fiddling with the line while his wide-eyed son watched in fascination. "Catfish are bottom feeders," Jay was saying, "so you have to make sure the lead weights are fastened at least a foot from the hook end of the line. That way when the sinker hits bottom, the bait floats up right in front of their fishy little faces."

"Wow," David whispered, with the reverent expression of one to whom the secret of universal wisdom had been revealed in stone. "That's, like, totally awesome. How'd you learn that, Dad?"

Fairly puffing with pride, Jay twisted the bill of his ratty, good-luck fishing cap to shade the back of his neck, then gave his son an affectionate just-between-us-real-men wink. "Dads have to know these things. It's the law."

David accepted that pronouncement with a solemn nod.

From her eavesdropping vantage point, Bethany managed to suppress a tickled snort. David was so much like his father, a contrary combination of imperious humility and cynical naïveté unique, she suspected, to this rare and undeniably exceptional gene pool.

At that moment, David snatched one pole from his father's lap and dug a fat larvae out of a nearby bucket. "I'm gonna catch a monster," he announced. "It's gonna be so big, it won't even fit in Mom's frying pan."

Cocking a brow, Bethany issued a gentle reminder. "Don't forget our agreement, gentlemen. Mom will not cook anything that isn't presented to her already cleaned, boned, skinned and dewhiskered."

"We know," David replied, flinging his line into the center of the two-acre pond. He looked over his shoulder, grinning. "Can we have 'em for supper tonight?"

"Since you haven't caught anything yet, that question may be a bit premature."

"Oh, we're gonna catch some, all right. Dad knows everything about catfish, don't you, Dad?"

Jay managed a sheepish shrug. "I don't like to brag—"

"Sure, you do," Bethany teased. "And what's more, you're exceptionally good at it."

Jay brightened. "Yes, I am, aren't I?"

"World's champ," she assured him. "But be that as it may, anything edible you two manage to coax out of that pond will have to wait for another day to be a guest in my frying pan. Tonight we're having hot dogs. Assuming, of course, I can coerce the green monster into spitting something resembling flame."

The final statement was issued while casting a skeptical eye at the temperamental, two-burner camp stove on which Bethany had prepared more outdoor meals than she cared to remember, most of which had been woefully undercooked or burnt beyond recognition. Usually, she'd considered such cooking arrangements as an enjoyable challenge. Now, however, the primitive appliance seemed a poor substitute for the perfectly good kitchen that was less than two hundred yards away.

But a promise was a promise, so Bethany pumped the propane fuel tank, grumbling, and after a few tries was able to ignite one of the burners. The other remained hopelessly clogged. She was studying the problem when she felt a peculiar tingle on her neck and looked over to see Jay watching her, his eyes soft with memories.

She held his gaze tenderly, sharing his silent reminiscence of happy moments they'd had as a family. Her heart swelled until she feared it might burst, not from happiness, but from regret. This was all an illusion, after all, a temporary game of make-believe conjured by children who were destined for disappointment.

Despite the laughter, the memories and the pretense, the sad truth was that they weren't a family anymore. And never would be again.

"Careful, Nathan. If you don't keep an eye on your marshmallow, it'll melt and fall onto the burner."

Taking his mother's warning to heart, the toddler tightened his two-fisted grip, mesmerized by the bubbling blob of white goo drooping from the tip of a straightened coat hanger.

David, sitting cross-legged on the ground, reached into the bag for his sixth marshmallow. "I don't know why we couldn't have a real camp fire," he groused. "Who ever heard of roasting marshmallows over a stupid stove?"

"It's fire season," Bethany explained for the umpteenth time. "Open camp fires aren't allowed. No, Nathan... here, let Mommy help."

"No want help!" Nathan whipped the hanger away from Bethany's extended hand, flinging the melting goo ball, which flew past his startled father's head to splatter against the tent. The toddler emitted a horrified shriek, dropped the coat hanger in the dirt and would have peeled the sticky mass off the canvas had his father not intercepted him.

As the distraught youngster darted past, Jay looped an arm around the child's fat tummy. "Whoa, tiger. That marshmallow is history. What say we start over with a brand new one?"

"New one?" Lip quivering, Nathan wiped his teary eyes, seeming mollified by the realization that the gummy glob now fused to the tent wall could actually be replaced.

Moments later, Nathan, having charitably accepted his sister's assistance, was happily chewing his first toasted marshmallow.

Bethany sat on the ground, hugging her knees and feeling more content than she had in a very long time. Crickets chirped softly. Darkness cooled the humid air to cottony softness. A sprinkle of shimmering stars peeked between cloud layers, competing with the flickering circle of flame around which the make-believe campers were gathered.

Beside her, Jay settled back in a lawn chair, his plastered leg propped on the ice chest, which had been converted into a temporary resting place for the only catfish the anglers had managed to drag out of the pond.

Thankfully the fish was large enough for a meal, although Bethany doubted that Nathan would partake. After one look at the spiny-faced monster nested in ice, the child had proclaimed it yucky and slammed the cooler lid.

Jay, who'd taken the rejection personally, made a special point of offering his youngest son a biology lesson on the miracle of catfish, expounding their wiles and prowess until even Bethany was convinced the creatures possessed magical powers.

Nathan, however, had listened intently, then waddled off to catch polliwogs in a paper cup.

Jay's crestfallen expression had been both poignant and amusing, although he'd recovered quickly and was feeling jovial enough to lead the children in a rousing sing-along, which Bethany, despite having been saddled with a singing voice Jay once compared to the croak of a dying toad, joined with unbridled enthusiasm.

For a while, the makeshift campsite was filled with music and laughter. Then the stars disappeared and the rumble of distant thunder suggested that it was time to retire.

After the children had been tucked in, Bethany was patting her way through the darkness toward her sleeping bag when Jay let out a curdling bellow and reared up so fast he almost knocked the tent over.

Bethany grabbed a flashlight and aimed the flickering beam toward the far side of the tent, where Jay was thrashing his way out of the flannel folds. "What it is, Jay, what's wrong?"

Muttering under his breath, Jay dragged his cast out of the bag, then flipped the top flap open. "That is what's wrong," he growled, wiggling a finger at the slimy catfish nestled in the center of his sleeping bag.

Bethany groaned, then shifted the flashlight beam to illuminate Nathan's innocent little face. "Fishy sleeping," the child announced.

Somehow, Bethany managed to maintain a calm voice. "I can see that, Nathan. The question is, why is he sleeping in your father's bag?"

Emitting a long-suffering sigh, Nathan adopted the pained tone children are so fond of using with unenlightened adults. "Him was cold."

"Ah." After biting her lip for a moment, she angled a glance at her indignant ex. "It seems your efforts to humanize catfish were more successful than you thought."

Jay was not amused. Grabbing the fish by its tail, he hobbled out to return it to the cooler while Bethany calmed the concerned toddler, explaining that catfish really *like* sleeping on ice cubes.

"Yeah," David added dryly. "'Specially if they're dead."

Bethany quelled her oldest son with a look, then tucked Nathan into his tiny, cartooned bag.

Moments later, Jay returned, still scowling, and flopped down on the outside of his fish-dampened bed. Bethany flipped off the flashlight, and an uneasy hush fell over the darkened tent.

Jay didn't know how long he'd lain there listening to the rhythmic sounds of his sleeping family. Perhaps an hour or more. He wasn't particularly worried about the encroaching thunder, or the fat raindrops that had just begun to beat on wind-whipped canvas. He was worried about Bethany.

She'd changed.

Her lovely skin was tight with constant fatigue, and her eyes, once so soft and nurturing, now held a spark of toughness he'd never seen before.

Perhaps it was simply a manifestation of his own frustration at feeling hobbled and helpless, but Jay couldn't shake the sensation that this strong, independent woman bore little resemblance to the emotionally needy wife he remembered. He wasn't the least bit comfortable with this unsettling evolution, despite a grudging admiration for her tenacity and resourcefulness in dealing with rural problems that were clearly beyond her experience.

Jay tilted his head, listening. He could distinguish between the sounds of his children's slumber and the familiar rhythm of his wife's breath. God, he'd missed that sound. How many nights had he lain awake like this, wishing and praying he'd hear it again? But not like this, not as part of a make-believe game for the benefit of their children.

Still, he was comforted by her closeness.

As he pondered that, he felt an odd vibration in the earth. A moment later, something crashed outside the tent. He jolted into a sitting position and was wondering if lightning had struck nearby when something hit the tent walls with enough force to snap one of the guide wires.

A canvas corner collapsed on Laurel, whose startled shriek woke everyone else.

"The tent's falling down," David screamed.

"We're going to die!" Laurel wailed.

Nathan sat up and burst into tears.

"Shh, everything's fine," Bethany whispered, crawling to calm the terrified children. At that moment there was a loud metallic clanging outside the tent. Bethany's head snapped up. "Did the camp stove blow over?"

"It's not that windy," Jay muttered, hauling his leg around so he could stand up.

David grabbed his flashlight and leaped to his feet to unzip the entrance. He stuck his head outside and hollered. "Oh, my gosh! C.J.'s loose!"

What followed was a chaos of flashlight beams and stumbling bodies struggling to exit the tent. Jay was the last to emerge, whereupon he froze, aiming his flashlight at the furious beast that was indiscriminately head-butting every item in its path.

Bethany dove for a rope handle dangling from the animal's collar, missed and landed face down in the mud. Propping herself up, she called to David. "Watch out!"

David swiveled to one side just as the goat sped past, head down, its flared nostrils illuminated by Jay's flashlight. "Good Lord," Jay mumbled. "That damned goat really is crazy."

"He's not so bad," Bethany said, futilely wiping mud off the front of her sweatshirt. "Apparently he doesn't like thunder. Don't worry. David will catch him."

"If he doesn't catch David first."

Bethany shrugged. "C.J. has knocked a few people over, but he's never really hurt anyone. I guess you could say that his bark is worse than his butt."

"Tell that to the camp stove," Jay said, aiming his flashlight at the crumpled hunk of green metal.

"Oh, dear."

A victorious shout captured their attention. "Got him!"

Jay tottered forward, squinting toward the snarled silhouettes at the edge of the pond. "Careful, son—"

"Oops. Lost him."

The silhouettes parted as C.J. bolted through a tangle of wild berry bushes and made a clean getaway.

"Hold on," Jay called, hobbling a determined path toward his son. "I'll give you a hand."

"No, wait, Jay." Bethany ran up beside him. "Why don't you take Nathan inside the tent? David and I can handle this."

"I'm not completely useless, you know."

"Of course you're not. It's just that—"

A huge hairy shadow came out of nowhere and rammed into Jay's stomach. As he flew backward, he glimpsed the tip of the moon peeking from beneath a cloud a split second before hitting the frigid water with enough force to knock his breath away.

He blinked in surprise. Bethany was on the shore, reaching out to him, screaming his name.

It was the last thing Jay heard before the heavy leg cast pulled him under, and he sank to the bottom of the murky pond.

Chapter Five

"Ninety-nine bottles of beer on the wall, ninety-nine bottles of beer," chimed the back seat choral society.

"Take one down," Bethany croaked happily. "Pass it around—"

"Ninety-eight bottles of beer on the wall," came the baritone finale from the passenger seat.

Picking up the pace, David and Laurel continued the lyrical chant, their voices rising to a piercing crescendo. "Ninety-eight bottles of beer on the wall, ninety-eight bottles of beer!"

"Take one down," Bethany sang, adjusting the rearview mirror. "Pass it around—"

"Ninety-seven bottles of beer on the w-a-all," Jay boomed, thrusting his arms out as if belting out a soul-wrenching aria.

Wincing, David and Laurel waited until their father's heartfelt stanza vibrated into silence before sucking simultaneous breaths for the next round. "Ninety-seven bottles of beer on the wall—"

"You know," Bethany interrupted, frowning, "I'm not sure encouraging children to revere alcoholic beverage in song is proper, parentwise. Why don't we sing about bottles of milk instead?"

David moaned. "Aw, Mom, that's so lame."

"Milk is not lame. It's chock-full of vitamins and minerals and all kinds of good things that are certainly worth singing about." After flipping off her bright beams for a passing car, she angled a glance to her right. "Back me up here, Jay."

"Hmm? Oh, your mother's right, kids. Milk is good for you."

"That doesn't mean we gotta sing about it," David grumbled. "Besides, our ranger troop always sang the beer song on field trips. Sometimes we got all the way down to ten bottles."

Jay leaned over, whispering, "Which explains why the troop leader had a nervous breakdown last year."

"Shh." Issuing a covert glance in the mirror, Bethany lowered her voice. "That had nothing to do with the boys. It was the corporate embezzlement charge that pushed the poor man over the edge."

Chuckling, Jay straightened in his seat, glancing toward the slumbering toddler slouched in his car seat. "I can't believe Nathan can sleep through this bedlam."

"Nathan could sleep through a tornado," Bethany mumbled, steering onto the familiar gravel drive. "Fortunately, he can spend what's left of the night in his own bed. We're home."

Unsnapping her safety belt, Laurel lurched forward and poked her upper body over the console between the front bucket seats. "But what about our camp out? You promised we could sleep out *all night long*."

"Yeah, Mom," David added, reinforcing his sister's argument. "It's not raining anymore, and C.J.'s locked in the barn, and Dad's got himself a brand new cast, so why do we hafta sleep in the house?"

"Because the tent is nothing but a collapsed heap of canvas, and since the sun will be up in another two hours, I consider the night to be officially over." She pulled up in front of the farmhouse and turned off the ignition. "Besides, I think it's only prudent to keep your father as far away from the pond as humanly possible. Even if his poor leg could tolerate the trauma of a third cast in as many days, I don't think the emergency room staff bought that tired old 'goat butts man into pond' story."

"They did when they found a polliwog in the old cast," Jay pointed out. "As for those—pardon the pun—fishy stares you were getting, I hastened to assure everyone that our divorce was amicable, and that you had pulled me out of the pond, not pushed me in."

"Did they believe you?"

"Let's just say that the nurse was looking at you when she asked if I wanted to press charges against, ahem, the goat."

"Oh, swell." Bethany shoved the door open, exited and rounded the van to the passenger side, where David and Laurel were piling out, still complaining. "Run upstairs and get ready for bed."

The children complied, albeit unhappily, and Bethany entered the van to remove the sleeping toddler from his car seat. Nathan stretched sleepily, grumbling, then pressed his face against his mother's shoulder and drifted back to sleep.

As she emerged from the van, Jay extended his arms. "Let me take him."

She hesitated, eyeing his cast. Both crutches had been discarded, and she had to admit he'd been walking fairly well without them, but she was still nervous about handing over the sleeping child. "Are you sure you can manage? There are stairs involved, you know."

"Hey, I've got this thing down to a science." He bent to tap the plaster as if the gesture would somehow convince her. Straightening, he reached out again, eyes softening as he gazed at the bundle of slumbering innocence that was his son. "Please. I promise not to drop him."

After a brief pause, Bethany laid the sleeping child in his father's arms.

Tenderly cradling his son, Jay kissed the baby's silky cheek, then turned carefully and carried him up the steps. Bethany opened the front door for him, then followed closely enough to steady him if he should falter.

But he didn't. Ascending the stairs with a gait that was firm, if slightly awkward, Jay tucked Nathan into bed, turned out the light and met Bethany in the hall. Together, they went into David's room, then Laurel's, and after all their children were safely nested into their own little beds, Jay and Bethany went downstairs.

"Do you want something to drink?" Jay asked as Bethany passed the sewing room heading toward her bedroom.

She paused at the doorway. "All I really want is some sleep."

"Oh."

Touched by his disappointment, Bethany leaned against the doorjamb. "I take it you're too wired to sleep?"

"I suppose so."

Rubbing the back of her neck, she blinked her grainy eyelids and stifled a yawn. "You've always been a night owl."

"Hazard of my profession," he confessed with a smile that was, Bethany thought, oddly sad. "I've been on second shift for so long I don't even get tired until sunrise."

"Yes, I remember." She glanced away, recalling a thousand lonely nights waiting for the telephone to ring, waiting for that horrible moment when a strange voice would announce that her husband had been killed in the line of duty.

In the line of duty.

God, she hated that phrase. And what did it really mean? That a dead hero was better than a live husband and father? That a policeman had a duty to his job, but not to his family?

According to the force, that's exactly what it meant. Jay had once told her that a good cop was married to his job.

Any woman with an ounce of sense would have been threatened by that. Bethany, however, had thought it terribly romantic. She'd imagined her swashbuckling man of valor donning a blue uniform to sweep the city clean, protecting life, liberty and the pursuit of happiness for thousands of grateful inhabitants. Even the police motto, To Protect and Serve, sent goose bumps up her spine.

During her formative adolescence, Bethany had dreamed of their future together, envisioning herself in a gingham apron as she ran to greet her happy husband at exactly 5:00 p.m. He, of course, would rush into her arms with triumphant tales of his day, stories of having rescued lost children and rushed pregnant women to the hospital.

Bethany had conveniently pushed away thoughts of muggers and bank robbers, and in her sheltered naïveté, had never even heard of the pimps and pushers and prostitutes inhabiting the sordid, seamy world that would eventually hold her husband captive, altering him forever.

Distracted by melancholy memories, Bethany didn't notice Jay moving closer until she felt a caress on her cheek.

She looked into his soft eyes, now dark with sensual promise. His fingers moved along her jaw, brushing aside wild spirals of still-damp hair clinging to her skin. His touch seared her, heating her inner core with a sense of peace and belonging that she'd never expected to feel again.

As Jay's palm gently cupped the back of her head, Bethany laid her cheek on his shoulder, melting against his strength. She could hear the reassuring pulse of his heart beating below her ear, feel his masculine warmth seeping in to fill the emptiness of her soul. She embraced him, sliding her arms around his lean waist to hold him close, as if her desperate grasp could recapture an elusive moment in time, a moment long past and forever mourned.

Jay touched her hair with his lips, then slipped his thumb under her chin, urging her to look at him. When she did, he kissed her, slowly, deeply, with aching sweetness.

Something cracked deep inside her, shattering like brittle glass and allowing a gush of liquid warmth to reawaken long-dormant emotions. She loved him; she needed him; she wanted him.

But she wanted all of him, his heart, his soul and his mind, things that were no longer his to give. He'd already committed them to his career, to a life she couldn't share and was too selfish to accept.

Turning her head, Bethany ended the kiss and broke the fragile bond between them. She placed her palms on his chest in symbolic withdrawal, although she didn't physically step away.

His muscles stiffened beneath her fingers, then quivered as he emitted a quiet sigh and nested his cheek in her hair. "What happened, Beth?" he whispered. "What went wrong with us?"

She closed her eyes for a moment. "We grew up."

"You don't believe that."

Hurt by his scolding parental tone, Bethany extricated herself from his embrace and stepped aside. With a safe distance between them, she steadied herself against the wall and spoke without looking over her shoulder. "If it soothes your conscience, I'm willing to accept full blame for the deterioration of our relationship."

"I'm not looking to place blame, Beth. I just want to understand."

She shrugged. "The truth is that I never really knew what it meant to be a policeman's wife, Jay. I simply couldn't cope. That was my failure, not yours."

In the stunned silence that followed, Bethany found the courage to turn and face him.

Jay stared at her for a long moment before speaking. "My father was a cop, and his father before him. Following them onto the force was all I ever wanted. You knew that. You've always known it."

"Yes, I knew it. I just didn't know what it would mean for me."

An angry spark lit his dark pupils. "What it meant for you was food on the table and a sturdy roof over your head."

"I don't want to fight, Jay."

"We're not fighting," he snapped while a muscle below his ear twitched wildly. "We're having meaningful conversation. Isn't that what you've always wanted, what you were always harping about? 'Talk to me, Jay. Tell me about your day.'" The twitching muscle nearly leaped off his face. "What in hell was I supposed to say, that I'd spent a hellish night holding a fifteen-year-old runaway's hand while she died of a drug overdose? Or did you want to hear about the twelve-year-old boy who'd rather sell his body to chicken hawks than go home and risk being beaten to death?"

"Jay, please." Bethany clutched her turning stomach, swallowing the vile surge that rose in her throat.

His anger instantly dissipated. "I'm sorry, baby. I never meant to upset you."

She backed away from his outstretched hand, holding her palms up as shields.

Jay's hand dropped to his side for a moment, quivering when he finally raised it to wipe his face. He shuddered once, then leaned against the wall, staring at his shoes before lifting his gaze to meet hers. "Forgive me, Beth. I had no right to say those things. You can't possibly understand that kind of inhumanity and horror, and I don't want you to understand it. I don't even want you to know it's out there.''

Bethany shook her head, realizing that he'd missed her point entirely, but unwilling to expose herself by attempting to clarify her meaning. Jay would never believe that despite being deeply affected by the horror he'd described, she wasn't the guileless schoolgirl he remembered. It wasn't Bethany's inability to understand human depravity that was at issue; it was her inability to accept the changes that dealing with such depravity had wrought on Jay himself.

''It's late,'' she said dully, hoping to end the unpleasant conversation.

Jay stepped forward to block her way. ''We can fix this, Beth. I'll do whatever it takes to make you happy.''

Blinking back tears, she raised her chin. ''Would you quit the force?''

He looked as if she'd struck him.

She sighed, wiping air with her hand as if the gesture could erase her foolish words. ''Forget I said that. It was cruel and stupid. I didn't mean it.''

As she spun toward the bedroom, Jay laid a hand on her shoulder. ''Please, I meant what I said. We *can* fix this. All you have to do is come home.''

A shiver rippled down her spine. Suppressing an urge to brush her cheek across his knuckles, she forced herself to meet his gaze. ''I *am* home.''

Then she went into her room and wept.

''Here's where he went over,'' Jay said, pointing to fresh hoofprints in the mud outside C.J.'s pen. ''Either he managed to get onto the roof of the lean-to and jumped from there, or he can do a five-foot leap from a stationary position. Either way, we've got a problem.''

"Aw, man." Kicking a pebble, David crossed his arms, staring glumly from the empty pen to the field behind the house, where the goat was tied beside a water bucket, enjoying a weed breakfast. "If Mom finds out C.J. can get out any time he wants, she'll sell him for sure."

"Not necessarily." Jay straightened, eyeing the pen's proximity to the barn. "If we can rig some bracing, we might be able to lay a chicken-wire ceiling over the entire pen. Then the only way that goat will get out is with a pair of wire cutters."

David considered that. "I dunno. Chicken wire is, you know, kinda flimsy. C.J.'s got real strong teeth."

"Granted, but to chew through the ceiling wire, he'd have to get to it. If we add some cleats to the barn wall, about eight feet above the lean-to roof, we can stretch the enclosure well above his reach."

A spark of enthusiasm flickered in the boy's dark eyes. "You think?"

"It's worth a try." Pushing back the bill of his cap, Jay gazed toward the house from which Bethany had just emerged lugging a basket of wet linens.

She hesitated on the porch, glancing toward the goat pen, only to look quickly away when she saw Jay watching her. Shifting her load, she hurried down the steps to an umbrella-shaped clothesline not far from the kitchen door and proceeded to hang sheets without another glance in Jay's direction.

David's worried gaze skittered between his parents. "Are you and Mom mad at each other?"

"Hmm? Oh, no, son. We're not mad."

"Are you sure? You guys have been, like, acting weird all morning."

Denial teetered on Jay's lips, but couldn't emerge because his teeth were so tightly clamped that his jaw ached. He forced his tense muscles to relax, managing what he hoped was a reassuring smile. "Your mom is just tired, son.

She only got a couple hours sleep last night, and now she's working hard trying to get your clothes ready for school tomorrow.''

At the reminder, David brightened. "Oh, yeah. School."

"Are you looking forward to it?"

"Sure! Mom took us to look at our new school a few weeks ago. It's really neat, with lotsa trees and basketball courts and stuff. Mom's gonna drive us tomorrow, but after that she says we can ride the bus with all our new friends. That's gonna be so cool."

Jay laughed, as pleased by his son's enthusiasm as he was concerned by his daughter's lack of it. Poor Laurel was terrified that no one at the new school would like her and feared spending the rest of her life languishing at the edge of the playground, friendless and alone.

Unfortunately, that was all too possible. Laurel was tremendously shy around new people. Always a timid child, she was further hampered by her poor eyesight and self-conscious about the thick glasses she'd worn since the tender age of three.

There was no doubt that tomorrow would be a tough day for his daughter. Jay wished there was something he could do to make it easier—

Bethany's voice broke the thoughtful silence. "David!" she called, ducking under the flapping drape of sheets as she hoisted the empty laundry basket under her arm. "I need you to do me a favor."

"Sure, Mom."

Although Jay hadn't been invited, he followed as David loped across the yard.

"I have to take Laurel into town to pick up some things she needs for school," Bethany told the boy without sparing her ex-husband a glance. "Nathan's taking a nap, so I'd like you to stay in the house until he wakes up."

Jay cleared his throat. "I can do that."

"I'm also expecting Mr. Morris to call," Bethany added without acknowledging Jay's offer. "I'm supposed to meet him in Sacramento first thing tomorrow morning for a breakfast meeting. If he calls while I'm gone, I need you to write down the address exactly as he gives it to you, okay?"

David, whose expression had soured the moment he heard Morris's name, assured his mother that he'd take the message, after which Bethany gave the boy a grateful smile and returned to the house.

Jay jammed his hands into his pockets, glaring at the back door through which she had disappeared.

David slid his father a slitty-eyed stare. "So, Mom's not mad at you, huh?"

"Oh, hush."

"What'd you do, anyway?"

"Nothing." Frustrated, Jay pivoted on his cast and hobbled toward the goat pen with his determined son dogging his heels.

"Maybe she's mad about, you know, you falling in the pond and everything."

"She's not mad," Jay said, teeth gritted, knowing that Bethany was quite clearly fried about last night's pitiful attempt to win her back. Not that he was willing to give up, of course. He just had to come up with another tactic, something a bit more, well, subtle. "I told you, David, your mother is simply tired. She's just working too hard, that's all."

"Mom always works hard," David insisted. "But she hardly ever gets mad."

"She's *not* mad!" Jay yanked his hat down, avoiding his son's reproachful gaze. "Hand me that tape measure, will you?"

Spotting the requested item in the mud beside a scattering of other tools, the boy scooped it up and plopped it in his father's outstretched hand. "You didn't make fun of her pumpkins, did you? Mom really likes her pumpkins."

"Oh, for—" Heaving a pained sigh, Jay focused on his son's somber face. "If you must know, I tried to talk your mother into coming back home, okay?"

David's eyes widened. "Uh-oh."

"Would that be so terrible? Coming home, I mean."

"Not really, only Mom hates living in the city."

A sick sensation settled in the pit of Jay's stomach. Over the years, Bethany had occasionally mentioned moving to the country. Once she'd gone so far as to bring home a stack of real estate magazine listings of rural properties. Jay hadn't bothered to look at them.

It wasn't that he hadn't cared. He simply hadn't taken her seriously, assuming the country-living thing to be a phase she was going through. After all, Bethany had been born and raised in Los Angeles. So had Jay, but if he'd realized how much moving had meant to her they could have looked for property outside the city, perhaps in the Chino area. It was a long commute into downtown, nearly two hours in peak traffic, which would have been difficult for Jay, but not impossible. Certainly he'd have considered such a move if he'd only known that's what she wanted.

Then again, he *had* known. She'd told him repeatedly. He'd simply chosen not to hear her.

"Mommy, can I wear this for school tomorrow?" Laurel held the flower-print jumper under her chin, using her free hand to smooth the ruffled bodice. "It's my very favorite."

Bethany glanced up from a sink filled with bubbles and dirty dishes to study the garment. "I think that would be lovely, Laurie, and you can wear that pretty white T-shirt with it, the one with the snap pockets."

The girl frowned, suddenly unsure. "Do you think it's too prissy?"

"Prissy?" Turning away from the sink, Bethany wiped her soapy hands on her apron, biting back a grin. "Now where on earth did you get an expression like that?"

She shrugged uncomfortably. "At my last school, there was this boy named Bobby who always called me Prissy Missy. He said only babies wore ruffly stuff."

"Oh, he did, did he?" Smiling, Bethany bent to hug her worried daughter. "Know what I think? I think Bobby teased you because he liked you."

"That's silly," Laurel muttered, flushing furiously. Tucking the jumper neatly under her arm, she squared her little shoulders and turned to leave, only to pause at the kitchen door. "Uh, Mom?"

"Yes, dear?"

"Is, uh, my white T-shirt clean?"

"Yes, dear."

Her freckled face split into a happy grin. Spinning around, she skipped through the living room, humming, and went upstairs.

A moment later, Bethany heard the living room sofa squeak. A soft canine growl was followed by a matching human one, after which a familiar ka-thunking sound moved toward the kitchen. Tensing, she continued to wash the dinner dishes, and when the sound stopped, she knew without looking that Jay was standing in the doorway.

"Do you need any help?" he asked.

"No, thanks. I'm almost done."

"Oh." Two more ka-thunks were followed by the scratch of wooden chair legs on linoleum. "Dinner was good."

"I'm glad you enjoyed it." After rinsing the final pot, Bethany laid it in the drainer and glanced around the spotless counter, looking for something else to clean. Seeing nothing, she finally drained the dishwater, washed down the sink and fortified herself to face her ex-husband, who was seated at the table.

Pasting on a pleasant but distant expression, she removed her apron and hung it on a hook beneath the sink cupboard. "David told me about your plan for C.J.'s pen. It's very clever."

"It ought to work well enough," Jay said, folding his arms on the table. "And the materials will be cheap, too."

"Labor isn't." Bethany leaned against the counter, hesitant to join Jay at the table because, well, she simply couldn't trust herself to get within touching distance. "I'll make a few calls tomorrow, and get a couple of bids for the job. Maybe it won't cost as much as I think."

Jay lifted his shoulders. "I figured David and I could handle it."

"Excuse me?"

Shifting restlessly, he raked his fingers through his hair, seeming surprised and a little hurt by her incredulous expression. "Well, sure. I mean, it's not much of a project. Hammer a few cleats and braces, then stretch the wire and fasten it down. We should be able to finish the whole job in a single afternoon."

She shook her head. "No, absolutely not. There's no way you can safely climb a ladder with that cast."

"Sure I can. After I make a snap brace for the legs, that ladder will be a sturdy as stairs. I have it all planned out."

"It's much too dangerous. I forbid it."

"Forbid?"

Jay's shock was evident. In all their years together, Bethany had never used that word, nor any like it, when speaking to her husband. She'd never contradicted him, never given him anything akin to an order, and she'd certainly never taken the liberty of informing him what he could or could not do.

For a second, Bethany thought he might rear out of the chair like a furious phoenix. Instead, he simply stared at her. After a long moment, a smile tugged the corner of his mouth. "You're right, of course. Maybe I'd better go back to my nice, safe little job."

The irony of that statement wasn't lost on Bethany, who instantly felt her face heat. Obviously a man whose career was fraught with desperate life-and-death situations wouldn't consider a weekend construction project to be a particularly hazardous activity. Such a man would, in fact, be amused by the notion.

She tossed up her hands. "Okay, fine, do whatever you want. David is perfectly capable of calling an ambulance, but don't come crying to me when you end up with *both* legs in a cast."

"No crying," he vowed solemnly, holding up his palm in a silent salute. "And when the job has been completed to perfection, apologies will be graciously accepted."

"Apologies for what?"

"For having doubted my ability."

Bethany covered her mouth to stifle a snorting giggle. "I've never doubted your ability, only your judgment."

"Ouch." Looking pained, Jay yanked an imaginary dart out of his chest. "You're a cruel woman."

"So I've been told." Glancing away, her gaze fell on a yellow scrap of paper taped to the refrigerator. Her smile faded at the reminder that she had to drive to Sacramento tomorrow, a trip that always made her nervous.

Jay followed her gaze. "Is that the message David took for you?"

"Yes." She licked her lips. "David forgot the name of the restaurant, but he wrote down the address, so I suppose I'll find the place."

Although Jay's nod seemed affable enough, Bethany took note of the telltale twitch of his jaw. "It seems a little odd that you'd have to go all the way to the city for a meeting when there are plenty of restaurants in Grass Valley."

"Apparently the client—or should I say potential client—owns a business in the downtown area. Roger says that corporate accounts must be wooed in their home territory."

Jay's frown indicated that he hadn't cared for the analogy. "I don't like the idea of you making that long drive by yourself."

"Well, it can't be helped. Roger spent part of the weekend in Fresno working on some deal or another, so he'll be driving up from there. We'll meet in Sacramento, have the stupid meeting and be back at the office before lunch."

"I could go with you."

Taken aback by the unexpected offer, Bethany stared in astonishment. "Why on earth would you want to do that?"

He shrugged. "In case you have a flat tire or something."

"I have an auto club card," she reminded him without pointing out that in light of his current physical restriction, he probably wouldn't be much help in the tire-changing department. "Besides, I doubt you'd be comfortable sitting in the car for hours."

"You mean you wouldn't even invite me into the restaurant?"

"Oh, for goodness sake. This is not *my* meeting, Jay, it's Roger's, and how on earth could I possibly justify an ex-husband tagging along?" Bethany cocked her head, regarding him thoughtfully. "You're not worried about being left alone tomorrow, are you?"

"Me?" He touched his chest, issuing a strained laugh. "Surely you jest. Why, there's not another soul in this world more capable of taking care of himself than I am. In fact, since Nathan will be in day care and the older kids off at school, I'm looking forward to a little peace and quiet, not to mention the thrill of having the television remote all to myself. I've always wanted the chance to get hooked on a soap opera."

"Sounds a little boring, if you ask me."

"Well, I didn't ask you." Awkwardly pushing away from the table, he hopped and heaved himself into an upright position. "I'll have you know that I've got a million things to do, not the least of which is calling the slow-motion garage to find out when my car will be ready."

"You might as well save yourself the aggravation," Bethany said. "I can tell you right now that the garage has been closed for the entire Labor Day weekend, so they won't even look at your car until tomorrow. In addition, the mechanic told me last Friday it would probably take days to track down all the parts they need, so you might as well spend the week relaxing and letting yourself heal."

"Well, darn." Jay sat down, eyeing her with what appeared to be a thoroughly satisfied expression. "I guess you're stuck with me for a while, huh?"

"I guess I am," she murmured, feeling an odd combination of relief and anxiety.

After running five hundred miles to escape temptation, Bethany couldn't suppress a surge of joy now that said temptation was residing under her roof. It was the joy that terrified her.

Chapter Six

"*But wait! Order now, and you'll also receive—*"

Click. "*Of course I love you, darling. I promise we'll be together as soon as my wife comes out of the coma—*"

Click. "*And the final question, for ten thousand dollars and a brand new automobile—*"

Click. "*Body-piercing transvestites—just plain folks or moral menace? Stay tuned—*"

Click.

Turning off the television, Jay tossed the remote on the cluttered coffee table, hobbled across the living room avoiding a clutch of colorful toddler toys and a wadded pajama bottom, and wandered into the kitchen. He passed the table, stained by spilled milk and strewn with sticky cereal bowls. Other than the crunch of a few stray flakes under his feet, the room was unnervingly quiet.

He stood in the deserted kitchen for a moment, then hobbled to the living room and retrieved the remote, turning the TV back on and flipping channels until he found a rerun of an old Western series he'd loved as a kid.

Ten minutes later, when the series credits rolled across the screen, Jay's thumb twitched over the channel button again. And again, and again, and again.

Well, hell, he thought. This relaxing stuff certainly wasn't what it was cracked up to be. A glance at his watch confirmed the worst. It was only ten o'clock, less than three hours since Bethany had rushed out the door on her way to drop Nathan off at day care, take the older kids to school, then fight rush-hour traffic all the way down the hill into the bustling heart of downtown Sacramento.

She'd promised to call home at lunchtime, just to assure Jay that she was okay and back in Grass Valley. Meanwhile, he had to figure some way to kill a couple of hours or he'd go stark, raving mad.

Having studied the inside walls until he was sick to death of them, Jay wandered out to the front porch, where Leon welcomed him with bared teeth and an irritated growl.

Jay glowered at the dog. "Give it a rest, you ugly, one-eyed mutt. Go bury a bone or something."

Leon pleated his muzzle, snarling and snapping air, but instead of joining the challenge, Jay ignored it. After a moment, Leon issued a disappointed whine, plopping his chin on his paws while Jay limped down the steps and wandered toward the goat pen.

He studied the enclosure for a few minutes, envisioning the completed project. He wished he could start on it now, but he didn't have the materials yet, and besides, despite his assurance to Bethany, Jay knew he'd have to wait until David could help him.

A glance at the rear pasture revealed that C.J. was relaxing in the shade, enjoying a respite from his weed-eating duties. Jay waved at C.J., calling out a cheery good-morning without noting that a conversation with a goat was probably indicative of severe social deprivation.

Then again, who'd ever know?

It wasn't as if anyone was around to hear him, unless one considered a thousand lumpy orange gourds an appropriate audience. Which Bethany no doubt would, since she treated those damned pumpkins as if they were fat little people.

Jay ambled to the edge of the fields, eyeing the pumpkins with a twinge of irrational jealously. Not only did Bethany spend more time talking with the stupid things than she did with him, she also showed them more affection than she'd shown him in years.

He grudgingly conceded, however, that it hadn't been entirely her fault. The few hours he'd spent at home after his transfer to the vice squad had been spent sleeping or ignoring Bethany's rambling litany of household problems.

Still, their life together hadn't been all that bad. There had been good times, too, lots of them. Jay couldn't fathom why Bethany had been so unhappy that she'd prefer a godforsaken wilderness where a person couldn't even pick up a loaf of bread without driving twenty-five miles to a block-long strip of buildings that was charitably considered a town. The fact that she loved living here was yet another indicator of just how much she'd changed.

Or perhaps of how little Jay had truly understood his wife in the first place.

Unsettled by that thought, Jay ambled to the house, wondering if he could speed up the passing hours by dragging out the kids' video game. Once inside, however, he couldn't bring himself to do so. It seemed so ... well, desperate.

Instead, he wandered to the sewing room and managed to kill an hour rearranging the few clothes he'd brought with him first by color, then by style. He was pondering whether he should switch the futon linens so he could sleep with his head pointing south instead of north when his eye fell on the lamp table he used as a nightstand and realized that Bethany hadn't set out his pain pills since Sunday morning, when he'd made such a big deal about not needing them any more. He glanced around and realized that the pill bottle was nowhere in sight.

Of course, he didn't really need the medication. Still, he really should know where the pills were, just in case. A glance at the clock confirmed that it was almost noon. Bethany should certainly be in the office by now.

Relieved by having concocted a semilegitimate excuse to call, Jay hurried to the kitchen and dialed the office number Bethany had posted by the phone. After a moment, a friendly female voice answered. "Morris Insurance Agency, may I help you?"

"Beth Murdock, please. This is her, uh, husband."

There was a strained pause. The woman mumbled something that sounded like, "One moment, please," then apparently covered the receiver with her hand, because all Jay could hear was whispered conversation.

A second later, Roger Morris picked up the line. "Jay, old chap, how are you feeling?"

Jay squeezed the receiver so tight his knuckles went white. "Just ducky," he snapped ungraciously. "Where's Beth?"

"I'm, ah, not sure."

A sick thud landed in the middle of Jay's chest. "What the hell is that supposed to mean?"

"Actually, I just got into the office myself. I was hoping Bethany would be here, since she never showed up at our meeting this morning."

"What?"

"Apparently she called in a couple of hours ago, saying she couldn't find the restaurant and wanted to confirm the address she had, which was, oddly enough, totally incorrect. The receptionist relayed the proper location, and that's the last anyone has heard from her."

"Oh, my God." Jay rubbed his face, feeling as if he was about to keel over in a dead faint. "She could have had an accident, been mugged . . . dear Lord, she could have been car jacked! We've got to call the police, issue an APB, put out missing person flyers—"

Roger interrupted with maddening logic. "Now, now, old man. That all seems a bit premature, don't you think? Bethany's a bright, capable woman. She probably just missed us at the restaurant and stopped for a quick bite before driving back up the hill."

"But—"

"I'm sure she'll be popping into the office any moment now," Roger continued smoothly. "I'll have her ring you up as soon as she gets in. Nice chatting with you."

"Wait!" Jay screamed at the dial tone buzzing in his ear. "Don't you dare hang up on me, you pompous—" Biting off the final insult, he slammed down the phone, his brain swirling with dread. Bethany was missing.

Missing.

He spun around, hobbling at top speed toward the front door. He'd have to find her, that's all. He'd drive every damn street in the city—

Except that he didn't have a car. He skidded to a stop and stood there, sick at heart. He was trapped, completely helpless, while the wife he adored more than life itself was God knows where, maybe kidnapped, maybe even dying.

There were no words to describe the terror Jay felt at that moment. His mind was swimming, swirling to another time, another place.

An image enveloped him, the memory of Bethany's terrified dark eyes. "I've been frantic, Jay. You were supposed to be home hours ago."

"Something came up," he'd replied in a flippant tone that in retrospect made him cringe.

He recalled her lip quivering with emotion. "Couldn't you have at least called? I was scared to death—"

"Look, I'm home now, all right?" he'd growled, ignoring her hurt expression. "I'm tired, and I'm not in the mood for another one of your interrogations."

Jay remembered turning his back on her and stomping away, filled with righteous indignation that she'd dared question his right to do what he pleased, when he pleased. He also remembered suppressing a twinge of regret that he hadn't told her about the deadly traffic accident that had sent every cop in the precinct scurrying into overtime.

At the time, Jay had assumed he was protecting Bethany from the ugliness of envisioning the bloody scene. Now he realized he'd simply been protecting himself from having to relive it.

But he hadn't understood the depth of her concern or the extent of her fear. He hadn't understood how her stomach must have tightened into a knot of pure, unadulterated terror. He hadn't understood Bethany's pain and worry and dread that something terrible might have happened to him. He simply hadn't been capable of understanding it.

Until now.

The next two hours were the most horrifying of Jay's life. He called the California Highway Patrol to describe Bethany's car and ask if such a vehicle had been involved in an accident.

It hadn't.

Then he called the Sacramento County Sheriff's Department to see if there was a crime report with a victim matching Bethany's description.

There wasn't.

He also phoned every hospital in three counties, and was fortifying himself to use his police credentials to check the county morgue when the telephone rang.

Snatching up the receiver, Jay screamed hello three times before the caller had an opportunity to respond.

"Jay? What on earth is going on? I've been getting a busy signal for twenty minutes."

"Bethany. Oh, thank God." He collapsed against the wall, wondering if the erratic pounding in his chest signaled a heart attack. "I thought you were dead."

"*Dead?* Oh, good grief, Jay, what in the world is the matter with you?"

"Just a minute." He patted his chest, gulping air until he had enough breath to speak. "I called the office—" He paused to pant for a moment. "Morris said you didn't make the meeting. No one knew where you were." Propping his back against the wall, he slid to the floor and sat there, shaking. "I was so damned scared, Beth. Where the hell have you been?"

A long-suffering sigh filtered over the line. "Do you know how many one-way streets there are in downtown Sacramento?"

"Huh?"

"There are dozens, probably hundreds, and not one of them leads to a recognizable freeway. By the time I learned that David had written A Street instead of K Street, I was hopelessly lost and circling the city like a starving vulture." She issued an indignant huff. "To make matters worse, I ended up stuck in a traffic jam in front of the Capitol because a bunch of environmental protestors decided to picket the state assembly on behalf of California's entire otter population. Now I like otters as much as anyone, but—" She cut off the tirade with an annoyed snort. "Oh, never mind. What was it you wanted anyway?"

"Wanted?" Jay repeated stupidly.

"You called the office," she reminded him, her patience thinning. "I assume you had a reason."

"Oh, yeah, well, sure." He cleared his throat. "I, uh, couldn't find my pain pills."

Bethany's voice changed instantly from irritation to concern. "Is your leg bothering you again?"

"Well, no, not exactly."

"Then why do you need the pills?"

"Because it might. Start bothering me, that is. And if it does, I figured I should know where the pills were. Just in case, you know?" Jay wiped his wet forehead, cursing himself for not having realized just how lame the excuse really was.

The silence on the line spoke volumes.

"Let me see if I have this right," Bethany said after a long moment. "You don't need the pain pills because you aren't having any pain, but you suddenly realized that you *might* have pain at some unforeseeable point in the future, so you felt compelled to call me immediately—at work, no less—to find out exactly where said pills were should that unlikely event occur. Is that what you're trying to tell me?"

"Ah, well, yes, I suppose."

"I see." There was a shuffling sound, as if she'd shifted the receiver. "Your pills are in the kitchen, on the top shelf of the cabinet nearest the sink."

"Oh. Okay, thanks." From his vantage point on the floor, Jay frowned at the cabinet in question. "Why didn't you just put them in the medicine cabinet?"

"Because Nathan can get into the medicine cabinet. In fact, Nathan can get into just about everything except the overhead kitchen cupboards. Now if there's nothing else, I have a ton of work to do, and for reasons that must be obvious even to you, I'm running behind."

"Sure, I understand. Uh, thanks for calling."

"You're welcome, Jay. Goodbye." The line clicked loudly enough to indicate that she'd cradled the receiver with more than the necessary force.

Jay dropped the phone in his lap, too drained to stand and hang it up. He'd just made a grade-A fool out of himself, but oddly enough, he didn't care. Bethany was alive; she was safe. Nothing else mattered.

Still, he couldn't help but wonder how many times during their marriage Bethany had suffered through the same ordeal that he'd just endured. Too many to count, he imagined, although he hadn't previously given credence to her concerns. Instead, he'd minimized her fear, even belittled it.

Now, for the first time in his life, Jay had experienced the emotional devastation to which she'd been repeatedly subjected. And he finally understood why she had left him.

At six-fifteen, Bethany rushed through the front door with Nathan tucked under one arm and a bag of groceries under the other. She lowered the toddler to the floor, swept the messy living room with a tired gaze and spoke to the three video gamers hunched around the television. "Dinner will be ready in an hour. David, will you please pick up Nathan's toys so I can vacuum later? And Laurel, honey, would you give Mommy a hand in the kitchen? I need some potatoes peeled."

Laurel instantly dropped the handset and stood, but David continued to stare trancelike at the television. "Yeah, Mom," he muttered. "Just let me finish this game."

Jay, who was also seated on the floor, pulled himself up on the sofa. "You can play another game later, son. Right now you need to do as your mother says."

"Aw, man. Drog's kingdom is almost wiped out. If I quit now, I'll hafta start all over again."

"Life's tough." Jay plucked the handset out of the boy's clutching fingers and turned the game off. Ignoring his son's furious muttering, Jay focused on Bethany. "Hi. How was your day?"

She slid him a narrowed look. "As if you didn't know."

"I meant, uh, after that."

Tossing her purse on the coffee table, Bethany managed a smile. "Sorry. I'm feeling a bit frazzled, but I shouldn't take it out on you."

Jay perched on the sofa, patting the cushion beside him. "Sit down and tell me all about it."

"I have to start dinner."

"But—"

"We'll talk later," Bethany mumbled, hanging up her blazer. "Do me a favor and keep an eye on Nathan, will you, please? He's trying to dismantle the video game handset."

Spinning around, Bethany hurried into the kitchen, where Laurel was somberly stacking potatoes beside the sink.

"How many should I do?" Laurel asked without looking up.

"They're fairly good size. I think six should be enough."

Nodding listlessly, Laurel turned on the faucet and picked up a plastic-handled safety peeler.

The child's somber mood didn't escape Bethany's notice. "So, how did school go?"

"It was okay, I guess."

"I imagine it was a little scary, though."

Laurel responded with a shrug.

"Do you like your new teacher?" Bethany asked, clearing the breakfast dishes.

"She's okay."

"And your new classmates?"

"They're okay."

Bethany retrieved a thawed package of chicken from the refrigerator, saddened by her daughter's somber mood. "I'd like to hear about your day, if you'd like to talk about it."

Frowning, Laurel dropped a peeled potato in the pot and poked her sliding glasses into place. "Teacher told us where to sit, then made us stand up and say our names, and then we had recess, and then we came home. Can I shake the crumbs on the chicken?"

"Yes, sweetie." Bethany sighed, recognizing the abrupt switch of topic as a thinly veiled request to drop the subject of school, at least for the moment. She hoped Laurel would be more communicative later. Meanwhile, Bethany had so much housework ahead of her that she'd be lucky to crawl into bed by midnight.

The next ninety minutes were a pressurized whirl of cooking, serving, eating and cleaning up.

Bethany had just filled the sink with soap bubbles when Jay hobbled into the kitchen. "I can wash those," he said, nodding toward the greasy stack of dinner dishes.

Surprised, she glanced over her shoulder. "That's not necessary. I don't expect guests to pitch in with the housework."

An irritated pucker settled between his tawny brows. "I'm hardly a guest."

"You don't live here," she pointed out. "That makes you a guest."

"I'm the children's father," he countered, ka-thunking across the kitchen to yank the dishwashing sponge out of her hand. "That makes me, uh, family."

She would have smiled if she'd not been too tired for the effort. Instead, she stepped away from the sink. "In that case, thank you. Leave the clean dishes in the drainer. David will dry them."

Jay stopped her as she turned to leave. "Wait a minute. I thought maybe we could, you know, talk."

"About what?"

"The kids, your day, my day... hell, we can even talk about your pumpkins, if you want."

Crossing her arms, Bethany regarded him with suspicion and disbelief. "If memory serves, you'd rather be tattooed with an ice pick than engage in mundane conversation, particularly with me. And as for your sudden helpfulness, I don't recall once in all the years we were married that you gave the slightest indication you ever knew or cared what a dish sponge was used for. What's going on, anyway?''

"I'm just trying to be friendly, okay?"

"No, it's not okay." Bethany tensed, rubbing the back of her neck. "I'm not going back to Los Angeles with you, Jay, so if that's what this is all about, you might as well go sit in front of the television and let me finish my work."

The disappointment in his eyes spoke volumes. Clearly she'd struck a nerve. He glanced away long enough to arrange a rinsed dinner plate in the drainer. "You don't like me very much, do you?"

A stabbing pain pierced her chest, then spread out in a throbbing ache of regret. The problem was that she liked him too much. She loved him. She'd always loved him, and she always would. But she simply couldn't be the wife he wanted, not any more. She had her own dreams, dreams that Jay hadn't been willing to share, or even to acknowledge.

Deep down she knew that the fault was hers and hers alone. Jay had dreams, too, dreams that Bethany couldn't live with any more than she could live with the person created by the fulfillment of those dreams.

"We may have our differences, Jay, but I don't dislike you. You're a good and decent man, and a wonderful father. I—" Bethany paused to choose her words carefully. "I admire you very much."

Jay stared at her for a moment. Their eyes met with an electric crackle that was nearly audible, definitely tangible. The lie stretched between them on that invisible wave, the lie of omission that Bethany had crafted with such care. She knew that Jay recognized the love in her eyes and prayed he wouldn't ask the question directly. If he did, she'd have to admit the truth, a truth that would give him false hope. That wouldn't help him, and it certainly wouldn't help her.

She held her breath, waiting.

Jay smiled. "Where do you keep the scouring pads?"

For the next two hours, Jay watched Bethany sweep floors, vacuum, pack lunches and put away clutter that he'd stepped over all day but hadn't really noticed. By the time Nathan had been hauled, kicking and screaming, off to bed, Bethany's eyes were ringed with fatigue and her shoulders slumped as if carrying the weight of a small planet.

A musical crescendo emanated from the television, capturing Jay's attention.

"Aw'right! That's my best score ever." Tossing the handset aside, David leaped up and flopped on the sofa beside his father. "Wanna play a game with me?"

"Maybe later," Jay said, distracted as Bethany rushed out of the kitchen and lugged a bucket of cleaning supplies up the stairs. "Doesn't your mother ever rest?"

David blinked, as if the question had never occurred to him. "I dunno."

"She's supposed to be off work by five," Jay muttered, more to himself than to the wide-eyed boy beside him. "But she doesn't even get home until almost six-thirty. It's only a twenty-minute drive. Why does it take so long?"

"She's gotta pick Nathan up from day care," David replied, startling Jay. "And sometimes she's gotta go to the market and get stuff for dinner."

A thought occurred to Jay. "But you and Laurel get home from school around three-thirty. Are you alone in the house until your mom gets home?"

"Nah. Mom said we could come straight home today on account of you being here. After you leave, we'll hafta stay at Mrs. Piper's house until Mom picks us up."

"Who's Mrs. Piper?"

"She's my friend Danny's mom. They live in that big white house with the horses out front."

"I see." Jay rubbed his chin, beginning to get the gist of how complicated the life of a single parent could be. He doubted Mrs. Piper would watch someone else's children for nothing, and Nathan's day care was certainly not a charitable institution. The total cost of child care must be enormous, particularly in comparison to the presumably modest salary of a clerk in a small rural insurance agency.

And there were plainly other pressures, as well. He regarded his oldest son, hating himself for what he was thinking. "By the way, David, you know, of course, that your mother had a pretty harrowing day."

David ducked his head. "Yeah, I heard."

"It was pretty frightening for her, driving around for hours looking for an address that doesn't exist."

The boy studied the hardwood floor without comment.

"I must admit, I was rather surprised that you made such a careless mistake writing down the message." Jay leaned back, folding his arms and propping his shoulders against the coffee table. "I'm going to assume that it was an accident, David, because even though you've made it clear that you dislike Mr. Morris, I can't believe you'd deliberately put your mother through that kind of grief just to keep her from meeting with him. Do we understand each other?"

Swallowing hard, David continued to avoid his father's gaze. "Yeah."

"Good. Now, let's get back to the original discussion about what we can do to make your mom's life easier."

At that, David finally looked up with a gleam in his eye. "Y'know, Mom would be home a lot sooner if she didn't have to go get Nathan first."

The thought had already crossed Jay's mind. "And she wouldn't be so tired if she didn't have to cook dinner as soon as she walked in the door."

David grinned. "Yeah, that'd make Mom real happy."

Absently hunching forward, Jay poked his finger inside his cast in a futile effort to reach an annoying itch. Despite the irritation, he couldn't help smiling. The opportunity of making Bethany happy was much too tempting to pass up, but beyond that lay a possibility even more enticing. Not only was Jay in the delightful position to ease Bethany's daily burden, but with a little extra effort he could actually make himself indispensable to her life.

And how hard could it be? Turn on the TV to entertain Nathan, then toss in a load of laundry, pick up a few toys and whip up a quick dinner. No problem. If he played his cards right, it wouldn't be long before Bethany discovered just how much she needed him and realized that the divorce had been a terrible mistake.

Chapter Seven

After pouring a dollop of milk on Nathan's cereal, Jay draped himself on a kitchen chair, feeling smug and confident. In the doorway, Bethany hovered like a worried honeybee, wringing her hands and biting her lower lip.

"It's not too late," she said. "There's still time for me to take Nathan to day care."

Jay grinned. "Nope. We've already discussed this. If you'll recall, we mutually decided that I'm quite capable of caring for my own kids."

Heaving a giant sigh, Bethany absently rubbed her upper arms, ruffling the silky material of an inexpensive dress that looked absolutely terrific clinging to her lithe frame. "We didn't mutually decide anything. You simply wore me down. The only reason I agreed to this insanity was a desperation for sleep, and I knew you wouldn't leave me alone until you got your way."

Hiking a brow, Jay managed not to leer. "You know perfectly well that if I'd really gotten my way with you, you'd be smiling this morning."

"Jay!" Bethany zipped a startled glance at Nathan, who was happily transferring wet little oat Os from his bowl to an abstract arrangement on the table. A crimson flush spread across her freckled cheeks. "This is your last chance. If I walk out that door without Nathan, life as you know it will never be the same. I will, of course, hold you financially responsible for any damage."

"Oh, ye of little faith."

"Faith has nothing to do with it," she muttered, shouldering a fat, woven handbag. "If you go through with this madness, I guarantee that by five o'clock this afternoon, your own faith will have been sorely tested." She turned, pausing to look over her shoulder with a final, pleading look.

Jay could barely contain his glee. "Tell Mommy bye-bye, Nathan."

"Bye-bye!" Nathan chirped with a wild wave of his spoon, the contents of which flew directly into his father's startled face.

Gasping, Jay lurched forward wiping milk and Oatie-Os out of his eyes. He skimmed a glance toward the doorway, chagrined that Bethany was still standing there, watching and grinning.

"Ah," she purred. "It's so reassuring to see that you have everything under control. Well, toodles, gentlemen. Have a wonderful day." Spinning on her sensible, low-heeled business pumps, Bethany strode away, chuckling.

Jay, still plucking cereal out of his hair, felt his heart sink as the front door closed and was overwhelmed by a brief surge of panic. Maybe Bethany was right. Maybe caring for a two-year-old *was* beyond his capability. Maybe he should charge outside screaming that he'd made a mistake—

A tug on his wrist captured Jay's attention.

"Look, Daddy!" Nathan proudly gestured to a twisting line of donut-shaped oaties winding a milky track across the table. "Choo-choo train!"

Chuckling, Jay decided that there was no way this adorably cherubic toddler could possibly live up to his mother's dire predictions. Bethany was, after all, prone to overreact and blow even minor incidents out of proportion. Besides, Jay could subdue hardened criminals spaced on PCP; he could hand-wrestle an armed suspect into submission; once he'd single-handedly arrested an entire roomful of drug dealers and held them for backup.

Surely he could manage one tiny two-year-old.

Thus fortified, Jay stroked his giggling son's head, which was a tawny, tousled replica of his own. "Nice job, tiger, but you're supposed to eat your cereal, not play with it. Okay?"

"O'tay." The child shoveled a giant spoonful into his mouth and chewed happily, cheeks puffed like the stuffed pouches of an overfed chipmunk.

"See?" Jay said to Leon as the dog ambled toward the kibble bowl. "Kids respond to common sense and reason."

Leon cocked his good eye with the same skepticism Bethany had expressed a few minutes earlier.

"So what do you know?" Jay argued. "You're just a silly mutt."

With what Jay could have sworn was a canine shrug, Leon wandered to his doggy bowls and began eating his own breakfast. Jay stood, stretching, and glanced around the room, rubbing his hands together as he planned his attack. First he'd clean up the kitchen, then he'd move into the living room, pick up a few toys and wipe a little dust. The way he had it figured, the whole place would be shipshape and shining by noon.

Optimistic to the point of cockiness, Jay scooped up the breakfast dishes, including Nathan's empty cereal bowl, and piled them in the sink, which he filled with a mass of soapy water. Humming loudly, he made a production out of washing the dishes, even juggling plastic bowls to show off for Nathan, who was watching from the table, giggling and clapping wildly.

In less than twenty minutes, the kitchen was swept and sparkling and Nathan was happily playing with a herd of colorful plastic dinosaurs on the kitchen table while his whistling father headed into the living room armed with furniture polish and a dust rag.

Jay hustled around, spritzing and buffing until every stick of wood in the room gleamed with a brilliant luster.

As he straightened, admiring his handiwork, an odd hiss emanated from the kitchen. When he went to check it out, he found that Nathan had pushed a chair over to the kitchen sink, turned the faucet on full blast and was in the process of washing his dinosaurs.

"Diny-sores want bath," the child insisted when his father turned off the water.

"Actually, they'd probably rather have a shower," Jay mumbled, scooping the plastic creatures out of the sink and drying them with a tea towel.

"Chow-er?"

"Yeah, shower. Real men don't take baths."

Seeming thrilled by that juicy tidbit of information, the child made no protest as Jay carried him into the living room and deposited him in front of the TV. "Here you go, sport. Cartoons."

Hooking a finger over his lower teeth, Nathan gazed up in wide-eyed wonder. "Real-man cartoons?"

"You bet. Nothing like an animated super hero to get the old testosterone pumping." Giving his son's head an affectionate pat, Jay glanced up in time to see Leon emerge from the kitchen, grumbling. A prickle of suspicion slid down Jay's spine. "Stay here, Nathan. Daddy will be right back."

As Jay headed to the kitchen, Leon trundled by with a woeful expression. A moment later, Jay saw why. When he'd carried Nathan away from the kitchen sink, he hadn't spotted the empty cereal box discarded on the floor, nor had he noticed that the dog's food and water bowls had been heaped to overflowing with tiny oat donuts. Jay moaned, eyeing the globs of partially soaked cereal and kibble, squashed and tracked across linoleum which had only minutes earlier been mopped squeaky clean.

Muttering to himself, Jay headed for the mop cabinet, wondering how in heaven's name Nathan had gotten into the pantry. Then he remembered Bethany's warning that only the uppermost kitchen cupboards were beyond the toddler's wily reach.

Clearly, that particular caution had been issued with unnerving acuity.

Sneaking a quick peek into the living room, Jay was relieved to see that Nathan was still sitting cross-legged on the floor, chewing his finger and thoroughly engrossed in watching super-hero cartoons. More confident, he began the cleanup by dumping the contents of Leon's bowls into the kitchen sink. He rinsed out the bowls, flipped on the garbage disposal and had just grabbed a shovel-shaped dustpan when a disturbing crunch emanated from the whirring disposal. He straightened, listening. In less than a heartbeat, the entire sink vibrated with a horrendous thwacking noise.

Dropping the dustpan, Jay leaped for the disposal switch, only to realize that smoke was wafting from under the sink. He yanked open the cabinet doors and issued a croak of dismay. The disposal motor was burning up.

He quickly unplugged the appliance, then hopped across the kitchen, head swiveling in blind panic as he searched for a fire extinguisher.

Where the hell would Beth keep it? Oh, Lord. What if she didn't have one? She had to have one. It was the law.

Frantic, Jay hobble-hopped to the broom closet, where he vaguely remembered seeing a red cylinder lurking behind a stash of cleaning utensils. It was, thank God, the extinguisher. He retrieved it just as the smoke alarm screeched loudly enough to stop traffic twenty miles away.

Coughing, Jay waved the smoke from the open cabinet, aimed the extinguisher and sprayed the overheated motor—not to mention the cleaning supplies stored in the cupboard—with a thick layer of gooey foam.

The motor sizzled once, then burped into benign silence.

With the threat of immediate immolation over, Jay dropped the spent canister, flung the back door open to air the place out and was desperately flapping a towel beneath the shrieking smoke alarm when Nathan toddled into the kitchen.

His little mouth moved, but his words were drowned out by the alarm's shrill screech.

"What?" Jay hollered, flapping frantically.

Nathan's mouth moved again.

"I can't—" the alarm suddenly stopped "—hear you!" Jay screamed at the startled child.

Nathan staggered backward, eyes huge, lip quivering.

Jay sighed, tossed the towel on the table and bent to give the frightened boy a quick hug. "Daddy wasn't yelling at you, son."

Seeming satisfied by the assurance, Nathan turned his attention to the foamy cabinet.

"Don't even think about it," Jay warned, following the boy's fascinated gaze. "Now, what were you trying to tell Daddy?"

"Me go potty."

Jay straightened. "Can you go by yourself, sport? Daddy's kind of, uh, in the middle of something."

Nathan's blue eyes lit like neon. "O'tay!" he chirped, then spun around and dashed upstairs, leaving his disgruntled father to ponder the wisdom of eschewed birth control.

Sagging against the broom cabinet, Jay's disillusioned gaze swept the room, which resembled a well-used artillery range. He figured it would take at least an hour to clean up the mess, and the garbage disposal was a total loss.

Bethany's words circled his mind. *I will, of course, hold you financially responsible for the damage.*

That assumed, of course, that Jay's lack of parenting skills was responsible for said damage, which in this case, it wasn't. Certainly, Jay couldn't be faulted because Bethany's decrepit old disposal happened to bite the big one on his shift.

At least, he didn't think the problem was his fault, but a niggling doubt pricked at him, so Jay ka-thunked his way to the sink, stuck his hand down the now-dead disposal unit and yanked out the chewed remnants of a red plastic dinosaur.

He groaned as dollar signs chinked in his mind. The good news was that he possessed at least one credit card that wasn't maxxed to its limit. The bad news was that the day had barely begun, a day that just might end up being the longest of his life.

Swallowing a frisson of pure dread, Jay squared his shoulders, gave himself a silent pep talk and located a screwdriver in a kitchen drawer. He was, after all, fairly adept with mechanical thingamajigs. Maybe he could fix the disposal himself, thus preventing Bethany from ever learning about this humiliating episode.

Buoyed by the thought, Jay tossed the foam-coated cleaning supplies into the sink, sponged the biggest globs off the disposal motor and awkwardly arranged himself so his upper torso was hunched in the cupboard. Behind him, the pipes whooshed, signaling that the upstairs toilet had been flushed.

Jay was too engrossed in his chore to pay much attention to rattling pipes. He removed several screws and eased off the metal motor cover. Immediately, a cascade of broken gear teeth fell from a mass of melted wire. Not a good sign, Jay thought as he glumly eyed the singed innards. In fact, it was a downright lousy sign. The garbage disposal was officially dead.

"Rest in peace," he muttered, scooting out from under the cupboard as the pipes whooshed and rattled again.

Cursing the entrapping leg cast, Jay used the counter to pull himself upright and was contemplating his options when he heard the upstairs toilet flush for the third time. He stood there, stunned, until the realization that the toilet was continuing to run filled him with utter horror. "Oh, Lord. *Nathan!*"

By the time Jay could hobble across the living room, a small river was flowing downstairs to join the expansive pool spreading over Bethany's lovely hardwood floor.

At the top of the stairs stood Nathan, grinning happily as water rushed around his fat little ankles. "Me go potty all by my-telf!"

Jay gritted his teeth, not trusting himself to respond, and heaved his way up the stairs, sloshing his way to the bathroom, where water gushed in a continual torrent out of the overflowing toilet bowl.

A moment later, after twisting the shut-off valve, Jay surveyed the chaos while Nathan, clearly delighted by the unexpected turn of events, toddled downstairs to float wooden coasters across the living room lake.

Jay stood there, bemused, benumbed and thoroughly bewildered. He'd always considered law enforcement to be the world's most challenging and humbling profession, but he'd been dead wrong. Parenthood, he decided, was clearly the most demanding career on earth.

It was also the most frightening.

* * *

Bethany's hand froze over the telephone. Flexing her fingers, she took a deep breath, retrieved her hand and turned away. Nope, she wasn't going to call. If something horrible had happened, she'd find out soon enough. Besides, there wasn't anything she could do except verify that her fire insurance and liability premiums were up to date. And she'd done that first thing this morning.

Hunching over a statistical report, Bethany propped her chin on her hands, forcing herself to stare at the blurred columns. Her eyes shifted toward the phone.

It was nearly noon. She'd been certain that Jay would have called by now, frantic because he'd turned his back and Nathan had emptied his milk glass on the kitchen table or stuck an apple slice in the VCR.

Maybe she *should* call home, just to make sure everything was all right.

Of course it was all right. Otherwise the fire department would have notified her.

But what if something had happened to Jay? Maybe he'd tripped on the stairs and knocked himself unconscious, and maybe Nathan had tried to wake his daddy up by pouring water in his face and ended up drowning him. Or maybe C.J. got loose and butted down the back door and went on a mad rampage through the house, and Jay couldn't get to the phone because the goat had him trapped in the bathroom—

Her fingers twitched toward the receiver.

"Bethany!"

She spun around, startled and feeling ridiculously guilty. "Ah..." She swallowed hard, forcing a thin smile. "Yes, Roger?"

"This policy analysis is excellent!" he gushed. "My stars, you are the bright one, aren't you?"

Bethany managed not to wince. "Thank you, Roger, but it's just a combined comparison study. The computer printouts are bulky and cumbersome, so I thought a simpler format would be easier to use."

"It's brilliant, my dear, absolutely first-rate." Dropping the report on her desk, he absently smoothed the thick silver-blond hair of which he was inordinately proud. "In fact, it proves my theory that your talents are being wasted on a hum-drum clerking job."

Her startled gaze snapped around. "You're not going to fire me, are you?"

"Fire you? Oh, good heavens, no. Why on earth would you think such a thing?"

Limp with relief, she propped her elbows on her desk and sagged forward. Bethany wasn't exactly in love with her job, but it did offer some satisfaction, and she certainly needed the money. "I guess comments about wasted talent strike me as a politically correct prologue to termination."

Roger flashed an amused smile, then perched on the corner of her desk. "Rubbish, my dear. Surely you're aware of the high esteem in which I hold you. It's been years since I've seen anyone with such impeccable instincts. You could go a long way in this business, Bethany." He leaned uncomfortably close. "Which is why I'd like you to join me for dinner this evening."

A gentle toe push rolled her chair back, putting more space between them. "I'm sorry, Roger. You know I always have dinner with my children."

He frowned. "Yes, of course, but this is business, Bethany, important business. Now that your ex-husband is so conveniently available as a sitter, I'd hoped we could take advantage of the opportunity to discuss your career options in a more relaxed setting."

Unsettled, Bethany struggled to express herself in a manner that was tactful, yet firm enough to eliminate ambiguity. "Roger, I appreciate your kindness and I appreciate my job. But as we've discussed before, my family is my first priority, and time with my children is very precious to me. Unless it's totally unavoidable, I'd really prefer that business discussions not extend beyond business hours."

"I quite understand," Roger replied, looking stricken. "Please believe that it wasn't my intent to deprive you of time with your children. I had intended, however clumsily, to reward your outstanding efforts with an enjoyable meal. Perhaps lunch would be an appropriate compromise."

Bethany's tight muscles instantly relaxed. "That sounds lovely," she replied, smiling. "I'll look forward to it."

"Splendid." Standing, Roger composed himself by smoothing his immaculate lapels. "I'll check my schedule and get back to you."

Bethany held her smile until Roger had disappeared into his private office, then swiveled to her desk and focused on the telephone. There was no way she could call home without alerting Jay that she doubted his ability to keep things under control. She did doubt it, of course, but she certainly didn't want to hurt his feelings. Unfortunately, she'd never get any work done with images of imagined disasters flashing through her mind. There must be another way to alleviate her fears.

She snapped her fingers. Compromise was the key word here, finding middle ground that would satisfy Bethany that all was well at home without alerting Jay to her woeful lack of trust.

Taking a deep breath, Bethany snatched up the receiver and called the sheriff.

Jay sniffed the casserole, wondering why it was emitting such an odd aroma. Except for a few minor substitutions, he'd followed the cookbook directions to the letter. Of course, he hadn't been able to find any chicken gravy, so he'd used a can of asparagus soup, figuring that chicken and asparagus went together well enough. Problem was, he hadn't found any chicken, either. So he'd used hamburger. What the hell, meat was meat.

Then there'd been some leftover corn in the fridge, so he'd tossed that in for color. But he hadn't been able to find any bay leaf in the spice rack, so he'd figured a sprig of wild rosemary from the back pasture would be close enough. Herbs were herbs, after all, and just to be sure the dish had a zesty flavor, he'd also added a few shakes from every spice bottle in the cupboard. Except for cinnamon, of course. Even Jay knew better than that.

Shrugging off a niggling doubt about the results, he shoved the casserole in a properly preheated oven and crossed his fingers, fervently hoping that his very first home-cooked meal would be a roaring success. Certainly, it should be. After all, Bethany liked everything that he'd put in it—except maybe for the wild rosemary—so she certainly should like the finished product. Besides, it probably wouldn't smell so funny after it was cooked.

A clunk upstairs drew his attention. He followed the sound, pausing to wave at Nathan, who was playing in his bedroom behind the stretched fishnet hammock Jay had stapled across the open doorway. Continuing down the hall, he peered into the bathroom just as the plumber was reseating the toilet that had been removed earlier that afternoon.

"Did you find the problem?" Jay asked hopefully.

"Sure did." The athletic young man wrestled the porcelain appliance into position, then straightened, wiping his forehead with a rag. "A bar of soap, one pink washcloth, about a half a roll of toilet tissue, and this." He reached into a bucket and pulled out a blue plastic dinosaur. "Diplodocus, I think, but it could be a brachiosaurus, which was a slightly larger member of a closely related species."

Jay moaned, glancing from the empty soap dish to the bare space on the towel rack to the spent cardboard tube still attached to the paper holder.

The plumber set the little dinosaur on the vanity. "I know how you feel," he said, chuckling. "I've got kids myself. Luckily, it doesn't cost me $168.95 every time one of the little rascals clogs the plumbing.''

"How much?"

After repeating the amount, the affable guy pulled a clipboard out of his tool chest. "Let's see now, we have the trip charge, same-day emergency-service minimum tacked on to nearly two hours labor, plus parts, of course—" He glanced up. "I saved the old trap, but the seal had to be replaced, and I was planning to use new flange bolts, but if you're looking to keep the cost down, I can always put the old rusty ones back in."

"And how much would that save?"

He shrugged. "Four, maybe five dollars."

Jay sagged against the doorjamb. "Do you take credit cards?"

"Sure do."

Heaving a pained sigh, Jay pulled out his wallet and handed over his card. "Use new bolts."

The plumber grinned. "Yeah, I figured you for the extravagant type."

The witty retort rolling on Jay's tongue was never uttered because the front doorbell rang. He glanced toward the landing, irritated, then excused himself and left the plumber happily zipping the overused credit card though a portable reader.

As he passed Nathan's room, the child ran to the doorway to tangle his little fingers in the confining fishnet. "Want out," he announced.

"In a few minutes," Jay mumbled, casting a critical eye at the hardwood floors in the upper hall and stairs. No sign of warping, thank goodness. Apparently he'd gotten the water wiped up before it had a chance to seep through the varnish and cause any real damage. Now if only the runner rugs he'd hung on the clothesline dried before Bethany got home—

"Daddy!" Nathan screeched. "Want out *now!*"

"All right, son," Jay called, limping down the stairs. "Just let Daddy answer the door."

The child replied with an earsplitting wail that reached a crescendo as Jay threw open the front door and found himself staring at a fat chest and a badge. He looked up, startled. "Archie. Uh, hi."

Hoisting a thick eyebrow, the deputy pulled his gaze from the plumbing truck in the driveway and peered into a living room that was completely bare except for a pile of furniture stacked in the only corner that had escaped the flood. "Thought I'd drop by to see if you needed anything."

"Oh. That was—" Jay winced as Nathan's shrill screams vibrated the walls "—nice of you, but, ah..." He paused, waiting for his son to take a breath before continuing. "Everything's under control." The words rushed out a moment before Nathan let another series of indignant shrieks fly. Jay managed a sick smile. "Excuse me. I'll be right back."

Archie blinked, craning his thick neck to peer inside the doorway. "Sure, son. Do what you have to do."

Jay spun around just as the uniformed plumber came down the stairs and strode toward the front door.

"Sign here," he said, holding out a clipboard.

Angling a glance at the deputy's amused face, Jay scrawled his name on the credit card slip.

"I wrote my home number on the work order," the plumber said, handing over Jay's copy of the paperwork and grinning broadly. "Under the circumstances, I figured you might be needing it." Ignoring Jay's withering look, the plumber hoisted his tool case, nodded to the bemused deputy, then strode to his truck, whistling.

Eyes twinkling, Archie hooked his thumbs on his holster belt, rocked back on his heels and offered a knowing wink. "Plumbing troubles, hmm?"

Jay sighed. "I'll pay big if you'll forget you saw that."

"Bribing an officer?" Archie clucked so loudly his belly wiggled. "That's a crime, son. Why, I could arrest you on the spot."

"Da-a-a-dy!" came the plaintive wail from upstairs. "Me want *out!*"

"Child abuse, too? My, my, you *are* in a heap of trouble." Archie paused, sniffing. "Good Lord, what's that smell?"

"Dinner," Jay snapped, heading toward the stairs.

A few minutes later, he returned with his placated youngest firmly in tow and found Archie standing in the living room eyeing the pile of furniture. "Guess I can figure out why all those skinny rugs are hanging on the line. Looks like you've had yourself quite a day."

"And I'd just love to chat about it," Jay muttered, rubbing his aching head while casting a grim glance at his watch. "But I've got to put this furniture back before the kids get home from school."

Laughing, Archie unfastened his cuff buttons and rolled up his sleeves. "Well, then, we'd best get to it. When I drove past the school bus, it was only a few miles up the road."

Jay gave the deputy a grateful smile, then moved forward to drag a lamp table into position.

The two men worked feverishly, hauling the sofa and love seat into the center of the room, struggling with the television cabinet, rearranging the stereo and speakers, and had just replaced the coffee table when the front door burst open.

"Hey, Dad, guess what? I tried out for the track team and—" David skidded to a stop and screwed up his face. "Phew, what stinks?"

"Never mind." Jay glanced toward the front porch. "Where's your sister?"

"She's coming." The boy stared toward the kitchen. "Did Leon throw up again?"

Archie turned away, pressing his palm over his quivering mouth.

Skewering the deputy with a warning stare, Jay spoke to his son. "Don't you have chores to do?"

"Yeah, sure." David dropped his knapsack on the sofa, wrinkled his nose and retreated out the front door.

As soon as David's footsteps faded from the porch planks, Archie straightened, struggling for composure. "Well, guess I'd best be heading out. I've got a load of kitty litter for the Jamison place."

"Since when does the sheriff's department deliver kitty litter?" Jay asked politely.

Archie shrugged. "Ida Jamison broke her hip a few months back. She can't get around too well, so I try to help out as best I can."

Jay smiled, intrigued by the notion that around here, local deputies were an important and integral part of the community. Although delivering pet supplies to incapacitated residents had never been part of Jay's police training, it certainly appealed to his belief in the most basic tenant of law enforcement—to protect and serve, a concept severely degraded by the gritty survival mode urban cops were forced to adapt.

"Thanks for the help," Jay said, following Archie to the front door. "And, ah, there's no need to mention any of this to Beth, is there?"

"No need at all. Oh, by the way." Rummaging through his breast pocket, Archie pulled out a small card. "You might want to give these folks a call."

"Why?" he asked, when a quick glance indicated that the business card belonged to a restaurant located a few miles up the road.

"Because they deliver," the deputy replied with a wink, then he sauntered away, chuckling.

Chapter Eight

"Don't worry about it, Jay," Bethany told her glum ex-husband as he emptied the untouched contents of five dinner plates into the casserole dish. "It's the thought that counts, and besides, soup and tuna sandwiches comprise a very nutritious meal."

Jay looked like a beaten man. "Yeah, but you had to fix it. The idea was to have a nice dinner all ready when you came home."

"I know." She patted his arm. "It was very sweet of you."

"That's me," he grumbled, carrying the remains of the disgusting casserole to the trash container. "Sweet."

Bethany frowned. "Wait, don't dump it in there. It'll smell up the entire kitchen. Use the garbage disposal."

He paused, staring into the trash with a sheepish expression. "I, uh, heard that kitchen scraps aren't good for septic tanks. The fat clogs them up, or something."

"Where did you hear that?"

"You know, around." Swallowing hard, Jay quickly dumped the greasy casserole contents into the trash before Bethany could protest, then he quickly removed the plastic trash liner and shuffled backward toward the kitchen door. "I'll take this outside to the garbage, so you won't have to worry about the, ah, smell."

Bethany laid the sponge on the counter, crossed her arms and watched Jay practically slither out the back door. He was behaving rather oddly, she thought, although she couldn't understand why. The house was immaculate, the floors had never been cleaner and, despite her fears, Jay had obviously managed far better than she'd dreamed possible. She'd expected him to gloat about his success. Instead, he'd seemed unduly embarrassed by her praise, which she had to confess had been grudgingly offered.

Bethany had never doubted Jay's ability to protect and care for his children. He was undeniably a wonderful father, compensating for a lack of hands-on experience in mundane, day-to-day child rearing with an abundance of patience, love and unerring parental instinct.

Maintaining a household, however, was another matter entirely. Once, when Bethany had been felled by the flu, Jay had tossed in a load of laundry and ended up with an entire drawer full of passion-pink underwear. On another occasion, a not-too-clever attempt at carrying a dish drainer stacked with clean china had resulted in six smashed glasses, three shattered dinner plates and four cracked bowls.

There were other such examples, more than Bethany cared to remember. When it came to household chores, Jay had always been a walking disaster. Bethany had no reason to believe that today would have been any different.

But it *had* been different. The house had been polished and thoroughly scrubbed, Nathan was safe, clean and happy, and with the exception of a certain inedible casserole, the household had apparently been run with incredible expertise despite her absence. Or perhaps, she thought unhappily, because of it.

Not that she'd wanted to find her home in ruins, of course, but discovering that her ex-husband was a more effective housekeeper than Bethany was herself had done little to bolster her quavering self-esteem.

Issuing a nervous sigh, Bethany finished stacking the dinner dishes by the sink, then turned on the faucet and as always, flipped the disposal switch to clear the line before filling the sink with dishwater. Nothing happened. She flipped the switch twice more, then knelt to open the sink cabinet, assuming the reset button had somehow been tripped.

The back door flew open. "Don't do that!" Jay shouted, startling her. He hobbled across the room to plant himself between Bethany and the sink cupboard. "I mean, I'll wash the dishes. You go put your feet up or something."

She sat on her heels, staring up in total bewilderment. "You don't have to wash the dishes."

"I insist." Reaching down, he helped Bethany to her feet.

She brushed off her knees, regarding him skeptically. "Do you feel all right, Jay?"

"Never better."

"Are you sure?"

"Of course I'm sure." A stiff smile cracked his cheeks. "Why?"

"Because you're all sweaty."

"It's, ah—" He coughed into his hand. "I ran to the garbage can and back, that's all."

Her gaze slipped to his cast. "That must have taken quite an effort. And speaking of garbage, did you know that the disposal isn't working?"

His shoulders slumped. "Darn. You've gone and ruined my surprise."

"What surprise?"

Spinning her around, Jay escorted her out of the kitchen. "The thing is, I realized that I'd flat forgotten to get you a housewarming gift. Rude, huh? Anyway, that old disposal of yours was a real clunker, you know?"

"Actually, it worked quite well."

Ignoring her comment, Jay flashed the same smile he'd once used after backing the family car into a tree. "Your new one will be here tomorrow, so, uh, happy housewarming."

By now, Bethany had been ushered to the living room and Jay was blocking entry into the kitchen. A rivulet of moisture slid a wet track from his brow to his jaw, where it dangled like a transparent truth bead. His eyes were bright but shifty. He couldn't meet her gaze yet somehow managed to maintain that silly, don't-believe-a-word-I'm-saying grin.

Bethany cocked her head, regarding him thoughtfully. "You broke the disposal, didn't you?"

His grin faded. "I'm hurt, Bethany, hurt and dismayed that you could believe me capable of such duplicity."

"So you didn't break it?"

"That's not what I said," Jay replied, with a forced haughtiness that nearly made her laugh out loud. "But your lack of trust is like a dagger in my heart. Besides, that disposal was a cheap piece of junk. I'm surprised it didn't burn up months ago."

"Burn up?" Bethany nearly choked on the words. "Good grief, Jay, what on earth happened today?"

"It didn't exactly burn up," he assured her quickly. "It just got a little warm and, well, it kind of starting smoking. No flames, honest."

Pressing a palm against her pounding heart, Bethany was at a loss for words, an admittedly unique situation that Jay apparently mistook as evidence of appreciation rather than a manifestation of abject horror.

He offered a relieved smile, spreading his hands in a gesture that was both supremely confident and strangely submissive. "So you can see there was never anything to worry about."

Since his fervent assurance was issued in a voice cracking a notch above normal, Bethany remained unconvinced, but decided that asking more questions was bound to reveal other details she suspected she'd rather not know. "Maybe I should just go upstairs and start getting Nathan ready for bed."

"Great idea," Jay mumbled, backing into the kitchen. "You do that."

With a final curious glance into the kitchen, Bethany crossed the living room where all three children were engrossed in watching television. "Nathan, sweetie, come upstairs as soon as your program is over. It's bath time."

"O'tay," Nathan mumbled without tearing his rapt gaze from the screen.

Bethany stood at the foot of the stairs for a moment, noticing that the flickering light from the TV was reflected in the gleaming surface of a coffee table that had quite plainly been polished within an inch of its life.

In fact, the entire room appeared to have been scoured by a team of professionals. Even the hardwood floor on which every speck of dust usually beckoned like neon was absolutely spotless, as if it had been thoroughly scrubbed and buffed dry. It was a chore Bethany knew from experience took hours, even for one not hampered by the inconvenience of an awkward walking cast.

The sad truth was that despite the dead disposal incident, Jay had nonetheless accomplished more in one day than Bethany could manage in a month. Feeling pathetic and inadequate, Bethany trudged upstairs, glumly noting that even the runner carpet on the stairs looked as if it had been steam cleaned.

Still fretting about Jay's superhuman achievements, Bethany went to Nathan's room, which was cluttered with the usual assortment of scattered toys. Jay had apparently missed at least one area, and Bethany felt a guilty pleasure at the small imperfection. She quickly tidied the space, then gathered clean pajamas for Nathan to slip into after his bath.

When Bethany exited the room, however, a metallic glint in the wooden door frame caught her eye. Closer examination revealed the object to be, of all things, a staple. As she studied it, she noticed a peculiar line of punctures encircling the door, pairs of tiny holes that were precisely the same length as the staple she'd found.

Frowning, she stepped back, wondering if the odd holes were a new addition or whether they'd been there all along and she simply hadn't noticed them. It was an old house, after all, and the woodwork, particularly around doors and windows, was already badly chipped when she'd moved in. Much of her furniture had also come with the house, except for the children's bedroom furnishings and a few pieces that Jay had insisted she take when she'd moved out.

The memory of that heartbreaking afternoon slipped into her mind, distracting her attention from the scarred doorjamb.

They'd both been so gracious to each other, and so stoic. Everything had been divided without the pitched battle over possessions that so many divorcing couples endured. Jay had helped her load the U-Haul. She'd insisted that he keep the microwave, fearing he'd starve without the ability to nuke himself a quick meal.

It had all been very polite and proper.

Then again, Jay and Bethany had always treated each other with kindness and respect. That had never changed. When Bethany left, Jay had fretted about her safety; she had worried about his ability to care for himself and the house they'd shared.

Clearly her concerns had been unjustified. Jay was quite obviously more capable in that regard than she'd given him credit for. That realization, however, was not a particularly pleasant one.

Preoccupied, Bethany continued down the hall, entering the bathroom to prepare for Nathan's evening ritual. She hung his pjs on a hook behind the door, set out his little toothbrush and the special striped toothpaste he favored, then retrieved his floaty toys and a clean towel from the linen closet. As she arranged the items on the vanity, a rubber squirt frog slipped from her hands to bounce beneath the commode. She bent to retrieve the item and noticed an odd smear around the porcelain base.

Plumber's putty? She eyed it critically, smiling. Yes, it was indeed plumber's putty. That clue, along with the two shiny new flange bolts, was a powerful indicator that Jay's day hadn't gone quite as smoothly as he'd led her to believe.

Bethany couldn't have been happier.

Jay tossed the sponge on the edge of the sparkling sink, then went to join David and Laurel in the living room. He sank onto the sofa, exhausted and feeling as if he'd dodged an entire clip of speeding bullets. Even though Bethany had accepted the disposal incident better than expected, Jay still feared that, if news of the other disasters leaked out, she'd never let him watch Nathan again. How could he possibly become indispensable to a woman who couldn't trust him any farther than she could fling an elephant with a slingshot?

Tomorrow, Jay vowed, would be different. The first order of business would be to dig the restaurant business card out of the trash and—

"Jay!"

He leaped from the sofa, spinning around as Bethany stomped down the stairs carrying a grinning, naked two-year-old. A nervous prickle slid down his spine. "Is something wrong?"

Bethany's face was like chiseled granite. "Nathan insists on taking a shower because—and I'm quoting here—'*real* men don't take baths.'"

"Chow-er," Nathan agreed, clapping his hands.

Jay felt like he'd swallowed a rock. He tried to smile, but his teeth stuck to his lips. "Gee, I wonder where he heard that."

"Yes, I wonder." She thrust the giggling toddler into Jay's arms.

He shifted slightly, adjusting to the child's weight. "What am I supposed to do now?"

"Give him a shower," Bethany snapped.

"Me?" Jay heaved a pained sigh. "All right, Beth, you've made your point. In the future, I'll watch what I say when Nathan's around."

"Good. His towel is on the vanity. Be sure to mop up the floor when you're done."

"Oh, for heaven's sake, you can't be serious."

"I'm very serious, Jay. If you think I'm going to drown myself trying to shower a rambunctious two-year-old because his father has a machismo complex, you're very much mistaken."

As she turned to leave, Jay panicked. "Wait! How am I supposed to do this without getting my cast wet?"

She tossed him a sour look. "That, Mr. Real Man, is your problem."

Before Jay could do more than stretch out a pleading hand, Bethany spun on her heel and marched away. A moment later, her bedroom door slammed.

David, who'd been watching the parental exchange from his position in front of the television, sadly shook his head. "Man, you're in big trouble now."

* * *

Bethany emerged from her bedroom to edge silently down the hall. For the past hour, a constant stream of footsteps had rumbled overhead, along with voices, the sound of running water and an occasional panicked shout. The house was silent now, and she was finally beginning to fret about the consequence of her anger.

A wedge of light streamed from the sewing room where the door had been left halfway open. She slipped along the wall and peered inside. A lump of pure guilt stuck in her throat.

Jay was slumped on the futon looking sad and vulnerable with his droopy shoulders, tousled, damp hair and water-splotched clothing. There was a childlike quality to his handsome face, a poignant ponderance that chinked at the emotional armor Bethany had so carefully constructed to protect herself from exactly what she was feeling right now.

Her heart felt swollen, exquisitely tender. Dear God, how she loved this man, a man who seemed paradoxically unchanged yet displayed none of the brooding arrogance she remembered. The person she was covertly observing seemed strangely subdued, almost humble, as he awkwardly attempted to unwind what appeared to be an entire roll of plastic wrap, apparently used to protect his cast from the shower spray.

While he grappled with the crinkly mess, Bethany cleared her throat, alerting him to her presence. "Do you need any help?"

He spared her a glance. "No, thanks. I think I've got it."

Hovering in the doorway, Bethany felt like an intruder in her own home. After a moment of watching the poor man struggle to unhook the tangled wrap from the metal base of his cast, she entered the room without invitation and knelt to examine the problem. "Hold still," she murmured, untwisting the plastic knot. "Just one more second . . . there. All done."

Sitting on her heels, she plucked at the wadded pile, avoiding Jay's gaze. An unexpected tingle slid along her spine. The air thickened with electric intensity, along with a palpable current of sudden tension.

A covert glance revealed that Jay was watching her with eyes that smoldered darkly, with an expression of longing that took her breath away.

Only when she lowered her gaze did she realize that she was kneeling in the cradle between his legs, and she recognized the implied intimacy of her position.

Sweet memories engulfed her, an aching reminiscence of similar moments when their passion had been unleashed with wave after wave of spellbinding ecstasy. There had been no modesty in their lovemaking, no reluctance to perform any physical expression of the most profound love either had ever known or would ever know again.

An exquisite sense of loss brought tears to her eyes.

Bethany turned away, stood shakily and steadied herself on the sewing table. "I came to apologize," she whispered. "I lost my temper this evening and forced you into an inappropriate situation. I'm sorry."

"Don't be sorry, Beth."

The futon frame squeaked. She knew without looking that Jay was standing close behind her.

After a moment, Jay's voice broke the tense silence. "I'll admit that considering the consequence of my actions never occurred to me, since you'd never held me accountable for them in the past. I figured you'd run around after me, quietly mopping up my messes, just like you'd always done. But things have changed, haven't they? You've changed."

Bethany stared at the wall of snapshots, her cadre of colorful memories. "Yes, I've changed. I've grown up, Jay, and so have you."

"Is growing up the reason we're not married anymore?"

"I don't know. Maybe." She rubbed her upper arms, unwilling to turn and face him. "No, that's not true. I do know that I wasn't happy existing as an appendage in your life, a life I hadn't chosen and couldn't share. I didn't like the person I'd become . . . or perhaps I should say nonperson, because that's what I saw when I looked in the mirror."

"Did I make you feel that way?"

"No. I made myself feel that way." Bethany closed her eyes for a moment, struggling to express something that was too elusive for words. "I was always frightened, Jay, frightened of losing you, frightened of losing myself. There I was, having been tossed into a grown-up world about which I was completely clueless, and all the while I knew that I must be a terrible disappointment to you because I was such a disappointment to myself."

The final words had barely left her mouth when Jay took hold of her shoulders, spinning her forcefully around. "You were *never* a disappointment to me, Beth."

"I was never a wife to you, either."

His face, inches from her own, softened into bewilderment. "That's not true. You were a wonderful wife, a fabulous wife, the best wife a man could ask for."

Avoiding his pained gaze, Bethany focused on a water spot on the shoulder of his shirt. "I was many things, Jay—a lover, a maid, a surrogate child and the mother of your children. But I was never your wife, never your partner. How could I be? A partner is equal in strength and in courage, but I was more like a flimsy vine wrapped so tightly around you that I became too weak to stand on my own."

Jay released her shoulders, stepping back. The pain in his eyes sliced her like a blade. "You don't really believe that. You can't."

"I did believe it, Jay, but I don't anymore. I've learned to take risks, to confront problems and to solve them. Like I said, I've grown up."

A grudging admiration broke through his brooding eyes. "Yes, you have," he said quietly. "I'll admit that I'm not completely comfortable with that."

"I know." Because she couldn't stop herself, she reached out to stroke his wrist. "I'm not comfortable with some of the changes I see in you, either."

His gaze slipped down to where her fingers danced on his skin. "What changes do you see, Beth?"

"Well, you seem more flexible, less controlling."

"Controlling? *Me?*"

She replied with a furtive smile.

Frowning, Jay offered a limp shrug. "I like to be in control," he finally admitted. "But that's not the same as being controlling."

Her smile broke into a grin. "You're also more adaptable. The farm, for instance. You like it here, don't you?"

"It has a certain primitive appeal, I suppose. The kids seem happy."

Bethany's heart nearly leaped from her chest. "They *are* happy, and so am I."

You could be happy here, too.

The thought slipped unbidden into her mind and was so powerful that she had to bite her tongue to keep from revealing the secret hope she'd never even admitted to herself.

Deep down, Bethany believed that Jay's change in attitude had more to do with absenting himself from the pressures of a brutal job and the seaminess of a city that consistently overshadowed the goodness of a person's soul. If Jay left the force, if he moved here to the peace and tranquillity of rural living, perhaps they really could be a family again.

A dizzying surge of joy made her giggle. She covered her mouth and spoke through her fingers. "Sorry. I seem to be feeling a bit silly tonight."

Jay's quizzical expression melted into a smile. He slipped a thumb under her chin, tilting her face up. "Your laugh is adorable, kind of like the squeak of a tickled mouse. I've always loved it."

"Have you?" Barely recognizing the breathless voice as her own, she was only vaguely aware of her fingers sliding up his arm and resting lightly against his chest.

"Mmm. I love your hair, too," he murmured, brushing his lips over a flyaway strand at her forehead.

"It's too fuzzy." Her mumbled response could have been referring to the tightly curled tresses that she'd always despised, or to the sudden spinning of her incoherent mind. Bethany had no idea what she was talking about, or for that matter what she was feeling or thinking.

Jay didn't seem to notice her befuddlement, because his mouth had moved lower, stroking each of her cheeks before touching a gentle kiss to the tip of her nose. "And I love your freckles," he whispered. "Every single one of them."

She shivered. "They make me look blotchy."

"They make you look fresh and eager."

Lifting her gaze, she moistened her lips, wondering if he could hear the wild pounding of her heart. "Eager for what?"

"Eager for this," he whispered, a moment before their lips met in a kiss so achingly poignant that she was swept into a timeless infinity, a swirling sweetness of touch and taste and unfathomable wonder.

Through a love affair spanning more than a decade, they'd shared a million kisses, yet in an incomprehensible, almost mysterious way, this seemed like their very first. In a sense, it was. The lovers who'd shared those years, who'd shared those kisses, weren't here. They didn't exist any more, because two very different individuals had taken their place.

Now each of those new and different people was touched by wonder, by the excitement of sensual discovery and the first blush of nervous anticipation, as if they were strangers drawn by an attraction too passionate to be proper and too intense to be ignored.

Emotionally, Bethany was spinning out of control. Physically, she was ablaze with reawakened desire, her body responding without conscious thought—or perhaps in spite of it. Aware of nothing beyond the warm circle of Jay's arms, the demanding crush of his moist mouth on hers, Bethany clutched him, molding her body to his warm contours, parting her lips to draw him inside.

"Mommy!" came the plaintive wail from upstairs. "Me want story." Nathan's voice instantly penetrated his mother's passion-drugged mind as maternal instinct warred briefly with erotic impulse, then won.

Panting and shaken, Bethany turned away, grateful to be firmly ensconced in the circle of Jay's strong arms lest her own rubbery limbs reveal how deeply his kiss had affected her.

"I, ah, promised Nathan you'd read to him," Jay said finally, sounding no steadier than Bethany felt. "I guess I forgot to tell you."

"Well, then..." She paused to fill her lungs. "I suppose I'd better go read."

"Yeah." He allowed her to step away, noting that as she did so, she was forced to steady herself on the sewing table. "Bethany?"

Grasping the doorjamb, she looked over her shoulder, her mouth reddened and slightly swollen from his kiss. "Yes?"

Jay swallowed hard. "Nothing. We'll talk later."

She managed a wobbly smile, and then she was gone.

Jay wanted to shout, to run, to leap over tall buildings screaming that life was beautiful because his wife still loved him. Of course, she hadn't said as much, at least not with words, but Jay had read her feelings in her eyes, absorbed them with his kiss—a kiss she'd returned with a fervency and passion beyond any he'd ever experienced.

Bethany loved him, all right, and that was just the beginning. Jay knew as surely as he knew his own name that she wanted their marriage back; she wanted their family to be whole again.

She wanted to come home.

Chapter Nine

"Lovely lunch, Bethany." Opening the office door, Roger stood aside, allowing Bethany to enter. He followed close behind, chatting congenially. "The cafe has magnificent ambience, don't you think? Quaint, yet elegant. The owners are clients, of course. Wonderful people. They took out a seven-figure umbrella policy last year. Our commission will be enormous."

Smiling through a roaring headache, Bethany managed a halfhearted nod as she made a beeline for the sanctuary of her desk. "Yes, lunch was lovely, Roger. Thank you."

Roger stepped around a potted plant to cut her off. "I must admit that I'm a bit taken aback by your lack of enthusiasm. Most people would be utterly delighted by the opportunity to increase their earning power at their employer's expense."

Trapped, Bethany shifted her shoulder bag, crossed her arms and leaned against the wall, wishing she could put off this discussion. Clearly she couldn't. "I don't mean to seem ungrateful, Roger. I realize that moving into a sales position could be quite lucrative, but I'm not certain I can make that commitment right now.''

An annoyed frown puckered his perfectly combed brows. ''Your reluctance is bewildering. I'm not only offering you a promotion, I'm willing to pay your training expenses. What more could you possibly want?''

''Your offer is more than generous,'' she assured him. ''The truth is that I'm concerned about the increased hours the job would require. Sales personnel work evenings and weekends on a routine basis. I'm afraid I'd never see my children.'' What Bethany didn't add was that the job would also force her to neglect her pumpkins and dash her plans to attend evening agricultural classes at the local college.

There was no doubt in Bethany's mind that she didn't want the promotion. Unfortunately, there was also no doubt that her family desperately needed the money a sales position could provide, so she couldn't afford to turn down Roger's offer without careful consideration.

''This is a big decision,'' she told her plainly perplexed boss. ''I know you're anxious for an answer, but I really do need some time to think. Could I possibly have a week or so to make up my mind?''

Annoyance spread from his brows into his pale eyes, although his reply was impeccably gracious. ''Of course, my dear. I understand completely.''

Bethany doubted that. ''Thank you, Roger. Your patience and generosity are deeply appreciated.''

Seeming mollified by her gushing response, Roger flashed a confident smile. After a few minutes of small talk, during which he reminded her that she was to accompany him on a site check later that afternoon, he excused himself, slipping into to his plush office and allowing Bethany to return to her desk.

She'd barely had time to scoop the day's mail out of her In basket when the telephone rang. It was Jay, and he was clearly panicked.

"It's Nathan!" he blurted the moment she answered. "His face is all red and he can't catch his breath! What should I do?"

Bethany went rigid. "Slow down and tell me exactly what happened."

"One minute he was fine, the next minute he wasn't. Can you come home?"

"Jay...answer my question. What, exactly, was Nathan doing when he became ill?" She squeezed the receiver, frightened by his frantic tone.

"We were outside. I was measuring the goat pen and Nathan was playing tag with the dog." He paused for breath. "I watched him every minute, Beth, honest to God. He was running and squealing and having a wonderful time, and then he fell down, and when I ran over, his skin was all red and he was panting like crazy, and—"

"Wait!" Bethany moistened her lips, trying to focus on the details he'd just relayed. Since the temperature outside was in the mid-nineties, heat exhaustion or heat stroke were very real and frightening possibilities. "Listen to my questions, Jay, and answer very carefully. Does Nathan have a fever?"

"Uh...I didn't take his temperature."

"Does his skin feel hot and dry, or cold and clammy?"

"I'm not sure. Just a minute." There was a clunk as he set down the receiver, presumably on the kitchen table or counter.

Bethany covered one ear to reduce the distraction of office noise and listened intently to sounds emanating from the telephone. In the distance, she heard Jay talking.

"Nathan...hold still. Let Daddy feel your head."

"No want to!" A childish giggle filtered through the line. "Want cookie."

Bethany's stiff muscles instantly relaxed. That definitely did not sound like a child in the throes of a medical emergency.

In the background, Jay continued to mutter aloud. "Later, Nathan... C'mon, sport. Please hold still...that's good. Uh-huh. Got it." A moment later, he returned to the phone, speaking more loudly to be heard over Nathan's repeated cookie requests, which were becoming increasingly vehement. "His skin isn't exactly hot, but he feels warm and kind of sweaty."

"Is he still out of breath?"

"Hmm? Well, no. He seems to be breathing okay now, but he *was* panting."

Bethany smiled. "I imagine so. If I'd been playing tag in ninety-degree heat, I'd be panting myself. Sponge him off with a wet washcloth and give him some juice. I'm sure he'll be just fine, but if he gets nauseous or suddenly becomes drowsy, call emergency immediately."

The line fell silent for a long moment. "Are you sure he's okay?"

"Da-a-a-ddy!" wailed the indignant toddler. "Want cookie *now!*"

Somehow Bethany managed to swallow a chuckle. "Trust me, Jay. Nathan is just fine."

After a few more minutes of reassurance, Jay reluctantly hung up, allowing Bethany to take a deep breath. She dabbed her moist forehead. At least this latest call had a basis in reason, which was more than she could say for the other calls Jay had made today, the most crucial of which had been a query as to whether dishwashing liquid could be used as a substitute for laundry detergent.

The man was driving her crazy. How was she supposed to get any work done with Jay bugging her every ten minutes to ask if Nathan could wear pull-up training pants with blue jeans, or informing her that the VCR clock was two minutes off and asking how to adjust the time?

But at the same moment she was seething with righteous frustration, an image flashed through her mind, the memory of similar telephone calls she'd made to Jay over the years. She, too, had rationalized interrupting his day with questions that, in retrospect, seemed embarrassingly trivial.

If she'd been honest, Bethany would have admitted that she'd called Jay out of loneliness and to secretly assure herself that he was still alive and well. Unfortunately, she hadn't been honest, not with herself and not with Jay. Their entire marriage had been based on delusion, a foundation of false expectation and pretense that had eventually cracked into a shaky pile of rubble on which no relationship could possibly survive.

That old foundation could never be rebuilt. But maybe, just maybe, they could start from scratch and construct a brand-new one.

By midafternoon, Jay felt like a wrung-out mop. He'd never recovered from the scare Nathan had given him earlier, when he'd been absolutely convinced that his child was dying. Jay couldn't remember ever being more frightened in his life and would rather face a junkie waving a shotgun than go through that again.

Shuddering, Jay collapsed on the sofa, keeping an eagle eye on the youngster who was at the moment contentedly watching a televised preschool program. He couldn't believe how much energy it took to keep up with someone so small. Every time he'd turned his back to sweep a floor or pick up a discarded toy, Nathan had either dismantled something or emptied its contents on the furniture.

In the space of six short hours, Nathan had managed to disembowel the vacuum cleaner, spread a trail of dog kibble from the kitchen to the upstairs bath, clog every sink in the house with clay, and prune Bethany's favorite pothos with a pair of plastic scissors.

On the positive side, the new garbage disposal had been delivered, although Jay dared not take his eyes off Nathan long enough to install it. He'd finally decided he'd have to wait until tonight, after everyone was asleep. With a little luck, he could get the damn thing in and working before dawn.

No wonder Bethany always had panda-bear eyes. She probably hadn't had a decent night's sleep since David was born. Given the extent of Jay's fatigue after only a couple days of handling responsibilities that Bethany had managed for years, it was amazing she'd been able to function at all.

And when he thought how irritated he used to get just because she called him at work once in a while, well, he felt like a real heel. He wished he'd been more patient, more understanding of what she was going through—

The thought was interrupted by what sounded like a herd of water buffalo stampeding onto the porch. Before Jay could get to his feet, the front door flew open. Laurel rushed inside, her magnified eyes huge and terrified.

She stood there gasping, a rush of tears streaking her freckled cheeks.

"My God," Jay muttered, pushing himself into a standing position. "What is it, honey, what's wrong?"

"T-the school bus."

Jay's heart nearly stopped. "What about the school bus? Was there an accident?"

"The school b-bus," she repeated, her voice quivering. She gulped air, then looked up with the most pathetic expression Jay had ever seen. "I-it ran over Leon."

At five-thirty, Bethany pulled into the driveway and saw the front door standing open. As she exited the car, an unnerving prickle slid down her spine. There were no sounds emanating from the house, no television, no voices, nothing.

"Jay?" she called, glancing around the deserted acreage. She turned toward the barn, cupping her mouth as she shouted for David and Laurel.

There was no reply, and she noticed that C.J. hadn't been returned to his pen, a chore David normally took care of as soon as he got home from school.

Suddenly frantic, Bethany dashed up the porch steps, ripped open the screen door and flew into the house, still shouting for someone, anyone. Still no answer.

She ran upstairs, checking the children's rooms and finding them empty. She ran downstairs, this time looking for blood. Thankfully, there was none. The living room was neat and tidy, as was the kitchen, except for the juice glass in the sink.

There was no overt evidence of disaster, yet clearly something was very, very wrong. Jay had no car, and as far as Bethany knew, no other means of transportation. Even if he'd asked a neighbor to drive him and the kids to the store, he would have left some kind of note.

And he certainly would have closed the front door.

Bethany's legs nearly gave out. Clutching the counter, she gazed out the kitchen window at the most frightening sight that could greet a frantic mother. A sheriff's unit was cruising up her driveway.

A sob choked her. Pushing away from the counter, she spun around, stumbled through the living room and out the front door just as all three of her children clambered from the back seat of the squad car. They all looked somber and unhappy, but didn't appear to be injured.

Bethany's heart pounded once in relief and once again in renewed apprehension when she saw Jay in the front passenger seat, his head slumped forward with his chin resting on his chest. She couldn't see his face, but his profile was grim. He looked . . . wounded.

At that moment, Archie Lunt stepped from the driver's side, ambled around the vehicle and leaned in the open passenger window, apparently speaking to Jay. The children clustered by the deputy, listening intently to whatever conversation was taking place.

No one noticed Bethany standing in the open doorway until she stepped forward to steady herself on the porch rail. Her voice, when she finally found it, was little more than a raw whisper. "What's going on?"

Laurel spun around and managed to croak out one word. "Mommy!" The distraught child dashed up the steps and flung her arms around her mother's waist. Her eyes were red, her pale cheeks streaked with dried tears.

A lump of icy fear was wedged in the center of Bethany's chest. "Oh, Laurie, sweetheart . . . what is it? What's wrong?"

"It was s-so awful," Laurel stammered, squeezing Bethany's waist with painful desperation. "It was the awfulest thing I ever saw in my whole entire life—" A hiccup interrupted her, and the remaining words were muffled by her mother's breasts. "I was so s-scared."

Fighting to suppress her growing terror, Bethany stroked her daughter's hair. "Scared of what, sweetie? Did Daddy get sick or hurt himself?"

All Laurie could manage was some vaguely intelligible garble about a bus, which meant less than nothing to Bethany, whose frenzied gaze was riveted on the squad car even though her view of the passenger window was still blocked by Archie's ample frame. Frustrated and fearing that Jay had been hurt, Bethany called out to the deputy. "Archie! What's happened?"

Archie looked over his shoulder, tipped his hat in acknowledgment, then stepped back and opened the passenger door. From her vantage point by the front door, Bethany still couldn't see inside the car. She did note, however, that Jay's emergence from the vehicle was awkward but apparently unassisted.

After prying herself from Laurel's clutches, Bethany moved to the porch steps just as Jay completed his exit. He straightened, shifting his weight to accommodate the furry bundle nestled in his arms.

"Oh, no." Bethany pressed both hands to her mouth, whispering against her palms. "Leon."

Jay looked up, stricken. "I'm sorry, Beth. He ran in front of the school bus. I should have been watching him closer—"

With a soft whine, Leon lifted his head and licked Jay's chin.

"Doggie's foot broke," Nathan announced importantly. "Doctor fixed it all better."

Bethany's gaze fell to a sparkling white cast on one of Leon's rear legs. "Oh, Leon, oh, you poor little thing." She hurried down the steps, rushing over to stroke the animal's soft fur. He cocked his head, blinking groggily.

"The vet gave him a tranquilizer," Jay explained, tenderly cradling the injured dog in his arms. "That's why he's so sleepy now, but he should be okay in a couple of hours."

As David stepped up to close the squad car door, the trauma of what he'd seen was reflected in his troubled eyes. "Man, it was, like, totally unreal. Leon was all happy, running around and barking and stuff, and then the bus drove away and Leon started yelping and crying, and I didn't know what to do, 'cause I thought he was, you know, hurt real bad, so Laurie ran to get Dad—" he paused for a gulp of air "—and we tried to call you at work, only you weren't there, so we called the sheriff, and then Archie came, and he drove us to the vet—"

"And Leon's leg was broke in *three* places," Laurel blurted. "Isn't that the awfulest thing? It must have hurt real bad, too, because he was crying really, really loud." Clearly distressed by the pain her beloved pet had suffered, a fresh spurt of tears trickled down her face.

"Hey there, princess," Jay said as Bethany comforted their tearful daughter. "Leon's going to be just fine. He's going to have to wear a cast for a while, that's all."

Laurel sniffed. "Just like you, huh, Daddy?"

"Yeah, just like me." Jay sputtered as Leon presented him with another juicy kiss. "Okay, boy, okay. Let's keep our tongues to ourselves, shall we?"

"He's just showing how much he likes you," David explained.

Jay cocked a brow, skeptically eyeing the animal that was gazing up with huge, adoring eyes. "*Now* he likes me?"

"Sure. I mean, he probably figures that it's on account of you his leg got fixed and stuff." David reached out to scratch the sleepy dog's head. "I'll bet he's real mad at the school bus, though."

"Good. I hope he'll give it a wide berth from now on." Shifting the limp animal in his arms, Jay turned to Archie. "I don't know what we'd have done without your help."

The deputy shrugged. "Glad to be of service," he said, preparing to enter the patrol unit. "I'll be going now, but if you run into any more problems, just give us a call."

"I will," Jay assured him. "And thanks again."

After adding her own expression of gratitude to Archie, Bethany waited until he'd driven away before following Jay up the steps and into the house.

Nathan dashed past them, hollering, "Me go potty."

"Laurel," Bethany mumbled, pushing a curly strand of hair out of her eyes. "Will you take Nathan upstairs, please?"

The girl nodded, scooping up her baby brother's hand as David made a beeline for the kitchen.

Bethany watched Jay carefully deposit Leon on the doggy bed in the corner of the living room. "I'm sorry I wasn't in the office when you called. There was this site check...." The words evaporated in a cloud of guilt. She expected Jay to tell her that she shouldn't have gone, that she should have stayed by her phone in case she was needed at home.

To her surprise, he simply said, "You've got a job to do. I understand."

"You do?"

"Sure." Jay straightened, brushing his palms. "I work for a living, too, remember? You have to go where the job sends you."

Sighing, Bethany sat heavily on the sofa. She propped her elbows on her knees and leaned forward, shaking her head. "I wish I'd been as understanding when . . . when we were together. It pains me to admit that sometimes I actually wondered if you turned off your beeper just to spite me. Now I realize that it was probably the only way you could get anything accomplished."

"I never turned off that pager unless I was working undercover, Beth. Playing the role of a transient street addict gets a little dicey if you have to interrupt the performance and run to call your wife." Jamming his hands in his pocket, he angled a sheepish glance in her direction. "Actually, though, I did think you were overprotective of the kids."

That came as no shock, since he'd told her so by word or deed dozens of times over the years. "You were probably right. Looking back, I suspect that there were more instances than I care to admit when I deliberately embellished my concerns so that you'd give them more credence. It was childish, I suppose, but I wanted you to worry about us because in my mind, worry was proof that you cared."

"I always cared." Looking pained, Jay scoured his forehead with his fingertips, seeming oddly reluctant to meet her gaze. "I just didn't understand that when it comes to kids, there's no such thing as being too careful. I had no idea how many things can go wrong with these tiny people. I mean, one minute Nathan is a perfect little angel and a split second later, he might be emptying the medicine cabinet, or playing with razor blades, or burning up with fever—'' He tossed his hands up in complete frustration. ''How did you do it, Beth? How in hell did you stay sane?''

Leaning against the sofa arm, Bethany absently smoothed a wrinkled doily. ''If I recall, my sanity or lack thereof was a subject of some debate.''

A covert glance confirmed an embarrassed flush darkening Jay's jawline. ''Words spoken in anger,'' he said softly. ''My ego couldn't accept that a sane woman would want to leave me.''

''I never wanted to leave you, Jay. I just wanted to find me.''

''And did you? Find yourself, that is.''

''Yes, I think so. The problem is that the person I found can't live in your world.'' Bethany didn't look up, unwilling to face Jay's disappointment. ''But as long as we're playing true confessions here, I should probably admit that I never understood how difficult it was to juggle the pressures of work and family. I remember that you used to walk through the door only to be greeted with a barrage of household complaints. At the time, I was frustrated to tears by your apathy. Now that I realize how long it takes to unwind and mentally move from office mode to family mode, I can understand why you barricaded yourself behind a newspaper and pretended I didn't exist.''

''I never did that!''

Bethany raised a brow, sliding him a quizzical look.

He glanced away, tempering his response. ''I never meant to do that.''

''I know.'' A flush of water upstairs drew Bethany's attention. ''Nathan seems to have recovered quite well.''

''Huh.'' Appearing lost in thought, Jay blinked from Bethany to the stairwell from which the echo of childish giggles was emanating. ''Oh, yeah. You were right. He was just a little overheated from playing too hard.''

"You were right, too," Bethany assured him. "If you hadn't brought him in the house and immediately cooled him down, he could have become seriously ill."

"So we're both right. How very civilized." Turning away, Jay hobbled over to flop on the love seat, which was situated across from the sofa on which Bethany was sitting. He snatched up the remote, absently flipping channel after channel.

Bethany watched warily. "Have I made you angry?"

"Of course not," he mumbled, pushing the remote buttons so hard that the screen flickered with the effort. "Angry people have real feelings for each other. But we don't, do we? We're like cordial strangers, issuing cardboard smiles and gushing worthless praise. Who the hell cares which one of us is right? I'll go back to my life, and you'll stay here with yours, so tell me, Beth, what difference does it make?"

"None, I suppose." She leaned back, regarding him thoughtfully. What she read in his sour expression was actually hope—hope that his frustration was a symptom that he didn't want to go back to his old life, that he wanted to stay and share hers.

From Bethany's perspective, Jay was a brilliant, talented man who could achieve success in any field he chose. He didn't have to waste his life chasing criminals, immersing himself in the grit and filth of human misery. After all, he'd already graduated from college with honors. A few more credits in science or business administration would qualify him for dozens, perhaps hundreds of careers.

Her contemplation was interrupted by movement from the corner of the room as Leon wobbled out of his bed. Ears perked, he cocked his head to focus on Jay, then used an awkward, three-legged hop to cross the room, settling in front of the love seat. With a contented sigh, the dog lay down, resting his chin on Jay's sneaker.

Bethany smiled. "It seems Leon has undergone a rather profound attitude adjustment."

"Or he could be getting into position to chew through my ankle," he muttered, reaching down to scratch behind one floppy black ear. "I never let my guard down around anything with teeth bigger than mine."

"You're such a skeptic."

"Don't knock it. A healthy dose of skepticism has kept my butt out of a sling more than once."

David's head popped around the kitchen door. "Are we gonna have dinner pretty soon, or what?"

Jay patted his shirt pocket. "Oh, geez, I forgot to call— I mean, cook. I forgot to cook."

"That's all right," Bethany said, standing. "I'll fix something."

"No!" Jay stood so quickly that Leon's chin bounced onto the floor. "I mean, I'll take care of dinner. After all, you've been working all day."

Bemused, Bethany rubbed the back of her neck. "And you haven't? Been working, that is."

"Well, it's not the same."

"Work is work, Jay. I would think you'd have figured that out by now."

"Yeah, but—"

"Why don't we just do it together?"

"Together?"

"Yes, Jay, together. It means jointly, by combined action, as a unified force."

He stroked his chin, smiling. "Together, hmm? Actually, I kind of like the sound of that."

"So do I," she whispered, then cleared her throat and looked away. "It's settled, then. You peel potatoes and I'll fry up the burgers."

"Now, wait a minute. Why can't you peel potatoes?"

"Because I don't like to peel potatoes."

"Well, neither do I," Jay complained, following her toward the kitchen. "So how come you get to be kitchen general?"

She spun in the doorway, facing him. "One word, Jay—casserole."

"That's not fair. It was my first time."

"My point exactly. Generals have to earn their stripes."

"I *have* earned my stripes," Jay countered. "Do you know how long that casserole took to prepare?"

"I shudder to think."

"Hey, it wasn't *that* bad."

David stepped aside to let his bickering parents enter the kitchen, followed by a limping but determined Border collie. The boy stood there for a moment, listening to the squabbling adults, then spun and dashed upstairs to his sister's room.

"Guess what?" he chortled. "Mom and Dad are fighting about what to fix for dinner!"

Laurel leaped from her bed, her face shining with excitement. "That means—"

"Pizza!" they hollered in unison, then shared a high-five and scurried downstairs to place their order.

Chapter Ten

By the end of Jay's second week at the farm, life had settled into a comfortable system of organized chaos. Bethany had to admit that her former husband had managed to keep a controlling rein on their curiously exuberant youngest while maintaining a living environment that was tidy enough to be sanitary, if not absolutely sterile.

That alone was a surprising development, but Bethany had been most astonished by Jay's sudden prowess in the kitchen. For the past week, Bethany had been greeted by perfectly prepared meals that were delicious by any standard. Not only had her former husband instantly evolved into a true gourmet, the clever fellow had also figured out the secret of frying chicken without soiling a pan and baking meat loaf in a cold oven. Truly amazing. Suspicious, of course, but nonetheless amazing.

Certainly Bethany hadn't questioned the unexpected appearance of this previously unknown talent. Whatever Jay's secret, she wasn't about to jeopardize the luxury of having a hot meal ready the moment she walked in the door.

Now, however, as Bethany cruised the rows of her pumpkin fields with the ever-present *Agricultural Encyclopedia* tucked under her arm, she shaded her eyes, looking toward the barn where Jay and David had nearly completed the goat pen enclosure.

Leon was hobbling at Jay's side, his injured leg still encased in a cast matching that of his now-beloved rescuer. Since the accident, the adoring dog had been Jay's constant companion. Refusing to let his human hero out of sight, Leon had even taken to sleeping on the foot of the futon. Jay, of course, pretended to be annoyed, issuing muttered complaints at the same time he was sneaking Leon the juiciest tidbits from his dinner plate.

Bethany was amused by the transformation of her grumpy male animals and amazed at how quickly the goat pen project had evolved. They'd made remarkable progress, having started first thing this morning and finished framing by lunchtime. It was barely two in the afternoon, and the chicken wire had been stretched to form a peaked roof over the entire compound.

From Bethany's vantage point, the project looked complete, although Jay and David were still hammering away. She hoped they'd soon be finished and have the remainder of their Saturday for some well-deserved rest and relaxation. David wanted to go fishing again, and despite the original mishap, Jay had seemed receptive to the idea.

In fact, David and Jay had become nearly inseparable, and David had blossomed in the light of his father's attention. Nathan, too, had seemed happier, although he occasionally asked about his friends at day care. Now that the repairs on Jay's car had been completed, Jay had promised to take Nathan over next week for a visit.

Both of the boys were happy as worm-fed larks, but Bethany was deeply concerned about Laurel, who followed her daddy around and clung to him yet still seemed distant and moody. Bethany suspected that her daughter's unhappiness stemmed from problems at school, problems the child steadfastly refused to discuss. Probing questions had been met with sullen silence, and Bethany's attempt to glean information from David had been just as fruitless, since the swaggering fourth-grader paid no attention to the goings-on of his sister's lowly second-grade class.

A glance toward the front porch revealed that Laurel was still sitting on the steps, coloring, as she had been for the past hour. Bethany was fretting about what she could do to cheer her morose daughter when she saw Jay walking toward the porch.

He sat down beside Laurel, who held up her coloring book, presumably to show off her work. Jay nodded, smiling, and slipped a fatherly arm around the girl's shoulders. A moment later they were engrossed in serious conversation.

Bethany hesitated, not wanting to intrude yet dying to know what was being discussed. Of course, she wouldn't actually be intruding if she passed by on her way into the house for, say, a cold glass of water.

Suddenly beset by uncontrollable thirst, Bethany dropped her book and tool bucket, then followed a circuitous route toward the house. She edged along the side of the porch where she couldn't be seen from the steps, but was close enough to overhear Jay and Laurel's conversation.

"Your teacher sounds like a very nice lady," Jay was saying.

"She's okay," Laurel agreed. "Sometimes she lets me pass out papers."

"That's an important job. She must like you a lot."

"I guess."

He laid the coloring book in his lap. "Tell me about your classmates. Are they nice, too?"

Frowning, Laurel retrieved her coloring book and flipped idly through the pages. "There's a girl named Karen. I kind of like her because she lets me play kickball with her friends. Sometimes she lets me sit next to her on the bus, too."

"So you like Karen?"

"I guess so. She has pretty hair."

Jay smiled. "Have you made any other new friends?"

She shook her head without looking up. "I don't like anybody else."

"Why not?"

"They're mean."

"All of them?"

Fidgeting with the corner of a page, Laurel squirmed away, shrugging her father's arm off her shoulders. "Some of the girls are okay, but all of the boys are mean. I hate them. I wish they'd just die."

The venom in Laurel's voice shook Bethany to her toes. She gripped the base of a porch rail, stunned that a child so sensitive she refused to swat a housefly was even capable of expressing such dark hatred.

Jay, however, merely leaned back, using his rejected arm as a prop. He gazed across the pumpkin fields, appearing unconcerned about the child's vehement vilification of his gender. After a long moment, he spoke in a voice that was deceptively casual. "What mean things are the boys doing?"

Laurel shrugged without looking up. "They're always saying stuff."

"What kind of stuff?"

"Mean stuff." She scratched a chewed fingernail across the page. "They call me, you know, bad names."

When Laurel's gaze shifted toward the corner of the porch, Bethany pulled back for a moment, then peered between porch rails and saw the angry twitch of Jay's jaw.

To his credit, he managed to keep a light and even tone. "What bad names do they call you, sweetie?"

She shrugged again. "Stupid names, like geek and dweeb and—" her voice broke "—and bottle face."

Jay quickly turned away to cough into his hand. When he straightened, an amused glint lit his eyes. "Bottle face?"

"Uh-huh," Laurel replied miserably. "On account of my glasses being fat as bottles. They all hate me because I'm so ugly."

"Oh, Laurie, you're not ugly." Jay straightened, hugging her fiercely. "You're beautiful, honey."

The reply, muffled by her father's shoulder, was barely audible. "No, I'm not."

"You most certainly are beautiful, and do you know what else? I'm willing to bet that those boys don't hate you at all. In fact, judging by what you've just told me, I think those boys like you a whole lot."

Bethany swallowed hard, wishing she could clue Jay that she'd already tried that tactic, and it had failed miserably.

It was clearly doomed to fail again, since Laurel had already pulled away and was rolling her eyes. "That's dumb."

"Sure, it's dumb," Jay agreed affably. "But that's how little boys act around little girls they like."

"How do you know?"

"Because I used to *be* a little boy."

The girl blinked, seeming stunned by the revelation that her big, strong daddy had ever been anything but—well, a big, strong daddy. *"You?"*

"Yep, and I know from personal experience that when boys tease a pretty girl, it's because they want her to notice them." Jay leaned close, lowering his voice to a conspiratorial whisper Bethany could barely hear. "Do you know what I did the first time I saw your mommy?"

"Uh-uh."

Jay chuckled. "I threw a paper wad at her and called her Spot."

"Why'd you do that?" Laurel asked, clearly horrified.

"Because she had these adorable freckles all over her face, and because it was the only way I could get her to notice me."

"So what did Mommy do when you, you know, called her that bad name?"

"She stomped my foot and emptied a can of soda over my head."

Laurel giggled, pressing her palms to her mouth. "She did not."

"No lie," Jay intoned, crossing his heart. "We were in high school at the time, so I was a lot older than the boys in your class, although sadly, I didn't act any older."

"What happened, Daddy?"

"Well, let's see. I think it was lunchtime, and your mommy was in the quad with a group of her friends. I'd been watching her for days, but she never even looked in my direction. She didn't know I was alive."

Listening, Bethany smiled, wishing she could interject that she most certainly *had* noticed him. She'd had a crush on Jay Murdock for weeks, and her carefully choreographed nonchalance had been part of a scheme her girlfriends insisted was absolutely foolproof. Boys, they'd announced, were egocentric creatures that could tolerate anything except being ignored.

As it turned out, they'd been right, although Bethany still winced at the memory of how horrified she'd been when the light of her young life had publicly dubbed her Spot. She'd been furious, and utterly humiliated.

Until now, Bethany had never understood that cruelty, which she'd eventually learned was diametrically opposed to an otherwise kind and sensitive nature. Odd, she mused, that after all these years, she was still learning about the man with whom she'd spent most of her life, and he still had the ability to surprise her.

The sound of Jay's voice caught Bethany's attention, and she strained to hear.

"So first I did a handstand, then I did so many push-ups my arms felt like spaghetti, but she still wouldn't look over at me, so I finally wadded some paper into a big fat ball and bounced it off the back of her head. Then I puffed up my chest and loped over, real jocklike, to retrieve my paper ball."

Laurel's eyes were enormous. "What happened then?"

"Well, I slipped her my best come-hither look and drawled, 'Hey there, Spot, what's happening?'" Jay chuckled, shaking his head. "As it turned out, that probably wasn't the world's best idea, because she gave me a look that could freeze meat and stomped my toe as hard as she could. Then while I was yelping and hopping around, she poured a soda over my head, pushed me on my keester and marched away. It was six months before I could convince her to speak to me again."

By the time Jay finished his story, Laurel was folded over, hugging herself and giggling madly.

He feigned indignance. "Hey, do you think your poor old dad's bruised ego is funny?"

"Uh-huh," Laurel replied, laughing so hard her breath came in little pig snorts.

Jay shrugged. "Okay, so maybe I asked for it. The point is that the boys in your class are doing the same thing I did, which is trying to get the attention of a girl they really like."

Reaching under her spectacles, Laurel wiped her moist eyes. "But how can I make them stop?"

"By being friendly and flashing that pretty smile at them. Trust me, sweetie, you'll make 'em melt."

She heaved a giant sigh. "I'd rather make them dry up and blow away."

"I'm sure you would," Jay said, giving her shoulders a fatherly squeeze. "At least for the moment. But some day you'll learn to appreciate boys, just like your mommy did."

Bethany emitted a snort of laughter, drawing Jay's attention. Their eyes met, their gazes warmed. He winked. She blew him a kiss. Then, her thirst forgotten, she slipped around the corner and returned to her pumpkins, brooding about how Jay had been able to get through to Laurel when Bethany's repeated attempts to do the same had failed miserably.

Pondering that, it occurred to Bethany that she hadn't realized just how much the children needed their father or how much she needed her husband.

Peeking out the living room window, Jay assured himself that Bethany was still toiling in the fields a safe distance from the evolving conspiracy. "Okay, so we've got it under control, right?"

"Right," David said, snapping to attention. "I'm gonna handle the stereo—"

"And I picked a whole bunch of pretty wildflowers for the table," Laurel blurted.

David slid his sister an annoyed glance. "And then we're supposed to keep Nathan upstairs, so it'll be nice and quiet down here."

Jay nodded. "Can you two get Nathan to bed by yourselves?"

"That's easy," David replied, grinning. "We'll just tell him to keep his eyes closed for ten whole minutes and he can have all the cookies he wants. It works every time."

"Is that what your mom does?" Jay asked, astounded by the devious plan and annoyed that he hadn't thought of it himself.

"Oh, no." Primly straightening her spectacles, Laurel gave her brother a withering look. "Mommy says it's not right to trick people and make bad promises."

"And your mommy is right," Jay mumbled, absently patting his daughter's head. He glanced at David. "Works every time, huh?"

With a shrewd grin, the boy rocked back on his heels. "Every time."

Laurel's self-righteous smile faded.

Jay cleared his throat. "We'll, uh, talk about it later. Meanwhile, I'm going in to town and pick up the rest of the things we'll need. You guys stay inside in case Nathan wakes up, but remember..." He placed a finger in front of his lips. "This is our secret, right?"

"Right!" came the simultaneous reply, along with a pair of matching salutes.

"At ease," Jay barked, returning the salute. "Assume command position—" he paused, glancing at his watch "—now!"

The youngsters scurried away, giggling.

Rubbing his hands together, Jay hobbled outside. Leon yawned, stood and hopped across the porch. Jay smiled, scratching the dog's head. "Hey, old man. How's it going?"

Whining, Leon leaned against Jay's knee.

"Yeah, I know. My leg itches, too."

Leon cocked his head and sighed.

Jay continued to scratch the dog's ears as he glanced around the fields, finally spotting Bethany, who was hunched over, as usual, with her nose practically buried in a vine.

Pride swelled inside his chest, along with a sense of wonder. Over the past week, he and Bethany had recaptured the closeness they'd once shared, allowing Jay a glimpse of the vivacious girl he remembered mingled with a strong, capable woman he couldn't help but admire. His sweet young wife had grown up when he wasn't looking, and unsettling as that was, Jay nonetheless liked what he saw.

He only wished he'd seen it sooner.

Jay swallowed a surge of regret, and he and Leon wound a hoppity path through the irrigation furrows. They reached Bethany just as she stood to dust off her knees. "You look grim," Jay told her. "More bugs?"

"No. At least, none that I see." She frowned at a lop-sided pumpkin. "It's just that they don't seem as big as they should be. I don't know why. I've been fertilizing like crazy. They should be big as barns by now."

Jay glanced around. "They look fine to me."

"I just hope they look fine to the canner's rep," she mumbled. "He'll be here tomorrow. It's the final assessment before harvest next month."

"Canner's rep?"

"Mmm." Bethany chewed her lower lip, obviously distracted. "It was the bank's idea."

"What has the bank got to do with pumpkins?"

"Uncle Horace took out a loan to plant," she explained. "When I took over, the bank was nervous about my lack of farming experience. They insisted that the crop be periodically assessed."

"Kind of like checking out the building site after issuing a construction loan?"

"I guess." A worried frown creased her forehead. "Only I think building a house would be easier. At least there are blueprints to follow."

Jay studied a few of the deformed little gourds and silently agreed that some of them didn't look much like the pumpkins he recalled carving for Halloween. "Maybe pumpkins are like babies," he reasoned. "Maybe they gain most of their weight during the last month before birth...or in this case, before harvest."

"Maybe." A limp shrug indicated that she remained hopeful but unconvinced. Pulling off a glove, she wiped her moist face, spreading a dirty smear across her cheek.

Smiling, Jay used his thumb to remove it. "I've got to run into town," he told her. "Nathan's taking a nap, but if he wakes up before I get back the kids will keep an eye on him."

"What do you need in town?" she asked, clearly surprised.

He shrugged. "Stuff, you know. By the way, don't worry about dinner tonight. I'll pick something up."

Her nervous gaze fell to his cast. "Are you sure you can drive? I mean, if you need something, I can go get it for you."

"I can drive," he assured her. "My car's an automatic, so my left foot doesn't have anything to do anyway. I'll be fine." Backing away, he snapped his fingers and spoke to Leon. "C'mon, boy. Want to go for a ride?"

Leon barked happily.

"Jay, I really don't think this is a good idea—"

"We'll be back in an hour or so," he called, hobbling through the furrows with Leon hot on his heels. "Remember, don't start dinner."

"Jay!" Bethany jammed her hands on her hips, watching him wave over his head as he navigated through the field as fast as his walking cast would allow. A few minutes later, Jay's car rolled out of the driveway and disappeared down the road. Sighing, she tossed her gloves on the ground and glared at a puckered pumpkin. "What are you looking at?"

The pumpkin didn't reply.

"Oh, yeah? Well, what do you know about men, anyway? All you had to do was sit there and wait for a pollinating bee."

Bethany sat heavily on the dry earth, watching the dust settle at the end of the driveway and contemplating how different Jay seemed. Different, yet familiar. He was, she realized, more like the spontaneous prankster with whom she'd fallen in love so long ago. And yet the youthful exuberance she remembered was now blended with a man of strength and honor, a man who, if she hadn't allowed herself to become tainted by years of hurt anger, Bethany would have loved even more.

She hadn't appreciated her husband. Even worse, she hadn't appreciated herself. But perhaps it wasn't too late. Perhaps they could mend their differences and become a family again—

Her wishful contemplation was interrupted by another rise of dust at the end of the driveway. Relieved that Jay had come to his senses and returned home, Bethany stood, shading her eyes, only to moan in disappointment. The car cruising down the driveway wasn't Jay's.

It belonged to Roger Morris.

Jay steered his freshly repaired utility vehicle down the deserted rural road, whistling and patting the precious bulge in his shirt pocket. Beside him were grocery bags filled with items needed to complete his plan—a romantic evening in celebration of what would have been his and Bethany's eleventh wedding anniversary.

Although disappointed that Bethany hadn't mentioned the significance of today's date, Jay consoled himself by mentally rehearsing what he was certain would become a memorable, if not downright unforgettable night.

But his happy mood popped like a wet bubble when he pulled into the driveway and saw Morris's car.

"Damn." Jay slapped the steering wheel, infuriated by the intrusion. Swerving into his parking place beside the barn, he snatched up his parcels and climbed out, fuming. After Leon leaped out, Jay slammed the car door and stalked toward the house.

No way was he going to let his wife's pompous boss screw up his plans. He hoped the jerk would leave peaceably. If not, Jay would bury his body in the back pasture, and there wasn't a jury in the state that would convict him.

Jay had nearly reached the front porch when David rushed out, slamming the door behind him. The boy dashed down the steps with worried eyes and a grim expression. "Guess who's here?"

"Yeah, I know." Jay aimed a slitty-eyed stare at the front door. "But he's just about to leave."

David took a relieved breath. "That's good, 'cause he's been trying to get Mom to, you know, run away with him."

Jay tripped on the step. *"What?"*

"To a hotel," David added with a knowing nod.

Stunned, Jay stood motionless, closing his mouth only when a draft chilled his tongue. Without another word, he stomped up the steps and flung the front door open with enough force to rattle every picture on the living room wall.

Bethany, who was seated on the sofa, jumped as though shot, pressed a palm against her chest and stared at Jay in astonishment while Roger rose from the love seat, flashing his best salesman smile.

"Jay, old chap, nice to see you again." Roger stepped around the furniture, holding out a manicured hand that Jay would have ignored even if his arms hadn't been loaded with parcels. "Bethany tells me that you've healed splendidly, and have been immensely helpful. Jolly good, I say. After her promotion, Bethany will certainly need any assistance you can give her."

Promotion?

Jay blinked at Bethany, who immediately bent her head and covered her eyes with her hand.

David scurried inside, took the grocery bags from his father, then slunk into the kitchen, tossing a worried look over his shoulder while Leon hopped to his corner bed and flopped down, looking bored.

Meanwhile, Roger had retrieved his rejected hand and was using it to smooth his silk necktie. He angled a proud glance in Bethany's direction. "Isn't that right, my dear?"

Reluctantly raising her gaze, Bethany glanced from Roger to Jay and back again. "You know that I haven't made a decision about that."

"Of course," Roger murmured with a dismissive flick of his hand. Turning to Jay, his smarmy smile broadened. "With your vast experience, old man, I'm certain you've recognized the magnificent opportunity this advancement represents. Surely you've encouraged Bethany to take advantage of it."

From the corner of his eye, Jay could see Bethany's frantic hand signals but paid no attention to them. Instead, he stared straight at Morris and spoke without moving his jaw. "Does this have anything to do with a hotel?"

Bethany curled forward, moaning, and pressed her forehead against her knees.

Roger, however, beamed. "Why, yes, as a matter of fact. There's a three-day seminar next week in San Francisco. It would provide a marvelous introduction to business basics of the insurance industry. Since you are so graciously available and able to provide child-care assistance, I'd hoped to entice Bethany into joining me."

"Joining you," Jay repeated, his eyes narrowing into slits.

"Indeed." Roger skimmed a vain glance at Bethany, who was staring at the floor, shaking her head and apparently mumbling to herself. "I'm to be the keynote speaker."

Bethany looked up helplessly. "I've told Roger that the seminar is out of the question."

Jay folded his arms. "Have you?"

"Yes, of course."

"I'd hoped you could convince her," Roger interjected, plainly perturbed by her refusal. "After all, opportunities of this magnitude don't come along every day."

"No, I imagine they don't." Relief seeped through every pore of Jay's body. Somehow he managed not to grin. "But it's Bethany's decision, after all. If she doesn't want this promotion of yours, she doesn't want it. End of story."

Roger frowned and would have spoken if Bethany hadn't leaped to her feet.

"I won't be going to the seminar," she explained. "As for the promotion, I haven't made up my mind yet. I promised Roger that we'd discuss it later." She swallowed hard, twisting her hands into finger knots. "After dinner."

Jay's folded arms sprang apart. "After dinner... tonight?"

"I, ah, invited Roger to join us," she said miserably. "I hope you don't mind."

"Mind?" Jay's horrified gaze swept from Bethany to Roger, who was smiling pleasantly, blissfully unaware of the tumult his presence had caused.

"If it's a problem, old man, I'd be happy to take Bethany out to supper. There's a lovely old steak house in Roseville—"

"No! I mean . . ." Jaw aching, Jay forced a smile so thin his lips disappeared. "It's not a problem. I'll, ah, just set an extra place, that's all."

"Excellent." With a jovial grin, Roger sauntered to his place on the love seat, dismissing Jay as if he was a servant. "Now, my dear, where were we? Oh, yes. The pension plan, which you must agree is exceptionally generous, and for which you'd be fully vested in less than five years."

Only the silent plea in Bethany's dark eyes kept Jay from hauling Morris out the front door and kicking his arrogant butt halfway to Tahoe.

At that fortuitous moment, Laurel appeared at the top of the stairs. "Daddy, Nathan's awake."

Jay hesitated, reluctant to leave his wife alone with a man who had obvious designs on her, yet realizing that petty jealousy was absurd considering that Bethany dealt with this jerk on a daily basis. With a regretful sigh, he headed up the stairs to Nathan's room.

As Jay scooped the sleepy toddler out of his crib, David appeared in the doorway, obviously distraught. "That guy is gonna ruin everything. What are we gonna do, Dad?"

"I don't know." Jay sat in a nearby rocker and began pulling off Nathan's damp undershirt. "Let me think for a minute."

"I could take him out to see the new goat pen," David suggested. "If he was to go inside, you know, to look around and stuff, maybe the gate might blow shut or something, and maybe he wouldn't be able to get out."

Jay gave the boy a reproachful look. "You know better than that, son."

"Yeah, I guess," David said, hanging his head. "It wouldn't be a nice thing to do."

"True, but the point is that after the barn fiasco, he'd never fall for it." Reaching into an open drawer, Jay retrieved a fresh shirt for Nathan. "We need a new strategy, something Morris won't be expecting."

David brightened. "We could tie him up and lock him in a closet."

"Ah, I don't think so."

"How come?"

"It would upset your mother."

"Oh."

Laurel stepped forward. "Daddy, you know that name you used to call Mommy?"

Having completed the chore of tugging a too-small shirt over a too-fat head, Jay looked up with a curious smile. "You mean, Spot?"

"Uh-huh." A crafty gleam lit Laurel's shiny blue eyes.

Jay let Nathan climb off his lap, then folded his arms and studied the red felt-tipped pen his daughter was holding. He shook his head, grinning. "Sweetheart, you're a genius."

Laurel smiled. "I know."

* * *

Leaning forward with her hands clasped demurely in her lap, Bethany's body language expressed attentive interest despite the fact that she'd barely heard a word Roger had said. Her mind was replaying Jay's disappointed expression and the cold fury in his eyes when he'd learned that Roger would be staying for dinner.

Somehow she had to find a way to let Jay know she'd had no choice but to invite him. Roger had this way of backing people into a corner, forcing them into decisions they wouldn't otherwise make. It was a talent that made him a top-notch insurance salesman and a personal boor.

"Don't you agree, my dear?"

Blinking, Bethany struggled to focus her mind. "Excuse me?"

"Don't you agree that a deferred compensation account subsidized by the agency would assure your family a secure financial future?"

"Well, yes, I suppose so."

"An astute observation, Bethany. Why, the tax savings alone would net a tidy sum in later years, perhaps even enough to cover college tuition for your children." Eyes glittering, Roger leaned in for the kill. "Deferred compensation is an exquisitely lucrative investment. Sadly, it's available only to our marketing professionals."

Bethany hoped she was smiling, but her face was too numb for her to tell. "I realize that sales positions provide more financial incentive than administrative work, but—"

"Have we discussed commissions? You'll receive a percentage fee for both new policies and renewals."

"Yes, you mentioned that," she murmured, distracted by a stomping on the stairs as Jay and the children descended.

The first thing she noticed was Jay's peculiar expression; then she saw that he was carrying Nathan, who appeared limp and abnormally lethargic, with his little face pressed against his father's chest. She stood, instantly wary. "Is something wrong?"

Jay entered the living room, pausing several feet away from the area where Bethany and Roger had been talking. "Nothing serious," he replied. "I'll just start dinner. Oh, by the way..." He whispered something in Nathan's ear to which the child responded by turning his red-speckled face toward the living room.

Ignoring Bethany's startled gasp, Jay regarded Roger with a cheery smile. "By the way, old chap, you *have* had chickenpox, right?"

"My God!" Roger sputtered, backing away. "I, ah ... My God!"

The sound of a slamming screen door was quickly followed by the screech of tires. David ambled over to glance out the window. "Gee, you were right, Dad. He really did leave skid marks."

Chapter Eleven

"I can't believe you did this," Bethany mumbled, scouring the crimson splotches off Nathan's grinning face.

Jay leaned against the downstairs bathroom's shower frame, reading aloud from the package of colorful kiddie pens. "Non-toxic and safe. Approved for preschool use."

"That's hardly the point." Bethany rinsed the soapy washcloth, then went to work on a circle of red dots extending down the child's fat little neck. "What kind of example are you setting for our children? I mean, faking a disease, for goodness sake. You frightened poor Roger half to death. It was devious, Jay, and it was cruel."

"Cruel?" Jay tossed the pen package on the back of the john. "I'll tell you what's cruel," he fumed. "Cruelty is having to share my special anniversary dinner with a pretentious Prince Charles wannabe that has romantic designs on my wife. That's not only cruel, it's downright inhuman."

"Anniversary?" Stunned, Bethany dropped the wash-cloth and sagged against the vanity. "Oh, good heavens. I can't believe I forgot."

"Neither can I," Jay muttered, sullenly kicking at the fuzzy blue throw rug. He angled a pouty glance upward. "You hurt my feelings."

"Oh, Jay, I'm so sorry. That's the last thing I'd ever want to—" She straightened. "Hey, wait a minute. First of all, we're divorced, and anniversaries aren't supposed to count for divorced people."

He shrugged. "A mere technicality."

"And second, *I'm* the one who's supposed to be angry here."

"Yes, well..." His sullen expression melted into a sheepish grin. "I was hoping to distract you from that."

Unable to maintain her gruff expression, Bethany felt the smile ease across her face without permission. She turned away, hoping to conceal her amusement, which was none-theless exposed by her mirrored reflection. A covert glance revealed that Jay was indeed watching her in the mirror, and seemed quite pleased with what he saw. She sighed. "You know, of course, that you're absolutely impossi-ble."

His smug smile widened. "You wouldn't have it any other way."

"As if I had a choice," she muttered, scooping Nathan from his perch on the sink vanity and standing him on the floor.

"Me got chicken-pops," Nathan announced happily.

Bethany gave Jay a rueful look. "Now see what you've done?"

"I'll deal with this." Squatting, Jay feigned a serious expression. "You didn't really have chicken pox, sport. We were just, ah, playing a game, remember?"

"Uh-huh. Cookies now?"

With a nervous eye shift, Jay leaned close to the toddler and whispered, "Later."

"You promised," Nathan insisted, his lip quivering with indignance.

Bethany folded her arms. "Bribery, too?"

Flashing a nervous smile, Jay wiped his forehead, then stood, scooping up the irritated toddler. "Hey, there, little man, what's your very favorite dinner in the whole wide world?"

"Hot dogs!"

Jay frowned. "I thought it was tacos."

"Hot dogs," Nathan insisted.

"Oh. Well, we'll have hot dogs another time, but Daddy went to the Taco Hut this afternoon, so tonight you're going to have tacos."

Nathan considered that. "Want cookies."

"My, my," Bethany crooned, flashing her sweetest smile. "We do have a problem here, don't we? And a special anniversary dinner of precooked tacos? Yummy."

"Tacos are for the children," Jay explained patiently. "You and I will dine later. Alone."

The final word was issued with a seductive wink that made Bethany's stomach quiver with anticipation. At a loss for words, she simply turned away and made a production out of wiping down the puddled vanity while Jay carried his frustrated son into the kitchen.

After he'd gone, Bethany pushed aside the damp cloth and stared into the mirror, grimacing at her grimy reflection. She looked absolutely horrible, wearing grungy overalls smeared with field mud while her hair sprang from her scalp in a mass of electrified corkscrews.

Later, Jay had said. *Alone.* The implication gave her goose bumps.

A moment later, Bethany had ripped off her filthy clothes, grabbed the shampoo bottle and was stepping into a steaming shower. If Jay wanted their anniversary to be special, Bethany was more than willing to do her part.

Red was erotic.

Satin was a feast for the senses.

Therefore, scarlet satin swirling on bare thighs must be exquisitely provocative and irresistibly sexy.

At least, that's what Bethany hoped as she slipped into the sleek, spaghetti-strapped skimmer that she hadn't worn since before Laurel's birth. Classic lines and simple elegance never went out of style, although Bethany wasn't certain fire-engine red would actually qualify as elegant. Still, the dress was one of the few garments she owned that wasn't made of denim or compiled from her drab wardrobe of mix-and-match office wear.

And amazingly enough, it still fit.

Bethany critically eyed her reflection. The skimmer's built-in bra bodice, which seemed a bit snugger than she remembered, gave her a significant cleavage boost, clinging to her curves like a second skin then flaring at mid-hip into a swirling crimson cloud.

A pair of delicate gold hoops gleamed at her earlobes, barely visible beneath the billow of glossy curls tumbling to her bare shoulders and cascading down her back. To complete the sensual ensemble, she'd chosen airy sandals with dainty white filigree straps, casual yet infinitely feminine and, she hoped, alluring.

After applying a rich ruby lip color and a quick spritz of her favorite fragrance, Bethany decided that she was as ready as she'd ever be.

Inhaling as deeply as the dress would allow, she massaged her churning stomach, realizing that she hadn't been this nervous since her wedding night. Then, however, she'd been a nineteen-year-old virgin; now she was a thirty-year-old mother of three. Under the circumstances, a sudden burst of chaste apprehension was absurd, but nonetheless authentic. She was anxious and excited, fearful and impatient, just as she'd been eleven years ago tonight. Except that she hadn't been wearing red. In fact, she hadn't been wearing anything at all.

Bethany muffled a ditzy giggle, then gave her reflection a stern stare, reminding herself that she wasn't a girl any longer. She was a woman now. A woman of strength. A woman of fortitude.

A woman of red-hot passion.

Moaning, Bethany turned away from the beguiling stranger in the mirror and was reaching to unzip the dress when there was a timid knock at the door.

"Mommy?" Laurel called. "Daddy says everything is ready now."

Bethany's fingers froze on the zipper tab. For the past hour, every attempt at leaving her bedroom had resulted in a flurry of activity culminated by one of the children blockading the hallway, issuing a frenzied plea for her to wait just a few more minutes.

Another series of tiny taps vibrated the bedroom door. "Mommy, you can come out now. Honest."

Bethany sighed. "All right, sweetie."

At the sound of scampering feet, Bethany squared her shoulders and went into the hall.

The first thing she noticed was that the house seemed inexorably dark considering that it was still daylight outside. As she moved toward the living room, she realized that the drapes had been drawn, and the only illumination was emanating from a series of flickering candles strategically placed around the room.

"My goodness," she murmured, pausing while her eyes adjusted to the dim light.

"Over here, Mommy," Laurel called impatiently from the kitchen door. "Come look at the table."

Moving carefully, Bethany passed the stairs, crossed the living room and stepped into the candle-lit kitchen. Two silver candlesticks and a vase of colorful wildflowers decorated the table, which had been laid with her hand-crocheted, special-occasion tablecloth, her grandmother's antique china, and the two crystal goblets that had managed to survive a Southern California quake.

David's voice boomed from the shadows. "Do you like it, Mom?"

"Oh, yes," she whispered, touching her throat. "It's beautiful."

"I picked the flowers," Laurel announced. "All I could find were wild sweetpeas, but Daddy said you'd like them better than store-bought stuff."

Choked with a rush of emotion, Bethany managed a moist smile and an agreeable nod, at which point Jay suddenly stepped into the flickering light.

"For madam's pleasure," he murmured, gallantly pulling back a chair.

Bethany just stood there, feeling as if she'd been swept into a wacky, wonderful dream in which the ambience of her homey little farmhouse had been miraculously transformed into a romantic hideaway.

"You're supposed to sit down," David informed her.

"Oh, of course." Spurred by the reminder, Bethany stepped forward and allowed herself to be seated.

Jay removed an intricately folded napkin from a dinner plate, spreading the ivory linen across Bethany's lap with the panache of a five-star maître d'. He straightened, snapped his fingers and three small silhouettes leaped forward.

Laurel grabbed Nathan's hand, dragging the curious toddler upstairs while David scampered directly into the living room. A moment later, the mellow strains of Bethany's favorite interlude floated through the house.

David poked his head into the kitchen. "We're gonna go upstairs now," he said with pointed enthusiasm. "And we won't come back down!"

Bethany bit back a smile. "Not ever?"

"Um, maybe for breakfast."

"Ah. Well then, perhaps we should say our good-nights now."

"Yeah, okay. G'night." The boy flashed his parents an excited grin, then spun around and dashed upstairs using more energy than the average grown-up could muster in a week.

Struck speechless, Bethany leaned back in her chair, marveling at the delightful display of creative ingenuity. "I can't believe you went to so much trouble."

"You're worth it," Jay whispered, capturing her hand and raising it to his lips, where each knuckle was favored by a tender, unhurried kiss. He gently turned her hand, pressing her palm to his cheek. "God, you're so beautiful," he whispered. "You look like a goddess."

Worry that the brazen attire made her look like a two-dollar tart melted in the heat of her husband's reverent gaze. "You look nice, too," she murmured stupidly, unable to take her eyes off what appeared to be the bow tie from David's Dracula costume, which Jay was wearing with a white T-shirt.

His nervous smile shifted to the floor. "I couldn't find anything in my duffel that was appropriate to the occasion, but I did scrub behind my ears and press my walking shorts." Rubbing his palms together, he glanced around as if trying to remind himself of something, then spotted a towel-wrapped bottle nestled in Bethany's ice-filled mop bucket. "Ah. The wine." He hobbled to the counter, retrieving the wine with a flourish, then displaying the chilled bottle over his crooked arm. "The finest Chardonnay in our cellar, madam."

"There isn't any cellar."

"If there was, this would be the best Chardonnay down there. Actually, it would be the only one down there," he added, reaching for a corkscrew. "Are you aware that there isn't a single bottle of decent wine in this entire house?"

Bethany was painfully aware of that. In fact, there wasn't any wine in the house, decent or otherwise, although over the years, she and Jay had frequently enjoyed wine with their meals. It was a habit Bethany had discarded after their separation, having discovered that no matter how fine the vintage, wine had no flavor unless shared.

The same could be said of pink sunsets and panoramic dawns, of lazy weekend mornings dawdling over coffee and toast and of so many simple delights that became dry and tasteless when experienced alone.

Bethany had tried not to dwell on what she'd lost, reminding herself that the inability to independently enjoy life's little pleasures was yet another symptom of the clingy dependency that had been her greatest weakness.

She'd craved autonomy, and she'd achieved it. But the cost had been dear.

A muffled pop drew her attention to Jay, who tossed the impaled cork on the counter and moved quickly to fill Bethany's crystal goblet with golden liquid. He raised the bottle as if saluting, clicked his leather heel against his plaster one and issued a snappy bow. "Our specialty of the evening is a magnificent poached salmon in delicate herb sauce, served with a lovely rice pilaf and garden fresh vegetables steamed to perfection."

"That sounds—" the ceiling suddenly vibrated with scampering feet "—wonderful." Bethany angled a worried glance at the quivering light fixture.

Jay, also distracted by the noise, made a valiant effort to ignore it. "We'll start with a cool cucumber soup," he murmured, moving two bowls of creamy liquid from the refrigerator to the table. "Followed by crisp greens with special house dressing and—"

The menu dissertation was interrupted by a rambunctious thumping upstairs, followed by the sound of Laurel's exasperated voice and Nathan's shrill protest.

Bethany laid her napkin on the table. "Perhaps I should check on the children."

"No, no...everything's under control." Jay frowned up at the ceiling with a muttered, "I hope."

At that moment, something hit the stairs with the force of a small stampede. After a scurry of descending footsteps, David skidded into the kitchen.

"Sorry," he mumbled, edging toward the pantry. "Forgot something." He opened the cupboard, pulled out something that crinkled suspiciously like a cellophane cookie bag, then flashed a nervous grin, said, "Bye," and charged upstairs.

Bethany angled Jay a quizzical glance, to which he responded by dabbing his forehead and slipping into his chair. "Shall we begin?" he asked, holding up his spoon. "We wouldn't want our soup to get, ah, warm."

"Certainly not." She swallowed an amused chuckle with a spoonful of cold soup. "Mmm. This is wonderful." Jay's proud grin faded as she added, "You must give me the recipe."

"I can't," he mumbled, staring into his bowl. "It's an old family secret, and my great-great-great—" he paused to count on his fingers "—great-great Aunt Brunhilda issued a curse on any family member who dared to reveal it."

"A curse, no less." Since Bethany recognized the delicious soup as the unique specialty of a nearby restaurant, she wasn't fooled by the imaginative tale. "Well, we certainly can't allow you to be hexed by your own ancestors, can we?"

"No, we certainly can't." Visibly relieved, Jay lifted his wine goblet. "A toast," he declared, as Bethany raised her glass. "To us."

"To us," she agreed.

And with the melodic clink of crystal, the evening had officially begun.

Leaning languidly back, Bethany contentedly sipped fresh coffee while Jay cleared the empty dessert bowls. For the past hour and a half, the house had been miraculously silent. The stereo had turned itself off when the album of mood music had finished playing, and after a quick up-stairs kid check, Jay had returned to pronounce all three children officially asleep.

Throughout the evening, Jay had fussed around the kitchen serving and clearing, all the while insisting Beth-any not lift so much as a finger to help. She'd felt like a pampered princess.

It was a lovely feeling. Now, watching Jay wipe down the counters as if he'd done so all his life, Bethany was amazed and amused. He'd gone to so much trouble tonight, and she appreciated his efforts more than he'd ever know.

"The sorbet was marvelous," she told him. "In fact, everything was marvelous. I can't remember ever enjoying a meal more."

"I'm glad," Jay said, placing the rinsed bowls in the drainer. "I wanted tonight to be special."

"It was."

"It's not over yet."

"There's more? Oh, goodness, I'm so full I couldn't eat another bite."

"The meal is over. The evening has just started." Jay re-trieved something from a drawer, concealing the item in his palm as he crossed the kitchen and settled into the chair beside Bethany. He absently tugged at the silly bow tie, moistened his lips, smiled, then moistened them again. Fi-nally he held out his hand, revealing a small, gift-wrapped box.

"What's that?"

Jay placed the gift in front of her. "Open it and find out."

Bethany stared at it, biting her lower lip. "I don't have anything for you."

"You've given me the happiest years of my life," he said quietly. "Everything else pales in comparison."

A rush of hot moisture pricked her eyes. She looked away, deeply moved and riddled by guilt.

Jay laid a warm palm over her hand. "Open it," he whispered. "Please."

Unable to speak, Bethany nodded, still avoiding his gaze. Her fingers plucked numbly at the ribbon, which despite her awkward efforts eventually fell away. She took a cleansing breath, then peeled the wrapping off to reveal a small velvet box. Holding it tenderly, she stroked the soft surface with the tip of her finger, then carefully lifted the lid and gasped in amazement. There, nested in a soft bed of creamy white satin, was a tiny golden pumpkin suspended from a dainty gold chain.

Overwhelmed, Bethany stared at the pendant, fighting a rush of grateful tears.

"Do you like it?" Jay asked anxiously. "It was custom made, so there's not another one like it in the entire universe. I thought...I mean, I hoped that would make it special to you."

"It's the most special thing I've ever seen," she whispered.

His eyes lit with relief and pleasure. Pushing back his chair, he rose and moved behind her. "Take it out," he urged, his voice pulsing with excitement. "I want to see how it looks on you."

"I, ah..." The words evaporated as she struggled with fingers benumbed by shock. "I can't. I'm all thumbs."

"What an oddity," Jay murmured, taking the box and removing the precious pendant without the slightest hesitation. "A manicure must be quite a challenge. Can you move your hair aside?"

Bending her head forward, Bethany complied by sweeping the curled mass to one side. A moment later, she felt Jay's warm fingertips brushing her nape and a gentle tickle as the tiny golden pumpkin nestled in the hollow of her throat. With her free hand, she reached up to touch the little replica, which seemed to radiate its own tender warmth.

Behind her, she felt the clasp click into place, although Jay continued to stroke her bare neck and shoulders. "You smell good," he whispered. "I remember that scent."

"You gave it to me...for my birthday, I think." She shivered as he caressed a sensitive spot beneath her earlobes.

"Mmm, sexy." His lips brushed the fine hairs of her nape, arousing every nerve in her body with electric intensity. A tiny moan slipped from between her lips. Her eyes fluttered shut, and she gave in to the unique sensation of floating on a tingling cloud watching bolts of white lightning entwined in erotic splendor.

The delicious image dissipated with a cool draft on her neck. With some effort, Bethany opened her eyes just as Jay pulled back her chair and took her hand, helping her to her feet. His palms cupped her shoulders, caressing them as warmly as his gaze caressed her face.

He was so beautiful, with the rugged features of a warrior and the soft mouth of a child. The dichotomy mirrored a conflict raging inside him, the desperate struggle between idealistic dreamer and cynical pragmatist that had wounded his innocence and bruised his spirit.

Bethany longed to touch him, to stroke his hair, to trace every nuance of his body with her hungry fingers, then gather his gentle power in her arms. And yet she could not move. She was mesmerized by his nearness, barely able to breathe.

One of his hands slid from her shoulder, brushed along her collarbone and came to rest at the pulsing hollow of her throat. His thumb slipped beneath the golden ball, lifting it slightly away from her skin. "It looks pretty," he said, his eyes glowing with pleasure. "Like it was made for you. Which, of course, it was."

Bethany felt her lips move. "I'll cherish it forever."

Then a strange thing happened. The flickering candlelight seemed to swirl up, embracing them in a golden vortex of iridescent warmth and silent song.

Lifting her right hand, Jay slipped an arm around her waist, guiding her in a sensual love dance, their bodies swaying in place to the music of their minds. Bethany laid her cheek on his shoulder and felt the comforting press of his lips against her temple.

The world moved with them in that rhythm of oneness, the bonding of souls that, through good times and bad, had never wavered. It had always been special between them. It had always seemed right.

It still did.

There, engulfed by her husband's loving embrace, Bethany felt a sense of belonging that had eluded her since the day they'd parted. She was overwhelmed by the sweet homecoming, a contented combination of excitement and blessed relief one experiences at the end of a long and grueling journey.

Bethany's feelings ran even deeper, beyond emotion, beyond a spiritual connection, plunging into the secret recesses of her physical body. She ached for him, her breasts throbbed, hardened nipples straining against stretched satin, rubbing the familiar landscape of his chest with joyous abandon and wanton desire.

Before Bethany could mentally cope with her rising passion, Jay had recognized it and responded, lowering his palm to the upper slope of her buttocks to hold her firmly against his aroused flesh.

He moved slowly, seductively, his lean hips moving in a sensual simulation of lovemaking so intensely erotic that Bethany's legs went limp and her knees turned to butter. His body heat seared through clothing to bare skin and beyond, burning a path directly to her feminine core.

Clutching his shirt, she uttered a tiny cry of pleasure and would have dissolved like hot jelly had he not tightened his grasp to hold her upright.

"Beth, honey—" A ragged breath cut him off. It took a moment before he could speak again. "I'll stop if you want me to."

"No, please." She clutched his shirt, stretching the cotton knit into a twisted tangle between her fingers. "Don't stop. I . . . don't want you to stop."

He closed his eyes as if issuing a silent prayer. When he opened them, Bethany saw love, and she saw fear. He swallowed hard. "I, ah, don't know what to do." Appearing chagrined by her startled expression, he tried for a smile that ended up more like a grimace. "I mean, it's silly, isn't it? We've made love hundreds of times, maybe even thousands, and here I am acting like a high-school virgin."

"It's not silly at all," she whispered, laying a fingertip at the corner of his mouth. "I'm nervous, too."

"You are?"

"Yes." Demurely lowering her gaze, she focused on the center of his chest. "If you were to let go of me right now, I'm not certain I could stand on my own."

His eyes widened. "That might be a problem."

"What do you mean?"

"I know the Rhett Butler thing is romantic, but under the circumstances—" he gave a pointed nod at his injured leg "—I don't think it would be the wisest thing to try."

Bethany smiled, realizing that Jay hadn't been kidding. The poor man really *was* nervous. The thought sent a spurt of calming strength into her rubbery limbs. "First of all, there won't be any stair-climbing involved. My bedroom's on the first floor, remember? Just down the hall from yours."

A wave of relief loosened a web of stress lines bracketing his mouth. "Oh, yeah. That's right."

"And second, I think I can get there under my own power." She released his shirt, smoothed it, then took his free hand, sandwiching it tightly between her moist palms. "May I hold on to this . . . for luck?"

His sexy smile sent chills down her spine. "You can hold onto anything I've got."

"I'll start with this," she replied, squeezing his hand and offering a coy smile. "Later, who knows?"

Jay's Adam's apple gave a frantic bounce.

Suddenly feeling in control, Bethany lifted his hand to her lips. She kissed each knuckle, then turned toward the door, urging him with her eyes. He followed, almost zombielike, as she led him down the short hallway to her bedroom.

Once inside, he pushed the door closed with his hip, swallowed hard, then glanced around the room.

"You haven't been in here before?" Bethany asked.

"No. I wondered if I should, you know, vacuum or something, but the door was always shut and I didn't want to intrude."

"I wouldn't have minded." She gestured toward the center of the room. "Besides, there's nothing to hide. Uncle Horace's dreary old bed, a wooden chair, a beat-up dresser with crooked drawers and an old TV tray that serves as both a nightstand and a lamp table. Hardly the boudoir of a libertine."

A peculiar expression flickered across his face. It lasted only a moment but brought an unpleasant thought to mind. Lowering her gaze, Bethany posed a question she probably had no right to ask. "Since we've been apart, have you . . . I mean, has there been anyone else?"

Prodded by his silence, she looked up and saw sadness in his eyes, and disbelief. "No, never." He took a deep breath. "And you?"

She shook her head.

He simply nodded as if he'd known it all along, although she noted the subtle twitch of his lips as he reined in a smile.

She clasped her hands together, wondering what to do now.

He shifted his weight, fidgeting with the vacant belt loops along the waistband of his walking shorts. After a silent moment, he suddenly reached toward the light switch.

"No," Bethany blurted, surprising herself. "I want to see you."

Jay's smile broke free. "I want to see you, too."

They stood there another moment, grinning stupidly, then Jay freed the tucked hem of his T-shirt and tugged the garment over his head. He shifted the wadded shirt between his hands, then laid it over the chair.

Bethany watched, overwhelmed by a sense of wonder that she'd forgotten how magnificent he was. There wasn't an ounce of fat on his upper torso, and every muscle was sleek, smooth, sculpted to perfection. Except for a few tawny hairs glistening between dusky nipples, his golden chest was smooth as stone.

Puffing her cheeks, she blew out a breath, then reached behind her back, feeling around for the zipper tab. A soft rasping was testament to her success. She pressed her upper arms tightly to her body so the dress wouldn't fall off.

It was Jay's turn, and he knew it.

With a quick zip, his shorts plopped to the floor, forming a beige cotton puddle at his feet. He stepped forward, hesitating briefly before gently hooking the flimsy red straps with his fingertips and easing them off her bare shoulders. His eyes were so gentle, so reverent, that Bethany's nervous fears evaporated. She moved her arms outward, just slightly but enough to release the fabric. The skimmer floated to the floor, baring her breasts to Jay's appreciative gaze.

Bethany touched his chest, scanning each contour with her fingertips. He made no move to restrict her exploration, even when her hands rested at the elastic of his briefs. When she knelt before him, he tensed, shivering. She smiled, feeling powerful, in control.

She teased him, tracing the line of his underwear with her fingers, lingering just below his navel then slipping her fingertips beneath the fabric and drawing it downward. His masculinity sprang free, shining and erect, greeting her with an ardor that took her breath away.

Composing herself, Bethany continued to slide the briefs down his thighs, allowing her cheek to brush the sheath's silky surface. A shudder ran the length of Jay's body. He groaned, a sound that was barely audible, yet seemed to vibrate the entire room.

Trembling with excitement, Bethany hurriedly pushed the briefs down to join the crumpled walking shorts, then waited impatiently for him to kick the discarded garments away. The moment he'd done so, she cupped him reverently between her palms and expressed her love for him.

So engrossed was she by the joy of the experience that she barely noticed that as Jay was stroking her hair, his caress was becoming increasingly urgent.

Finally he reached down, lifting her to her feet. His eyes glittered like those of a starving man being offered a sumptuous buffet. "My turn."

The husky promise made her quiver. In less than a heartbeat, the promise was fulfilled.

Jay cherished her with his lips, touching and tasting his way from her rock-hard nipples to her soft belly and beyond, until the heat of his love ignited a fire storm deep inside her.

With a cry of completion, Bethany threw her head back, clutching his shoulders and gasping for breath. Jay stood quickly, slipping his arm around her for support. He lowered her to the bed, then joined her, using extra effort to hoist his weighted leg onto the mattress.

"Can you manage?" Bethany whispered.

"Oh, yeah."

"Your leg?"

"Not a problem."

"But—"

"If it gets in my way, I'll gnaw the damn thing off." Jay rolled over, silencing her with a kiss, then he whispered against her lips. "Do you still love me, Beth?"

Tears sprang to her eyes. "I've always loved you, Jay. I always will."

He kissed her again, sweetly, softly. Then he sheltered her with his body and filled her with his love.

Chapter Twelve

Drawn by the irresistible aroma of freshly brewed coffee and steaming waffles, Bethany staggered to the kitchen, fumbling with her cotton robe buttons. She propped herself against the doorjamb, yawning, blinking and otherwise trying to adjust to a waking state. Her mind was willing; her body, however, refused to cooperate, longing for just a few extra minutes of languid, love-nourished sleep.

The clinking of silverware and din of childish chatter, music to her mommy ears, aided a slow rouse to consciousness.

"Hi, Mom," David chirped, setting down a half-empty glass of milk. "Dad made waffles."

Laurel, not to be outdone, added, "And he said we could put jelly on them instead of syrup."

"So I see," Bethany replied, eyeing the sticky orange goo coating the lower half of Nathan's happy face. Stifling a yawn, she sat in a vacant chair, rubbed her eyes and blinked at her bright-eyed children. "Mmm, it smells wonderful in here."

Jay looked up from the counter where he was keeping watch on the steaming waffle iron. "Hey, sleepyhead. I thought farm folks were always up with the chickens."

"It's Sunday," she murmured. "Even chickens sleep in on Sunday."

"You never do," David reminded her. "Did you stay up real late last night?"

From the corner of her eye, Bethany saw Jay's satisfied grin. She looked quickly away, studying a crusty salt shaker while a slow flush crept up her throat. "A little late, I guess."

An understatement, of course. She and Jay had made mad, passionate love until two in the morning. Then he'd awakened her at four, and they'd started all over again. It had been a magical night, a shining night, a night of seeking lips and whispered promise, of spiraling emotions and sweet satisfaction. It had been the most glorious night of her life.

Her reverie was broken as a mug of hot coffee appeared on the table in front of her.

When she glanced up, Jay kissed her cheek and gave her shoulders an intimate squeeze. "A cup of twice-brewed java ought to jump-start your day," he whispered. "But if you'd rather have something more stimulating, I can certainly arrange it."

"You're incorrigible." She rolled her eyes toward the children, warning him that they were listening with acute interest, if not downright glee. Lifting the mug, she allowed herself a quick sip before guiding the conversation to a more appropriate breakfast-table topic. "I've got work to do in the fields," she said to no one in particular. "The canner's rep will be here before noon, and I want to make sure everything is perfect."

Jay, who'd taken her hint and started clearing the breakfast dishes, angled a skeptical glance across the table. "So what are you planning to do, sweep the furrows and polish the pumpkins with lemon oil?"

She set the mug down. "You're making fun of me."

"A little, maybe," he confessed with an indulgent smile. "But only because you're so cute."

"Hmm. Well, your assessment is fairly accurate. Pumpkin fields need housekeeping, too. Withered leaves have to be removed, and any vines that have shriveled due to lack of pollination—"

"You're kidding."

"The plants have to be checked for any stray insects that might have sneaked in since my last bug safari, and I want to make sure that the soil is properly damp but not soggy—"

"Good grief, Beth, the man doesn't give a fat rat's tail about the ground's moisture content. From what you told me, he just wants to make sure there's a large enough crop to collateralize the loan."

She shrugged, stung by Jay's incredulous expression and annoyed because she knew he was right. Unfortunately, a lack of confidence in her farming ability couldn't be eased by a single application of truth. "There's no harm in being tidy."

"There could be," Jay said, setting the sticky plates in the sink. "You need rest, honey. Why don't you just kick back and relax. The man will be out, he'll do his thing and he'll leave. No amount of leaf pruning is going to change his estimates, is it?"

Unable to meet his gaze, Bethany stared into her coffee mug without answering his question. Deep down, she knew as well as he did that at this stage of the growing season, it was much too late to make any meaningful change. What Jay didn't know, and what Bethany wasn't willing to tell him, was just how much this crop meant to her.

There was more than financial stability at stake. After last night, Bethany realized that everything she'd ever dreamed about was finally within her grasp. The past two weeks had been the happiest of her life. She suspected they'd been the happiest of Jay's, too. Once away from urban stress, he'd been different, more relaxed, more like the sensitive young man she remembered.

For the first time in years, Bethany had real hope that they could be a family again. They could build a life here, a good life, but the farm was the key. Without it, everything she'd strived for would be lost. Once back in the city, the fresh blush of renewal would become stale, and their lives would slip back into that fathomless existence of separate desperation. For Bethany, that was the most terrifying thought of all.

"Yeah, all right. Sure, I understand." Jay hung up the phone, scouring his forehead with his fingertips while suppressing a serious urge to pound his fist on the wall.

The call he'd been dreading couldn't have come at a worse time.

Jay stared at the phone for a moment, wishing it dead, then turned his attention to the kitchen window. He crossed the room, sweeping the gingham curtains aside to scan the fields for Bethany and the canner's representative, a friendly young man who'd arrived less than an hour ago. Bethany was nowhere to be seen. The canner's rep, however, was pulling out of the driveway, accelerating toward the main road.

Behind Jay, the clickety-hop of dog claws on linoleum announced Leon's arrival. "The crop review didn't last as long as I thought," Jay muttered, scratching one of the animal's floppy ears.

Leon glanced up, whining.

"Bad news, huh?" Jay frowned. "On the other hand, Bethany told me that the rep tagged sample plants on his first visit, so most of his calculations are created from a small percentage of the crop. That makes sense, I suppose, and it would be a heck of a lot quicker than trying to measure every stupid pumpkin in the field.''

Leon sat with an awkward shoulder motion that Jay interpreted as a skeptical shrug.

''Yeah, I guess so.'' Jay skimmed a glance toward the living room, where all three kids were safely ensconced in front of the TV, turning their brains to mush. ''Maybe we should wander out and see how things went.''

With tail-wagging agreement, the dog instantly stood, hoisted his injured leg and click-hopped to the back door, waiting patiently until Jay had opened it for him.

Once on the back porch, Jay studied the deserted fields with a sinking sensation. ''Where'd she go, boy?''

Leon cocked his eye at the barn.

''Oh.'' A twinge of apprehension skittered down his spine. If things had gone well, Bethany would have dashed into the house, cheeks glowing, and blurted the wonderful news. The fact that she had chosen seclusion didn't bode well.

Still staring at the open barn door, Jay was halfway down the porch steps when Leon emitted a cautionary yelp.

''What?'' He glanced over his shoulder and saw the dog seated stoically on the stoop. Leon barked again.

''No, she won't consider it an intrusion,'' Jay explained. ''Look at it this way, if you were feeling blue because, say, that sweet little spaniel down the street dumped you for a big, strong Rottweiler, wouldn't you turn to your loved ones for comfort?''

Leon scooted backward, baring his teeth.

''All right, maybe you wouldn't, but women are different. They need to share their feelings.'' As Jay chatted, he ambled toward the barn, knowing without a backward glance that the dog was doing a three-footed hobble directly behind him. ''Besides, it's not the end of the world.

Even if the crop isn't large enough to completely cover the bank's interest, there should be enough money left over from selling the farm to pay off the loan. If not, I've got a few bucks put aside—"

A frantic yip drew Jay's attention. He looked over his shoulder to see Leon hobble a few steps backward and plop his bony rump on the ground, whining pitifully.

"Hey, don't worry," Jay told him, squatting to ruffle the animal's furry neck. "You'll like Los Angeles. Our house has a big, shady yard, and there's a park down the street where you and the kids can go play. And there are dozens of other dogs in our neighborhood, so you'll make lots of new friends."

Leon bellied down, plopped his chin on his paws and emitted a pained sigh.

"Yeah, I know. It's a big move." Jay stood, smiling at the forlorn animal. "Trust me, boy, everything will work out okay."

That said, Jay continued into the barn, pausing in the doorway while his eyes adjusted to the dimness. The roomy interior was cluttered by tools, buckets, small carts and other farming paraphernalia. Bags of feed and fertilizer were stored in vacant animal stalls. Bethany was at the back of the barn, kneeling beside a bag that had apparently been dragged from one of the stacks into the shaft of light from the open barn door.

"Fertilizer, eh?" When she didn't respond, Jay sauntered further into the musky bowels of the ramshackle barn, hooked his thumbs in his pockets and skimmed a disinterested glance at the object of his wife's scrutiny. "What are you doing?"

She answered without looking up. "Checking the nitrogen content."

"Why?"

"Because the rep said that an improperly balanced fertilizer can shift nutrients from fruit to foliage." Sitting back on her heels, she propped her elbows on her thighs and hunched forward, looking miserable. "According to him, that could explain why the pumpkins put on so little weight these past few weeks and why the leaves are so lush and green."

"I thought you wanted lush, green leaves."

"My assumption was that healthy leaves were the sign of a healthy plant. I didn't realize that the vines were supposed to wither this time of year, because they should be sending nutrients to the maturing pumpkins." She was silent a moment. When she spoke again, there was a bitter edge to her voice. "If I hadn't been so inexperienced, I would have realized what was happening and made the proper adjustments. I should have known better."

Jay felt terrible for her. He struggled to say something, anything, that would put a smile on her lovely face. "Well, I don't care what that jerk representative said. Even if the crop isn't going to be large enough to pay off the loan, I still think you've done one hell of a great job here."

She did smile, but just barely. "The crop will be large enough to pay off the loan."

"It will?"

"There was never any doubt of that," she murmured, fingering a torn corner on the fertilizer bag. "But the profit won't be as large as I'd hoped."

"You're actually going to make a profit?"

Apparently taking umbrage at the shock in his voice, she scowled at him. "Of course I'm going to make a profit. Do you honestly think I'd go to this much trouble if I expected to lose money?"

"Not deliberately, of course." He shifted, unnerved by her squinty stare. "I mean, no one wants to lose money. Hell, I figured you were hoping to break even."

"Break even?" She stood slowly, her incredulous gaze locked on his face. "You think that I spent three months of my life toiling in those fields, fighting bugs, breathing dirt, straining my back, turning my fingers into blistered pulp, all in the hope that I would simply *break even?* How stupid do you think I am?''

"Look, honey, I don't think you're stupid. I think you're one of the smartest people I know, but you're not cut out to be a farmer, that's all, and nobody expects you to be.'' Trying to comfort her, Jay gave her shoulder a gentle squeeze and instantly realized that she considered the gesture condescending rather than consoling.

Dropping his hand, he struggled to come up with something soothing, optimistic and preferably brilliant. He favored her with his flashiest grin, the one that always made her crack a smile no matter how unhappy she was or how angry she wanted to be. "Hey, shouldn't we be celebrating here? All your hard work has paid off. You'll be able to wipe out the loan and pocket some change, to boot. I'd think you'd be thrilled to your toenails.''

"Well, I'm not.''

Jay's grin faded at the flat statement, issued without a hint of a smile. "I can see that. I just don't understand why.''

Whirling, she jammed her fists on her hips. "Because this year's profit combined with my line of credit at the bank still won't give me enough to prepare the back pasture for planting. I'll have to take that darned promotion now, because it's the only way I'll be able to plant the extra acreage. Unfortunately, that pretty well scuttles my plan to take night courses at the agricultural college—''

"Wait a minute.'' Jay cut her off, frowning. "What on earth are you talking about?''

"I'm talking about doubling next year's crop.''

"Next year's . . .'' The words died on his tongue. Holding out his palm, he shook his head. "This doesn't make sense. You won't even be here next year.''

"What are you talking about? Of course, I'm going to be here. Where else would I be?" She stiffened as if shot. "You can't possibly believe— Oh, good heavens, no."

Confounded, Jay stared at her, struggling to find his voice. "Last night, we talked. You said you still loved me. You said you wanted our family to be together."

"I do," she whispered miserably. "But I never meant that I would go back to Los Angeles. I thought you understood that."

If she'd reared back and gut-kicked him, Jay wouldn't have been more stunned. "Then all that talk about staying together was just a bunch of lies?"

"No! I never lied. I meant every word." Frustrated, she rubbed her face, then tossed out her hands and finally folded her arms, keeping him at a distance. "And what about you, Jay? Those things you said about how the farm was growing on you, about how you could understand why the kids were so happy here . . . were those all lies, too?"

"They weren't lies, Beth. I do like the farm."

Her eyes softened. "Then stay here. Stay with us."

As he looked away, his jaw locked. He stared mutely across the darkened interior of the barn, absently noting a plethora of shiny dust particles dancing in the light shaft from the open door.

After a moment, Bethany spoke softly. "Perhaps we should talk about this later."

"We can't." Turning to face her, Jay sucked in a resigned breath, held it a moment, then exhaled all at once. "I'm leaving tomorrow."

"Tomorrow?" She touched her throat, swaying slightly. "I don't understand."

"My watch commander just called. They're shorthanded. He needs light-duty coverage and wants me back on tomorrow's second shift."

A sheen of tears gleamed in her eyes. "I see."

"Come with me," Jay begged, taking hold of her shoulders. "The school year has just started, so the kids won't have much catching up to do. It's the perfect time, Beth."

She backed away, rotating her shoulders to shake off his hands. "And what about the farm, Jay, what about the crop? Do I just leave it to rot in the field?"

"Of course not. You can hire a caretaker until harvest."

"Then what?"

He didn't like the angry spark in her eyes. "I guess you'll have to sell it."

"The crop or the farm?"

The sharp edge in her voice made him wince. "Both, I suppose."

She held his gaze for a moment, then spun around, staring into the darkness.

"Maybe you won't have to sell the farm," Jay blurted, spurred by sudden panic. "I mean, it would be a great vacation place, right? You and the kids might even be able to spend summers here, and I'd fly up for weekends."

"No." She turned, facing him with a numb expression and eyes as dull as country dirt. "I won't sell, Jay, and I won't leave."

An icy pit opened in the center of his stomach, spreading a cold fury to the core of his soul. "I hadn't realized that a few acres of rocky ground meant more to you than our family."

A quiver slid the length of her stiff back. "This farm means as much to me as your job means to you, Jay. If our family is so important, would you be willing to give that up?"

"It's not the same, Beth, and you know it."

"It's exactly the same." She lifted her chin. "What about a compromise, Jay? I'll sell the farm. You quit your job. Then we'll throw a dart at a road map, and start over wherever it lands."

There was a plea in her dark eyes that would have seemed poignant had Jay not been so angry. "You're being ridiculous."

She stared at him without blinking. "Yes," she murmured. "I suppose I am."

They stared at each other without speaking, the silence creating an emotional distance far greater than the spacial one. Jay wanted to speak, but didn't know what to say. He was afraid, more afraid than he'd been since the day Bethany had told him she wanted a divorce.

Bethany gazed past his shoulder, presumably focusing on the well-nurtured fields beyond the open barn door. "I thought things between us had changed," she whispered. "I thought you had changed, but you haven't. You still don't understand."

A flash of white caught his attention as her teeth scraped her lower lip. He stared at her mouth, remembering its soft flavor, its honeyed warmth. "I'm trying to understand, Beth. God knows, I'm trying."

She heaved a sad sigh, folding her arms like a shield. "I know you are. I'm trying, too, trying to understand how people can have totally different personalities based on geography."

The observation was a bit too astute for comfort. "Life isn't static. Things happen. People react. I am who I am, Beth. That used to be good enough for you."

"I was talking about both of us, Jay. I don't like the people we used to be. I was claustrophobic and cowardly. You were distant and uncommunicative. We were both unhappy. Why in heaven's name would either of us want to be like that again?"

"We wouldn't, and we won't." Jay gripped her shoulders, turning her toward him. "Like you said, Beth, we've both changed. We've grown up. It has nothing to do with the city versus the farm. That's just an excuse, and you know it. If we wanted to succeed as a family, we could do it anywhere.''

She studied his face, as if contemplating his sincerity. After a moment, her dark gaze bored directly into his eyes. "You're right, the place doesn't matter. But your job does matter, Jay. I hate what it does to you, and I hate what it does to me. I'll go back to Los Angeles, if that's what you want, but I won't go back as a cop's wife.''

Jay yanked his hands away as if the flesh of his palms had been seared by the betrayal. Unable to speak, he stared at her, feeling furious, feeling deceived. Spinning around, he steadied himself on a splintering stall, staring sightlessly at the plank floor. Emotion crowded his throat, choking him. He turned feelings into words and spit them out. "I was a cop when you married me. You knew what you were getting.''

"I thought I knew," came her sad response. "But prowling the night streets did something to you, Jay. You changed into someone I didn't recognize. I didn't like that person, and I didn't like who I became when I was with him." Pursing her lips, she focused on his chest, choosing her words carefully. "I love you. I will always love you, but I can't go back to the way things used to be. I can't live with the fear anymore, and I can't live with the isolation.''

Bethany gently touched his arm, wishing there was some way she could reach him. When he turned his face, she saw the anger in his eyes and knew the battle was lost. Still, she couldn't give up. "Let's go inside and cool off," she said. "Then maybe we can talk this through rationally.''

"It doesn't sound like we have much to talk about.''

"Please, Jay. We're both saying things we're bound to regret. Promise me that for once, we can sit down and have a meaningful conversation about our future." She waited a moment, watching the telltale twitch of his jaw. "What have we got to lose?''

Reaching back, he massaged his neck, still staring at the barn floor as if fascinated by hay and dirt clods. "All right," he said finally. "We'll cool down and we'll talk."

Bethany exhaled all at once, issuing a silent prayer of thanks. Talking was the first step, and it was an important one. In all their years together, Jay had never agreed to participate in a serious conversation about their relationship. To Bethany, it was a small miracle.

Outside, Leon barked, alerting them to the sound of a droning engine. Neither Jay nor Bethany looked up until they heard the honking horn.

Jay shoved his hands in his pocket, gazing out the barn door. "It's Archie," he said dully.

Bethany moistened her lips. "I'd better see what he wants."

"Yeah," came the bitter response. "You'd better."

Squaring her shoulders, she lifted her chin and strode briskly into the yard, fighting tears. Weak women cried. Bethany wasn't weak anymore. She was strong.

Strong.

And alone.

Bethany's heart felt like lead as she went directly to the squad car, where Archie's elbow protruded from the open window. "Hey, there, Beth," he drawled, scratching his sparsely furred scalp. "Just dropped by to see how the party went."

"Party?"

"The party went fine." It was Jay who replied, startling her since she hadn't realized he'd followed her out of the barn. "Thanks for your help."

"Help?" Feeling like a dim-witted parrot, Bethany's quizzical gaze swung from Archie to Jay and back again.

Jay wouldn't look at her. "Archie steered me toward a place where I could have...something special made."

Automatically, Bethany reached up to stroke the golden globe resting below the massive lump that was forming in her throat. She closed her eyes, blocking the exit of threatening tears, and took several deep breaths to compose herself.

"That sure turned out pretty," Archie said, eyeing the tiny pendant. "Told you they did good work."

"Yeah, great work. Thanks again."

The crackling radio cut off Archie's reply. Immediately both Jay and the deputy fell silent, their attention riveted on the dispatcher's urgent message. "All units, 10-31 at the Combie convenience, east of Highway 49. RP reports shots fired, possible 417, barricaded suspect with hostages. All available respond with 10-20 and check back."

Archie grabbed the microphone and barked, "Unit 236, responding from McCourtney Road."

"What is it?" Bethany asked, alarmed by the deputy's grim expression.

"Robbery gone sour," Archie muttered, shoving the vehicle into reverse. "Gotta go."

"Hold it!" Jay shouted, rounding the front of the car and forcing Archie to jam on the brakes when he yanked open the passenger door.

"No!" Bethany screamed as Jay leaped inside. "Stay here, Jay, please! You promised we'd talk...you *promised!*"

But the squad car had already disappeared in a rising cloud of dust.

She stood there, numb, staring at the empty driveway. Then the anger swelled in her chest, the icy fury that once again, he'd chosen the thrill of the chase over his family.

Furious, Bethany marched into the house, made a quick phone call, then stomped into the living room to snap at her startled children. "Turn off the TV and get into the van."

"Where are we going?" David asked, grabbing the remote.

"To Danny's house. Have you seen my keys?"

"Over there," Laurel said. "By your purse. Is Mrs. Piper going to baby-sit us?"

"Just for a little while," Bethany muttered, herding the children outside.

This time, she wasn't going to sit idly home, waiting for the phone to ring. Jay had promised to spend the afternoon talking about their future. One way or another, that's exactly what he was going to do.

Chapter Thirteen

Two sheriff's units were already on the scene when Deputy Lunt screeched into the parking lot some twenty yards from the convenience store. Both vehicles were parked askew, doors open, out of sight of the convenience store occupants. One deputy was outside his unit, speaking with an agitated citizen. Another was squatting beside the second car, using its open door as a shield. The radio mike was in the deputy's left hand; a service revolver, pointed skyward at the ready, was clutched in his right hand.

Lunt pulled up in an adjacent gas station parking lot just behind the other units. Retrieving a riot baton from its holder, the old deputy simultaneously unsnapped his holster and hoisted his girth from the driver's seat with surprising agility. "Stay put, Murdock. This isn't your fight."

Since Lunt was too preoccupied to expect a reply, none was issued. Instead, Jay emerged from the passenger side, scanning the tense scene with practiced eyes. There were, he noted, four vehicles parked directly in front of the convenience store, an observation that could provide clues to how many people were still inside.

Lunt headed for the squatting deputy. Jay, assuming that the agitated civilian was the RP, police jargon for Reporting Person, swung his plastered foot over a concrete parking bump and moved quickly in that direction.

"So I was putting change in the machine to get my Sunday paper, you know?" The civilian, a compact, casually dressed young man who appeared to be in his late twenties, was shifting from foot to foot and frantically wiping his face while staring at the side of the convenience store as if expecting the wall to explode. "And when I looked through the front window, I saw George behind the counter, like always, only he's holding his hands up. I thought it was a joke, you know, then I saw this freaked-out guy waving the biggest gun I ever saw in my life. So I yelled, 'Hey! What's going on?' And when the guy whirls around, George dives down behind the counter. Then the alarm starts wailing, and the crazy bastard points the gun right at me and shoots the damned window out!"

When the interviewing deputy glanced up, Jay retrieved an identification wallet from a back pocket, flipped it open and held up his badge. "Murdock, LAPD."

The deputy's eyes narrowed, his gaze slipping to Jay's cast, then up again. Jay focused on the civilian, knowing that the situation was too critical for the deputy to interrupt the interview with questions about Jay.

The frantic witness was continuing his story. "The next thing I know, man, I'm licking pavement and there's broken glass all over and people inside are screaming and shouting and I hear this crazed voice yelling shut up and threatening to blow someone's head off. It was like a bad movie, you know? I couldn't believe what was happening."

The shaken fellow pulled off a blue baseball cap and set it on the hood of the squad car. He raked his hair, sucking a series of quick breaths, his face ashen, his eyes glazed. For a moment, Jay feared the poor guy would pass out.

Apparently, the deputy saw the same thing, because he laid a steadying hand on the frantic man's shoulder and spoke in a soothing voice. "You're doing fine," he murmured. "Can you remember how many shots were fired?"

Jay regarded the deputy with approval, recognizing and admiring the instinctive way he'd calmed a witness on the brink of emotional shutdown.

The civilian's breathing slowed slightly and his eyes focused. "I don't know. A couple, maybe...could have been as many as three, but real close together, like this—" he pointed his finger like a gun "—bang-bang-bang."

Nodding, the deputy scrawled on the notepad he held. "What happened next?"

"I crawled to my car—thank God I'd left the motor running—and I took off. I pulled in here—" he gestured to the gas station a few yards behind them "—and while I was dialing emergency on my cell phone, that guy—" he pointed to the squatting deputy "—drove up just as the guy with the gun ran out into the parking lot." The man paused for breath, angling a nervous glance at Jay. "I guess the deputy must have been on patrol or something—maybe he was driving by and heard the alarm, because I'd barely gotten through to the emergency dispatcher when he showed up. So anyway, the guy looks at the deputy, then does a one-eighty and hauls butt back into the store."

Jay nodded, then pointed toward a dusty black import parked askew beside the gas station phone booth. "Is that your car?" The man indicated that it was. "Other than the gunman and the counter clerk, did you see anyone else in the store?"

"No, but when the gun went off, I heard a woman scream, and...and—" The man wiped his face, his pale eyes wide with terror. "I heard a baby cry."

Jay's heart sank.

The deputy's head snapped up. "Are you certain about that?"

"Yeah," the guy replied miserably. "I'm real sure."

Behind him, two more squad cars arrived. When the interviewing deputy went over to brief the new arrivals, Jay nodded toward the convenience store parking lot. "Were all of those cars there when you first arrived?" he asked the shaken civilian.

"Yeah—no, wait. That blue pickup drove up after me."

"Did you see who was driving it?"

The man squinched up his face. "An old guy, I think. Yeah, that's right. White mustache, bald on top, wearing one of those Hawaiian-type shirts."

Jay mentally clicked off a list of at least four potential hostages—a woman, a child, an older man and George, who'd been behind the counter. "What could you see of the gunman?"

"Oh, he was skinny. Not very tall, maybe five-seven or five-eight. He was real pale, like he lived in a cave or something, and he was wearing one of those rock-band T-shirts."

"Did you hear his voice?"

"Well, yeah . . . when he was yelling for everyone to shut up."

"Did he speak with an accent?"

"I don't think so. His voice was kind of shrill, though. High-pitched."

"See anything else? Any scars, tattoos, that kind of thing?"

The man shook his head. "Like I told the deputy, I didn't see much of anything except this huge gun barrel looking right at me."

"What kind of gun?"

"Big."

"Could you tell if it was a revolver or automatic?"

"No."

"What did the man look like?"

"Hell, I don't know. He was kind of young, I think, with buzzed hair." The witness frowned. "Come to think of it, I remember that his eyes were weird, all red, like he'd just pulled an all-nighter or something. He was wild, that's all. That damned gun was shaking all over the place. Look, can I go now? I don't feel so good."

"You'd better stay around in case the deputies have more questions."

Muttering to himself, the frazzled witness wandered over to his car and sat in the passenger seat with his head in his hands.

Meanwhile, Jay took the civilian's cap from the hood of the patrol unit and mentally processed the information he'd gleaned about the suspect. Exceptionally pale skin, red eyes, jittery nerves, obviously inexperienced to target a store crawling with customers in the middle of the day. It was possible, even likely, that the robber was a strung-out hype, a situation that would up the ante, riskwise. There was nothing as dangerously unpredictable as a desperate, drug-fried brain.

Considering this, Jay went over to Archie, who was huddled with a group of deputies near the patrol unit that had been first on the scene.

Lunt glanced up. "Thought I told you to stay in the car."

"Is a negotiating team on the way?" Jay asked, ignoring the reprimand.

"Yeah, but it's scrambled out of Nevada City, so it'll take them a while to get here and set up the communications van."

Shifting the blue cap from his right to his left hand, Jay rubbed his neck, eyeing the sparkle of shattered glass strewn across the convenience store's parking area. In Los Angeles, the SWAT team would be in place by now and the negotiators would already be trying to establish a telephone link with the suspect. Then again, they wouldn't have to make a twenty-mile trip to the scene, either. In L.A., police stations dotted the landscape like gas stations.

"According to the witness, this guy's a ball of raw nerves," Jay said. "We know he's armed, and we know he's figured out where the trigger is. Several rounds fired in rapid succession, so it sounds like he's got himself an automatic. He's trapped, he's panicked, he's got at least four hostages, and he's not very bright. The way I see it, he's not the type to sit calmly and wait for the phone to ring so he can play let's make a deal. More likely he'll freak and start throwing bodies out into the parking lot."

"Maybe not," Lunt replied, although his grim expression revealed that he believed Jay's disastrous scenario was more than a slim possibility. "Right now we're hanging back, trying not to spook him. The longer he has to think about things, the more rational he'll become about his situation and what he has to do to get out of it alive."

"Yeah, well, I know that's what the book says. Problem is, most of these guys haven't read that book, and a fair percentage of them are suicidal, so getting out alive isn't a real big priority for them."

Lunt's jaw tightened, but he didn't disagree. He glanced toward an unmarked unit pulling into the parking lot. A man in plain clothes emerged, drawing uniformed deputies—including Lunt—like a human magnet, so Jay assumed the new arrival was the on-scene commander.

A distant sound caught Jay's attention. He cocked his head, listening, and was certain that the ominous crashing noise had come from inside the store. The thought crossed his mind that the guy might be barricading the door, which would completely isolate the innocent victims inside. At the same time, patrol units were moving out, preparing to encircle the building.

Jay had to act fast.

He tossed his badge and identification wallet into Lunt's patrol unit, then hurried around the back of the convenience store, circling to the side of the building away from the congregation of law-enforcement officers. Pausing at the corner just beyond view of both the deputies and the store's occupants, Jay bent forward to ruffle his hair, and since most locals wore T-shirts hanging loose, he tugged the hem of his T-shirt from the waistband of his cutoff blue jeans.

Then he put on the witness's blue cap, pulled the brim down to his eyebrows and, ignoring the startled shouts of deputies from the neighboring parking lot, Jay sauntered casually around the front of the building and walked into the store.

As expected, the counter was deserted. Tucking one hand in a pocket, Jay plastered a friendly grin on his face while his practiced gaze swept the cluttered but deceptively vacant store. "Hey, George! Those darn kids been throwing rocks at your window again?"

A nervous middle-aged man emerged from the back room, his eyes black with fear. Since the guy was wearing a short-sleeved white shirt and he had a head full of thick, dark hair, Jay presumed he wasn't the Hawaiian-shirted customer the civilian witness had described.

"Better sweep that mess up, George. Some old lady's bound to slip on that glass and sue your shorts off." Forcing a cheerful tone, Jay moved toward the counter, scanning the open doorway through which the older man had emerged. Since the outer portion of the store seemed vacant, Jay presumed that the customers had been herded into the back room.

The dark-haired man remained silent, but his eyes darted to the left, toward a row of stocked food aisles closest to the front door.

"Got any fresh sour cream?" Jay asked, slipping a quick look down each aisle as he moved by. "Tonight's poker night, and I've got me a hankering for onion dip. The wife makes a killer dip—"

A shadow loomed up from behind him, pressing cold steel against Jay's throat.

Jay slowly raised his hands, turning his head slightly. He saw the blur of clammy white skin and a bloodshot blue eye with a pinpoint pupil. And beyond his captor, he looked through the shattered window and saw patrol units positioned around the perimeter.

Then he saw something else, something that made his heart sink—Bethany's silver-gray minivan screeching onto the scene.

The store was surrounded. Riot guns were aimed and ready. A pall of tense silence shrouded the area, and the grim-faced deputies hunched in battle position.

Like a scene from a war movie, Bethany thought, the one used to build suspense before blood exploded across the screen.

Dazed, she clung to the open door of her van, searching for Jay. A sick sensation settled in the pit of her stomach. She stepped away from her vehicle, wringing her hands, feeling frantic. She'd never seen anything like this before, at least not in person. Nothing could have prepared her for the smell of fear in the air, the stench of terrified anticipation.

A movement caught her eye. She turned to see Archie Lunt running toward her, more quickly than she'd have believed a man of his girth could possibly move.

He snagged her arm, dragging her behind the van. "You shouldn't be here."

Bethany already knew that. "Where's Jay?"

"Go home, Beth."

"I intend to," she replied, turning to scan the tense standoff behind her. "And I intend to take Jay with me. Now, where is he?"

The deputy's silence was deafening.

Focusing her attention, she searched Archie's sullen face. A frisson of pure terror slid down her spine. "Something's wrong," she whispered. "Tell me."

Archie closed his eyes for a moment. "Please, Beth. Go home."

"I won't leave without him." She twisted out of the deputy's grasp. "Where is he, Archie? Where is my husband?"

There was no reply. None was needed, because when Archie's gaze slid toward the barricaded storefront, Bethany knew the answer. Jay was inside, facing an armed man with nothing more than his wits and his all-consuming machismo.

He could be injured; he could be dying; he could be dead.

That horrifying image was Bethany's final thought as she crumpled to the pavement.

"Well, hell," Jay mumbled, sitting on the concrete floor of the storage room with his back pressed against a stack of warehoused soda cartons. "I sure did pick a bad time to crave onion dip."

"Shut up!" The gunman, who appeared to be in his early twenties, wiped a bare forearm across his face, then used both hands to steady a .44 automatic that was shaking like a wind-whipped leaf. "I'll kill you . . . I'll kill you all."

The threat drew a muffled sob from the young mother who was hunched in a corner, her body protectively folded over a whimpering toddler with a head full of blond ringlets.

"Shut that kid up!" the gunman screamed, swinging around.

With the quivering weapon pointed directly at her face, the frantic mother tried to comply, issuing a series of whispered shushing sounds and covering the child's wet face with frenzied kisses. Fortunately, the baby sniffed, stuck a thumb in her mouth and burrowed quietly against her mother's breast.

George and the Hawaiian-shirted man were both seated awkwardly on the floor, their hands laced behind their heads. A new wrinkle had been added when Jay discovered that there were two more hostages than he'd expected—a pair of teenage girls, who were now cowering beside a stack of cardboard cartons, hugging each other and staring at their knees.

Leaning back, Jay adjusted the bill of the commandeered cap, scanning the storage room and sizing up options. As expected, there was a back door leading into an alley behind the store. Unfortunately, the exit was blocked by two stacked beer pallets, rendering it useless.

"Kids are a pain," Jay drawled, measuring the gunman's reaction. "That's why I don't have any."

The gunman swallowed hard, pacing from the storage room to the doorway leading into the store, then back again.

"By the way, my name's Murdock. My friends call me Jay. What do your friends call you?"

Ignoring the question, the frightened man looked over his shoulder, straining to see out the front window of the store.

"Ah. Well, you don't mind if the rest of us get acquainted, do you?" Jay asked brightly, hoping that the gunman would be less likely to harm people who'd been individualized, humanized and personalized by name. Before the nervous fellow could respond, Jay turned toward the counter clerk. "Everyone knows George here, and you're—" His gaze signaled the man in the colorful shirt.

"Uh . . . Gabe," the man stammered. "Gabe Stein."

"Nice to meet you, Gabe." Jay smiled at the teenagers, who glanced frantically around the room.

The spiky-haired blonde mumbled nervously, "I'm Veronica—my friends call me Ronnie—and this is my cousin, Joyce."

Joyce, a dark-eyed brunette, gave a jerky nod.

The young mother, however, was too terrified to speak or even to look up. Curled in a ball, she rocked back and forth, clinging to her child.

Jay turned his attention to the gunman, who was sweating like the proverbial pig. "You got any kids?"

"Shut up."

This time, the command was mumbled without conviction, which Jay took as a positive sign. "Just as well. They're always sniveling and cost a damned fortune. It's just a matter of time before that one's going to start whining again."

The gunman glanced at the teary-eyed toddler, whose tiny shoulders shuddered with intermittent remnants of earlier sobs.

Jay saw something in the guy's eyes, a softness, a flash of regret, perhaps. He took advantage by pressing his point home. "Personally, I can't think straight when there are crying kids around. Drives me nuts."

Ignoring the horrified stares of his fellow hostages, Jay rolled his head, massaging the back of his neck, and continued chatting in a calm, almost casual manner. "Right about now, I imagine you're trying to concentrate on how to get out of this situation. Like I said, it's hard for a man to think when there are crying kids around. If I was in your shoes, I'd send Mama and the kid packing."

"Nobody's going anywhere," the man mumbled, his reddened eyes darting around the room as if seeking his own place to hide.

Jay shrugged. "Up to you, man, but the way I figure it, you're keeping us as bargaining chips. Makes sense, of course, but hell, how many do you need? I mean, you'll still have five of us left. Besides, babies make bad hostages, you know? They cry whenever they feel like it, and nothing grates a man's nerves more than a sniveling kid, right?''

At that point, the telephone rang. The gunman nearly jumped out of his skin. Whirling, he stiff-armed his weapon, shifting his indiscriminate aim from person to person, his eyes wild. "Don't move!" he shouted. "Don't move or I'll blow your heads off, I swear I will.''

"Nobody's going to move,'' Jay assured him quietly.

By the fourth ring, the gunman was panting hard and blinking sweat out of his eyes.

"You might as well answer that,'' Jay told him. "I'm pretty sure it's for you.''

"Drink this,'' Archie said, handing Bethany a paper cup filled with steaming black liquid. "It'll make you feel better.''

"Thank you.'' Since her stomach was a quivering mass of nerves, she twirled the cup in her hand for a moment before setting the untouched coffee on the ground. Shading her eyes, she squinted past the circle of patrol cars that were at least fifty yards away and studied the storefront's shattered window for the hundredth time.

Over the past three hours, Jay had been acting as the middleman between the would-be robber and the sheriff's negotiating team. According to Archie, Jay had entered the store posing as a customer, apparently to facilitate negotiations and protect the people trapped inside.

Clearly, he'd been successful. A young mother had come out first, carrying a beautiful baby Bethany judged to be about a year old. An hour later, two teenage girls had been exchanged for a supply of hamburgers and French fries, and shortly thereafter, an elderly man in a gaudy shirt had emerged after feigning a heart attack under secret instructions from "some guy wearing a leg cast.''

According to Archie, who had—bless his heart—done his best to keep Bethany up to speed on the proceedings, there were now only three people still inside the store—the gunman, who'd been identified as Robert Sims; George Clarkson, owner of the establishment; and, of course, Jay.

But something had gone wrong over the past half hour.

No one had told Bethany as much, although she recognized renewed tension etched on the deputies' grim faces, and Archie was avoiding her frantic questions with uninformative, even evasive, replies.

To help Bethany avoid the media that had been crawling around the crime-scene perimeter for hours, Archie had garnered approval for her minivan to be parked inside the secured area, a safe distance away from the store itself. That kept reporters from shoving a microphone in her face, but it hadn't prevented them from leaning over the barricades, shouting questions. She had no idea how they'd learned who she was, but they knew, and they were constantly bombarding her with stupid queries about how it felt to know that her husband was being held hostage.

Well, it felt awful. Worse than awful. It felt . . . like her world was about to explode. Life without Jay was beyond her sphere of comprehension. Yes, she'd divorced him, but that hadn't meant she'd stopped loving him, only that she loved him too much to live with the fear.

So Bethany had left; but the fear had followed.

A few minutes earlier she'd overheard a couple of reporters whispering that communications from inside the store had inexplicably been cut off. After rushing to find Archie, Bethany had been repeatedly assured by the stonefaced deputy that Jay was unharmed and that the communications glitch was temporary.

Bethany wanted to believe that. Part of her insisted on believing it. Yet another surprisingly cynical aspect of herself whispered that if Jay had been hurt, no one would dare admit it for fear she'd lose what little sanity she had left.

If anything happened to him—

She squeezed her eyes shut, shaking off the horrible thought. Nothing would happen to Jay. He was a cop with years of undercover experience. He knew how to take care of himself. In fact, he'd probably survived dozens of similar situations.

Only Bethany hadn't witnessed any of those.

But she'd most certainly imagined them. Night after sleepless night, she'd envisioned her husband crumpled in some nondescript alley, drenched with his own blood.

Sagging against the minivan's hood, Bethany folded her arms, feeling desperately ill. In all the years she'd lived with Jay, she'd thought that worrying beside a silent telephone was the most terrible thing anyone could endure. She'd been wrong. This was far worse. Watching, waiting, seeing what police officers see, feeling what police officers feel, suffering the same unbearable tension, the same gut-twisting loss of control. In less than a heartbeat, any situation could instantly turn sour. People could be maimed. Lives could be lost.

And there seemed no way to stop it.

Bethany had always known that pressure and stress were a part of Jay's job. Until this moment, she'd never fully appreciated what that meant. She'd never understood what life as a cop was really like, had never realistically imagined constant tension punctuated by moments of sheer, unadulterated terror.

Now for the first time, she'd gotten a taste of that life, and she loathed it. The air was heavy, so thick with tension that she could barely breathe, so charged with electric anxiety that the hair on her nape stood on end. Even the blistering heat of a mid-September day couldn't warm her icy skin. She was dizzy with fear, her stomach churning with frigid terror.

Then without warning, the shroud of silence was snapped by a sudden shout. Bethany stiffened, vaguely noting that Archie had leaped from her side and was running toward the command circle. Since there was no one around to stop her, Bethany followed, slowly at first, then faster and faster still.

A man had stumbled out of the store, a man with thick black hair. He was wearing a white shirt. And he was bleeding.

Two officers in camouflaged fatigues swooped in to flank the staggering man and haul him to safety. An EMS unit, which had been on standby, went into action, surrounding the injured man by the open rear doors of the medical van while a cadre of deputies peppered the frazzled fellow— whom Bethany assumed to be George, the store owner— with sharp questions.

Bethany arrived, unnoticed, at the edge of the human circle.

"I don't know what happened," George was saying as paramedics tended the cut on his head. "Sims was talking rationally, telling the guy in the leg cast about how he'd gotten laid off from his job and moaning about his girl-friend walking out...that kind of stuff. Then the phone rang again and Sims went ballistic, ripping the cord out of the wall and throwing the entire phone across the room. The damned thing bounced off a wall, right into my nog-gin. Knocked me silly— Ouch!"

Shrugging an apology, the paramedic finished smooth-ing a bandage over George's brow while a deputy contin-ued the interrogation. "Did Sims say anything, make any threats?"

"Not then," George replied glumly. "He just ran around the store, waving the gun and smashing anything break-able. The other guy—Jay, I think his name was—he tried to calm him down and damned near got shot for his trou-ble."

Bethany grabbed her stomach, swaying dangerously. Swallowing the bitter bile surging into her throat, she forced herself to stay upright, refusing to faint. She leaned against the side of the EMS van, where the open rear doors obscured her presence.

"Everything just unraveled," George was saying. "Sims and this Jay fellow had been getting along real good, but all of a sudden, Sims went all freaky, screaming and hollering scary stuff about how he couldn't stand it no more. And while he was busy smashing bottles, the other guy—"

"Jay?" asked a deputy.

"Yeah, Jay... Well, he points toward the front door and tells me to get out. I didn't have to hear it twice. I spun my butt around and hit the door running." George paused a moment, and when he spoke again, his voice broke. "Just before I got out, though, Sims started screaming at me. He said—" a pained cough "—he said I should tell you guys that you had ten minutes to pack up and clear the parking lot."

"Did Sims say anything else?"

There was a long pause. Straining to hear, Bethany edged close enough to hug one of the van's open doors.

After a moment, George spoke again, his voice quivering with emotion. "He just kept saying that he couldn't take it, and if you guys were still here at three-fifteen—"

When the man's voice dropped, Bethany stretched forward, grasping the rear door handle for support when she heard his final whispered words.

"Someone was going to die."

A gasp of horror broke the subsequent silence. Bethany shook her head numbly, realizing that the sound had come from her. "No," she whispered, backing away from the van, from what she'd heard, from what she dared not believe. *"No!"*

A stunned face peered around the van door. In a moment, Bethany was surrounded by deputies hustling her toward her vehicle. She struggled against their grasp, screaming. "Do something, please... he's going to shoot my husband. You've got to stop him, don't you understand? You've got to *do something!*"

Then she heard it. Distant. Deceptively benign. A small popping sound, like a freed champagne cork.

Ripping her left wrist free, Bethany shot a terrified glance at her watch. She nearly fainted. It was only three-thirteen, but she knew without doubt that it was too late.

The fatal shot had already been fired.

Chapter Fourteen

The world became a red daze, a surrealistic environment of faraway voices, of people moving with jerky speed and speaking in agitated whispers. Bethany was vaguely aware that her body was supported, yet her mind floated free, morbidly fascinated by the hushed rush, the fleet of faceless uniforms converging on the silent store.

Jay.

Silently screaming his name, she cursed the courage that had taken him away from her. He'd chosen valor over his family, risking death rather than insisting on life with those who so desperately loved him. Yet deep down, Bethany knew that Jay could never have turned his back on people in trouble, regardless of the consequences. It was that protective compassion that made him the man he was, the man she loved more than life itself.

That knowledge provided no comfort. She was heart-broken. She was angry. She was numb with grief, shattered by shock.

Mere moments had passed since the shot rang out. It seemed like years. Bethany's world had slowed to a virtual crawl, a torpid filmstrip in slow motion. Uniformed deputies seemed to materialize from thin air, encircling the small brick building like a siege of camouflaged locusts.

Words of consolation were murmured in her ear. A familiar voice. A soothing voice. The voice of a friend.

Archie held her upright, grasping her torso firmly, tenaciously. Struggle would be futile. It didn't matter. There was nowhere to run, no one to run to.

Dear God, she prayed, *how could You let this happen?*

As if in response, a tingling warmth eased down her icy limbs. The feeling returned to her fingers. She was aware of her feet touching pavement, of legs that were intact and supporting her weight. Her eyes focused on the buzz of activity centered around the storefront door; her brain processed the information rationally.

Something had changed.

A shout emanated from the circle of armed men surrounding the store. Instructions, Bethany decided, issued to someone inside.

There was an electric tension in the air, an atmosphere of anticipation rather than of utter doom.

Bethany blinked, feeling dizzy, and realized that she'd been holding her breath. Her lungs contracted, spilling stale air in a massive rush, then gulping fresh oxygen to clear her fuzzy mind.

Squinting at the storefront, she noticed shifting reflections on the glass, a signal that the door was opening. Something flew out, a glint of steel that landed on the pavement, skidding at the feet of the nearest deputy. He quickly retrieved the item, examined it, then tucked it into his belt. It looked like a gun, although from her vantage point, Bethany couldn't be certain.

A moment later, a man emerged from the store, his hands high over his head. He was terribly thin, surprisingly young and appeared to be deathly afraid. The young man stood there like a terrified rabbit surrounded by a predatory pack. Deputies yelled at him, barking instructions. He seemed unable to move, as if frozen with fear. After a long moment, someone reached out, snagged his clothing and threw him to the ground.

The pack converged, swallowing him whole.

When the deputies finally dispersed, the terrified young man was upright and handcuffed. Attention was once again focused into the store. Oddly, the officers appeared to be speaking with someone inside.

But no one was in there except—

With superhuman strength, Bethany ripped out of Archie's grasp. She wavered a moment, clutching at her chest as if to calm the frenzied beat of a reawakening heart.

A second man emerged from the store, a man wearing a strange blue cap and cutoff jeans.

A man with a cast on his left leg.

Jay hobbled over to lay a hand on the cuffed man's shoulder. He spoke somberly to the skinny young fellow, who stared at the ground and nodded, then was led away to a waiting patrol unit.

Pressing her palms to her lips, Bethany stood there, swaying, silently issuing a prayer of gratitude and begging forgiveness for having doubted the power of divine destiny.

"Jay!" As the scream tore from her throat, her legs responded and she sprinted across the parking lot into his open arms. She hugged him fiercely, alternately laughing and crying. "Oh, Jay, oh, Lord, I thought we'd lost you."

"I'm fine, honey. I'm fine." His voice was firm, yet his convulsive embrace betrayed his own fears. Despite his habitual bravado, he was deeply shaken, and Bethany knew it.

And Bethany knew something else, something that was confirmed during the chaos that followed.

Over the next half hour, as Jay was being debriefed by on-scene commanders, Bethany saw the satisfied glow in his eyes, inner recognition of his accomplishment. Around her, deputies chatted about his heroism with unabashed admiration. No one doubted that Jay's decision to intervene had saved lives. If not for his action, someone would have died in that store—perhaps some of the hostages; most certainly the gunman himself, since the last shot had been fired as Jay wrestled the gun away from the suicidal man, who'd been pressing the weapon to his own temple.

The unerring instinct and depth of courage Jay had shown couldn't be taught in the police academy. It was a natural talent, possessed by those chosen few who were born for law enforcement.

Jay was one of those chosen few.

He was born to be a cop, and at that moment, Bethany realized just how much his career meant to him. If she asked him to give it up, he might eventually relent because he loved her. But she loved him too much to let him sacrifice a career that was his life.

Because she loved him, she had to let him go.

It was late afternoon when Jay and Bethany picked the children up from Mrs. Piper and returned to the farm. Although live coverage of the hostage standoff had been provided by several television stations, Danny's mother had thankfully monitored the children with an eagle eye, preventing a horrifying discovery of their father's perilous involvement.

So the family's final evening together was spent quietly, reflectively, with promises to tearful children that the next visit would be soon. Of course, "soon" didn't mean much to a pair of brokenhearted youngsters who understood only that their daddy was leaving again.

Jay tried to explain that he had to leave because of his job. Eventually he gave up, partly because the rationale had fallen on deaf little ears and partly because he wasn't certain he believed it any more.

Something had happened to him today, during the siege as well as afterward.

Inside the store, all Jay had been able to think about was Bethany and the children. He'd put himself at risk without considering how his behavior could affect his family's future. If anything had happened to him, Bethany would have had to raise their children alone, children who'd have grown up without the guiding hand of a father who loved them.

Of course, Jay realized that life itself was a mine field of danger. People died crossing the street, driving a car, and were unfairly struck down by deadly disease. Jay understood all that, but he also understood that thrusting himself into a hostage situation had been the equivalent of standing in front of a speeding truck with a blindfolded driver. It had been stupid, and it had been selfish.

He hadn't realized just how stupid and selfish until afterward, when he'd seen Bethany dashing toward him, screaming his name. Now, remembering the raw terror in her eyes, he was riddled by guilt at having put her through it in the first place. The worst part was realizing that this hadn't been the first time she'd endured that kind of terror. It had simply been the first time Jay had seen it.

It was no wonder she'd left him. Not only had he been blind to her suffering, he'd had the gall to ask her to return, to relive that agony over and over and over again.

That had been wrong of him, dead wrong. For the first time in years, Bethany was finally happy. She loved the farm, she loved her new life.

Jay loved her too much to let her give it up.

The freeway was deadlocked. In the distance, the vague outline of the downtown skyline was blurred by an ugly brown haze. Around him, Jay saw the grim faces of frustrated drivers, some pounding their steering wheels in anger, others staring with glazed expressions at the massive clogged artery in which they were hopelessly trapped.

Rush hour.

An odd title for a time when no one in the city was allowed the privilege of even moving forward, let alone rushing. It was, Jay recalled, one of the reasons—excuses, really—he'd used to justify working nights. In truth, he'd loved the action and excitement that geared up when the sun went down. Bad guys thrived in darkness. Jay went in pursuit of those bad guys, because he was, after all, a white knight of the people.

People who were too numb with fear to notice, let alone appreciate his role as their self-appointed savior. People who were so overwhelmed by crime and corruption that they were prisoners in their own homes. People who viewed cops with suspicion, because the only time they saw one was during a personal crisis.

In ten years, Jay hadn't changed that. Oh, he'd put his share of bad guys in jail. Pushers and users; prostitutes and pimps; scam artists; the occasional mugger.

Every last one of them had been back on the street by morning.

Meanwhile, normal citizens fitfully slept behind dead bolts and security bars, waking just as Jay slipped into the shadows like a vampire slinking from the deadly rays of a rising sun.

Jay had told himself that he was making a better world. He wasn't. Every day, people struggling to cope continued to file zombielike to their day jobs, unaware of and unaffected by the results of Jay's nightly prowl.

But Jay had been affected. He'd become hardened, cynical. He'd lost faith in humanity. He'd lost faith in himself.

Odd, he thought, gazing out over the smog-encrusted skyline, that he'd never noticed the stark poverty tucked between gleaming glass high rises, the grit of despair etched on the faces of a populace resigned to the stark realities of life.

A decade earlier, Jay had naively believed himself capable of changing all that. Looking back on his career, however, he honestly couldn't think of a single person whose life had been positively transformed by his efforts.

One could argue that taking violent felons off the streets spared potential victims, and that was true, as far as it went, but it wasn't the reason Jay had become a cop. He'd joined the force to help people, individual people with faces and names and families who were part of his own community. He'd envisioned himself cruising happy, tree-lined streets where kids waved and their parents greeted him by name. He'd imagined himself delivering groceries to an appreciative invalid or dropping by with a bag of kibble for a vacationing family's pet.

In point of fact, Jay had imagined himself doing Archie Lunt's job.

Over the past weeks, Jay had learned a great deal about himself, and even more about his wife. He *had* taken Bethany for granted, pulling her into a life she'd never chosen without giving a moment's consideration to her needs. He'd simply assumed that she wanted whatever he wanted. What gall.

Jay had never really understood Bethany, nor had he ever tried to understand her. That's why he'd lost her. And in the end, that's why he'd lost himself.

Dawn broke softly over the Sierra crest, bathing the foothills with a pink hush. Sitting on the front stoop, Bethany watched the awakening day with hot coffee and cool reflection. In the weeks since Jay had left, Bethany had finally allowed herself to grieve his loss and the loss of their marriage. In that painful retrospective, she'd also allowed herself to acknowledge her contribution to the breakdown of their relationship.

Over the years, Bethany had consistently tried to change her husband, altering those parts of his personality she'd fallen in love with in the first place. For instance, she'd always resented his take-charge attitude, despite the fact that it made her feel safe and protected. One moment she'd leaned on him, unable to stand on her own feet; the next, she'd pushed him away, accusing him of trying to control her.

If she hadn't known what she needed, how could she have legitimately expected Jay to know?

Bethany had thought she needed independence. In retrospect, she realized that all she'd ever needed or craved was respect, yet she couldn't expect Jay, or anyone else, to respect her when she hadn't respected herself.

That's why she'd left him. That's why she'd run to the farm. She'd been looking for a sense of independence and belonging. And she'd found it, but she'd found so much more.

Setting her coffee mug on the porch rail, Bethany wandered toward the fields dotted with shiny orange pumpkins ready for harvest. They'd been her babies these past months, her dearest friends, her salvation.

She loved them. She loved the farm.

Squatting in an irrigation furrow, she absently examined a wilting leaf for insects. There were a few, but it didn't matter now. The canner's crew would be here later today, and by the end of the weekend, the fields would be barren. It was the end of the season, the end of an era.

Bethany had learned much this summer, about pumpkins and about herself. Yet there was so much undiscovered.

She sighed, standing to brush the soil from her palms. Her soil. Soil she'd tilled and cultivated, watered and nurtured into a productive burst of plenty. She'd done it all by herself, and she was proud of her accomplishment.

Glancing around, her gaze settled on the barn and on C.J.'s new enclosure. The goat regarded her placidly, with trust and, she thought, a modicum of affection.

She'd miss him. She'd miss quiet dawns and the chirping cacophony of rosy sunsets; she'd miss the joy of watching delicate blossoms evolve into fat, sturdy fruits; she'd miss the smell of sun in the air, and the warm breeze caressing her face.

She'd miss it all, and she'd grieve its passing. But there was no choice now, because she had so much more to gain.

Self-respect, she'd discovered, was not determined by locale. The changes inside her were permanent. To her surprise, Jay had been willing to accept those changes, to demonstrate that they could both continue to grow as individuals and still be a family.

In the end, that's all Bethany had ever wanted. Yet she'd nearly thrown it away.

"Yep, he's a nice little billy," the old farmer drawled as he circled the wire enclosure. "Got me a sweet doe that'll make him feel right at home."

Through the fence, C.J. eyed the smiling stranger with an expression akin to homicidal rage. Snorting furiously, the goat ducked his head, churned his hoofed feet and rammed the gate with enough force to crack one of the support poles.

Bethany hugged David, who was on the verge of tears, and eyed the flimsy rope in the farmer's hand. "Maybe I should have taken the vet's suggestion and given him a tranquilizer."

The man took umbrage at the suggestion. "Why, I've had goats all my life, ma'am. Ain't no one in this county understands 'em better than me."

"I'm sure that's true, and I'm thrilled to have found such a wonderful home for C.J. It's just that—"

"C.J.'s special," David blurted, wiping a fresh flood of unmanly tears from his pale cheeks. "He likes apples for dessert. You'll give him apples, won't you? I mean, he'll be real bummed if he doesn't get any. He might even stop eating, on account of him being real stubborn and all."

Flashing a nearly toothless grin, the old man squatted down to David's level. "Well, son, if this here goat likes apples, I'll make darn good and sure that he gets as many of 'em as his fat tummy can hold."

Heaving a shuddering sigh, David cast his mother a pleading look. "C.J. doesn't understand why we're making him go away. Can't we keep him, Mom? Please?"

"Oh, honey, I wish we could, but you know farm animals aren't allowed in the city."

"Nobody would hafta know," the boy insisted. "Dad and I can make a real neat pen in the backyard, and C.J. will be real quiet, I know he will. Please, Mom."

Bethany felt like she'd swallowed a brick. "We've talked about this, David. You know we might not be living with Daddy."

"How come?"

"Because your father doesn't even know that we're moving back to Los Angeles. Now, let's go into the house and let this nice man get C.J. ready for his new home."

David kicked a pebble with his toe, reluctantly allowing himself to be led away from his furious pet's pen. Bethany, too, was deeply saddened by the goat's departure. The annoying creature had become, well, a member of the family. They'd all miss him. And they'd miss the farm.

Her gaze fell on the massive For Sale sign in the middle of the now-denuded fields, where only tattered remnants of her beautiful pumpkin vines remained. As always, she resisted the urge to rip the horrid sign out by telling herself that there was no other way to repair their shattered family.

A voice in the back of her brain whispered that it might already be too late. Telephone conversations with Jay over the past month had taken on a strange, evasive tone. When she'd tested the waters by commenting on her inclination to put the farm up for sale after harvest, Jay had insisted—roughly, she thought, and in no uncertain terms—that doing so would be a terrible mistake.

Bethany had taken that to mean that Jay had reconsidered his earlier request that she and the children return home. Maybe he didn't want her anymore. The thought was terrifying, yet she was nonetheless determined. Whether Jay wanted Bethany back or not, she knew that he wanted his children, children who desperately needed their father. It had been wrong of her to move them so far away from him. Even if it was too late for Bethany to save her marriage, she was determined to save her children's relationship with their dad.

Pressing a maternal kiss on the top of her son's head, she forced a bright smile. "Just think, in a few weeks you'll be back in your old school with all the friends you left behind. Won't that be wonderful?"

David shrugged, jamming his hands in his pockets and mumbling at the ground. "Yeah, sure, I guess so."

As they reached the porch, Leon sat up, shifting his weight from the rear leg that was nearly healed, yet still weak enough to favor. He whined pitifully, as if begging reassurance that he wouldn't suffer C.J.'s fate. David dropped to his knees, scratching the dog's furry ruff. "Don't worry, boy," he murmured. "You're gonna come with us."

Leon licked his young master's face.

Bethany glanced up and saw Laurel peering through the curtains, her face contorted in anguish as she watched the kindly old farmer struggling to harness their beloved goat. Bethany bit her lip, fighting her own tears. This was more difficult than she could have ever imagined. The fact that the children had agreed being with their father was more important than staying on the farm hadn't eased the trauma of leaving—for them, or for her.

Her sad thoughts were interrupted by a bellow from the goat pen. Whirling, Bethany realized that after managing to loop the rope around C.J.'s neck, the farmer had lost control, and the situation had deteriorated into a dangerous battle of wills. The furious animal had initiated a relentless attack on the hapless man, who was frantically dodging each vicious charge while struggling to hang on to his end of the rope.

"Oh, geez," David mumbled, his eyes huge. "C.J.'s gonna kill him for sure."

The melodramatic comment spurred Bethany into action. She and David dashed across the yard just as C.J. broke away from his captor. With a snort of pure triumph, the goat leaped through the open gate and scampered toward the back pasture with the useless rope flapping in the breeze. The unhappy farmer got to his feet, muttering, brushed off his coveralls and loped after the escaped goat with an expression of steely determination.

"Good grief." Bethany sighed, tossing up her hands. "He'll never catch him now."

"Nope," David agreed with a satisfied smirk. "He sure won't."

Jamming her hands on her hips, Bethany watched the frantic game of goat tag, wondering if she should call a halt to this pathetic effort and simply insist that C.J. be part of the deal for whoever purchased the farm. At least the poor animal wouldn't be forced out of his home—

"Mom." David tugged at her wrist. "Someone's coming."

Turning, Bethany shaded her eyes, gazing toward the road as a cloud of driveway dust announced an arriving vehicle. From this distance, Bethany noted only that the vehicle was white and assumed it was a sheriff's patrol unit. "Archie said he'd drop by this weekend."

"It doesn't look like Archie's car. It looks like—" David's scrunched face suddenly lit up. "Dad! It's Dad!"

Bethany went rigid. "David, honey, you know it's not your father. It's probably one of the Realtors—"

But David was halfway down the driveway, waving his hand wildly over his head. Behind Bethany, a delighted shriek emanated from the doorway as Laurel flew out of the house and charged after her brother, screaming with excitement.

Nathan toddled out to the porch, giggling madly and clapping his fat little hands. "Daddy home!"

Stunned, Bethany stood as if rooted to the ground, watching the familiar, square-shaped utility vehicle emerge from the dust cloud. A lump wedged in her throat as the vehicle shuddered to a stop. Jay emerged, surrounded by his laughing children.

Breath backed up in Bethany's throat. She could hardly believe her eyes, and yet she knew without doubt that this was no illusion. Jay was here. Dear God, he was here.

And he was the most beautiful sight in the world.

Scooping up Nathan, she rushed across the yard, stopping a few feet from where Jay and the older children were engaged in a rush of nonstop chatter. When he saw her, his eyes warmed. He stood, seeming oddly nervous, and gave her an uncertain smile. "Hi."

"Hi, yourself," she whispered breathlessly. "Why didn't you let us know you were coming?"

Avoiding her gaze, Jay took Nathan from her arms, tossing him into the air until he squealed joyfully. "I, ah, wasn't sure when I'd be here."

"Can you stay all weekend?" David shouted, frantically yanking his father's arm. "Are you gonna help us pack?"

Frowning, Jay lowered Nathan to the ground as his reproachful gaze settled on the For Sale sign. "What's that all about?"

Bethany glanced away. "I, ah, was going to tell you."

"Tell me what?"

When Bethany didn't answer, Laurel stepped forward. "We're moving back to L.A.," she announced importantly.

Jay went white. "Why?"

Bethany, whose attention was inexplicably drawn to a loose string on the pocket of her coveralls, cleared her throat several times. "We, ah, that is, the children and I, decided that we . . . uh, they . . . needed to spend more time with you."

"In Los Angeles?"

Nodding miserably, she shrank beneath his incredulous stare, certain that her fears about Jay having second thoughts regarding the renewal of their relationship had been justified.

Jay swallowed hard, shaking his head. "Well, that's going to present a bit of a problem."

"How come?" David asked.

He slipped Bethany an uncertain glance. "Because I just rented an apartment in Grass Valley."

"I understand," Bethany said quickly. "But we won't actually be interfering with your life, because—" Her head snapped up. "In Grass Valley?"

He shrugged.

Bethany blinked in bewilderment. "I don't understand. What about your job?"

"I quit."

"You *what?*"

"I quit." Casually, reaching inside his vehicle, Jay extracted a bulging department store bag and handed it to his excited youngsters. "A few extra school supplies," he explained. "I thought you guys could use them."

"Wow!" David dug through the treasure trove of fancy pencils and cartoon-studded homework folders. "Thanks, Dad!"

"Wait a minute," Bethany mumbled, massaging her forehead. "The police force has been your entire life. How could you just give it all up?"

"It wasn't my life, Beth. You are." He smiled at Laurel's beaming face. "You and the children. Once I realized that, there wasn't anything on earth that could keep me away. Oh. And I have something for you, too." Reaching into his pocket, he pulled out a small, folded sheet and handed it to her.

It was a check for a staggering amount, made out to Bethany. She stumbled back a step, staring in complete confusion. "What's this for?"

"I figured it would give you a head start on planting the back pasture without going to the bank for another loan. And you're going to need tuition money, for agricultural college." He glanced fondly around the farm. "With your grit and determination, once you get a Ph.D. in pumpkins, you're going to turn this place into a profit-making showpiece. I just wanted to do what I could to help a little, that's all."

Bethany was almost speechless. Almost. She licked her lips, casting another disbelieving glance at the check. "This is more than a little help, Jay. Where in the world did you ever get this kind of money?"

Ducking his head, he ignored the question by rifling through the cluttered back seat of his car.

A thought hit Bethany with the force of a speeding truck. "Oh, Lord. Oh, no, Jay. You cashed out your pension, didn't you?"

"It was just sitting there, gathering dust."

"Gathering interest," she corrected.

"Whatever." He slid her a sheepish grin. "Anyway, you're a good investment, right? And the way I see it, this kind of makes us partners."

"Partners," she murmured, still stunned by the shocking turn of events. "I like the sound of that."

Jay's smile glowed through his eyes. "So do I."

A soothing warmth trickled down Bethany's spine, chilled only by the reminder of how much he'd sacrificed for them. "But your job, Jay. You've wanted to be a police officer since high school. I can't let you give that up."

"I'm not giving anything up. I've already put in an application with the local sheriff." His sneakers shuffled the dirt, an endearing evasive maneuver that reminded her of David. "I know it's still law enforcement," he mumbled, avoiding her gaze. "And I know how you feel about that, but things are a lot different up here. What happened at the convenience store, well, it was a fluke, you know? From what Archie says, violent crime is pretty rare up here. He likes to think it's because the sheriff's department is on top of things."

Bethany smiled. "I suspect that he's right."

Jay, who'd been studying his shoes as if willing them to fly, angled a hesitant glance up. "So you wouldn't be too upset if I was to be accepted by the department?"

"No," she whispered. "I wouldn't be the least bit upset."

A proud gleam danced in his eyes. "There's nothing official yet, but Archie thinks I'm a shoo-in."

The comment drew David's attention from the new picture dictionary he'd been perusing. "You mean you're going to be a deputy, just like Archie?"

"It looks that way."

"Wow, that's too cool."

"But how come you're going to live in an apartment?" Laurel asked in wide-eyed innocence. "Why can't you live with us?"

Pursing his lips, Jay studied a grease smear on the hood of his car. "I, ah, figured maybe your mom would need her sewing room back."

Three pairs of quizzical eyes turned in Bethany's direction. "Actually, I do," she confessed, much to her children's dismay. Somehow, she managed to keep a straight face. "But since we're partners and everything, we might be able to work something else out."

Jay's tawny brow gave a hopeful hitch. "Like what?"

She shrugged. "Well, all the bedrooms are full, so I guess you'd have to share with someone."

David instantly announced, "You can sleep with me, Dad."

"Thanks, son," Jay replied, grinning. "I think I'll take you up on that."

Crestfallen, Bethany stammered, "That's not what I meant."

"I know," Jay whispered, caressing her cheek. "But we have to set an appropriate example for the children, until after the wedding."

"The—"

"Yay!" screamed Laurel and David in unison.

"Wedding?" Bethany finished lamely.

"It's only proper," Jay explained, grinning. Then he pulled her into his arms. "Mrs. Murdock, will you marry me again?"

"Yes, Mr. Murdock, I believe I will."

The children's joyous celebration of shouts was interrupted by an even louder scream from the back pasture.

Bethany pulled away. "Good grief! I forgot all about—"

At that moment, the farmer chugged past the goat pen, bellowing, with a rampaging goat hot on his heels.

"Holy cow!"

David shot across the yard, hollering at C.J. while Jay simply stepped back, stunned. "What on earth?"

"Don't even ask," Bethany mumbled, dashing after her son.

In the chaos that followed, the terrified farmer dived into his pickup truck and burned rubber all the way to the main road while C.J., with the hated rope still flapping around his neck, continued to express his indignance by butting everything in sight.

"Head him off by the porch!" Jay yelled.

David zigzagged around the obstinate animal, shooing him toward the barn, where Bethany made a futile attempt to corral the furious animal. "He's going into the fields!"

The entire family dashed on an intercept course, but C.J. had something else in mind. The goat skidded to a stop, cocked his head, then bent down, churned forward and felled the For Sale sign with a vicious head butt. The sign cracked, lurched over and plopped into the dirt.

C.J. stood over the sign, emitted a triumphant bleat, then casually trotted to his enclosure and stuck his head in the oat bucket.

"Well." Jay swallowed hard, eyeing the crushed sign. "I second that motion."

"So do I." Smiling, Bethany tucked her hand under her soon-to-be-former-ex-husband's arm. "Now about this wedding..."

Epilogue

David thought the ceremony was, like, totally cool. Of course, he'd never been to a wedding before, cool or not, but he figured his parents' wedding had to be the most special day there ever was.

First of all, he got to be his dad's best man, which was a real important job, even more important than Laurel's. She only got to be maid of honor. Being an honor person couldn't be nearly as good as being a best person, but David hadn't said anything to his sister, on account of him not wanting to hurt her feelings.

Besides, Laurel looked pretty good for a girl, all gussied up in the fancy dress Mom sewed for her. It was all fluffy and swirly, and Mom said the color made her eyes look like sapphires, whatever those were. Laurel complained it made her look prissy, but she was kind of grinning when she said it, and then Mom laughed, like they were sharing some kind of weird joke. David didn't see what was so funny, but Dad said that men should never try to figure out what women were talking about. David thought that was pretty silly, but he accepted it because his dad knew everything.

Besides, there was lots of other neat stuff going on that day. Everybody in town showed up for the wedding, and most of the ladies brought stuff to eat later at the reception. David helped set up the tables and chairs outside, in a park across from the church. It was hard work, but David didn't mind. He thought it was fun.

The only thing he didn't like was wearing a funny suit with a weird belt that Dad said was a cummerbund. It was stupid, because it just kind of hung there, useless. David only wore it because Dad had one, and so did Nathan, who was supposed to carry the wedding rings down the aisle on a lacy pillow.

The preacher was worried about Nathan, because he was so little and all. But David figured his baby brother did okay, except for when he saw his preschool teacher sitting in one of the pews. Then he got all excited and stepped on a bunch of people's toes so he could show off his pillow.

After his teacher told him that it was a real pretty pillow, Nathan got all giggly and ran over to Dad, which was basically where he was supposed to be in the first place, so even though everyone in the church started laughing, David supposed it turned out okay.

He thought the music was kind of boring, though, except when the organist started playing "Here Comes the Bride." Then everybody got real quiet and Dad started to sweat.

Standing at the aisle, Mom was wearing a fancy white suit she'd sewed out of something called brocade, and a floppy hat that made her look like a magazine model. David thought she was the prettiest mom in the whole entire world. Even Leon, sitting on the front pew wearing David's Dracula bow tie, must have thought she looked pretty, because he barked when she came down the aisle, and David had to tell him to hush up.

Afterward, everyone shook everyone's hand, and a weird guy in a sweatsuit was taking pictures like crazy while Dad's deputy buddies threw rice all over the place, which made Leon sneeze and growl. David figured Leon didn't like people throwing stuff at Mom and Dad, but he stopped snarling when Dad scratched his ear, so nobody got bit or anything. Mr. Morris didn't come to the wedding. Mom said that was because he'd opened a new insurance office in Sacramento. No one saw him much anymore. That suited David fine.

Anyway, after all the rice and stuff, everyone went across the street to the park. David thought the reception party was real fun, too, and the music was pretty nifty, even though it was just some taped stuff played on a big boom box.

But the best part came later that night, when Dad had hauled all his stuff out of David's room and moved in with Mom. That's when David knew for sure that everything would be okay. Dad was home for good. The Murdocks were a real family again. And that was the coolest thing of all.

* * * * *

Watch for BAREFOOT BRIDE, the next book in Diana Whitney's delightful PARENTHOOD miniseries, coming in December 1996, only from Silhouette Special Edition.

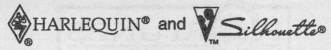

HARLEQUIN® and **Silhouette®**

are proud to present...

HERE COME THE GROOMS™

Four marriage-minded stories written by top Harlequin and Silhouette authors!

Next month, you'll find:

Married?!	by Annette Broadrick
Designs on Love	by Gina Wilkins
It Happened One Night	by Marie Ferrarella
Lazarus Rising	by Anne Stuart

ADDED BONUS! In every edition of *Here Come the Grooms* you'll find $5.00 worth of coupons good for Harlequin and Silhouette products.

On sale at your favorite Harlequin and Silhouette retail outlet.

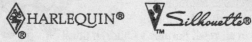
HARLEQUIN®   **Silhouette®**

The exciting new cross-line continuity series about love, marriage—and Daddy's unexpected need for a baby carriage!

🐛🐛🐛🐛🐛🐛🐛🐛

You loved

THE BABY NOTION by Dixie Browning (Desire #1011 7/96)
and
BABY IN A BASKET by Helen R. Myers
(Romance #1169 8/96)

Now the series continues with...

MARRIED...WITH TWINS! by Jennifer Mikels
(Special Edition #1054 9/96)

The soon-to-be separated Kincaids just found out they're about to be parents. Will their newfound family grant them a second chance at marriage?

Don't miss the next books in this wonderful series:

HOW TO HOOK A HUSBAND (AND A BABY)
by Carolyn Zane (Yours Truly #29 10/96)

DISCOVERED: DADDY
by Marilyn Pappano (Intimate Moments #746 11/96)

DADDY KNOWS LAST continues each month...
only from

Silhouette®
™

Look us up on-line at: http://www.romance.net

DKL-SE

This October, be the first to read these wonderful authors as they make their dazzling debuts!

Women to Watch

THE WEDDING KISS by Robin Wells
(Silhouette Romance #1185)
A reluctant bachelor rescues the woman he loves from the man she's about to marry—and turns into a willing groom himself!

THE SEX TEST by Patty Salier
(Silhouette Desire #1032)
A pretty professor learns there's more to making love than meets the eye when she takes lessons from a sexy stranger.

IN A FAMILY WAY by Julia Mozingo
(Special Edition #1062)
A woman without a past finds shelter in the arms of a handsome rancher. Can she trust him to protect her unborn child?

UNDER COVER OF THE NIGHT by Roberta Tobeck
(Intimate Moments #744)
A rugged government agent encounters the woman he has always loved. But past secrets could threaten their future.

DATELESS IN DALLAS by Samantha Carter
(Yours Truly)
A hapless reporter investigates how to find the perfect mate—and winds up falling for her handsome rival!

Don't miss the brightest stars of tomorrow!

Only from **Silhouette®**
™